The First Two

By
Adrian Mallabo

To Jenny!

I hope you enjoy

the book!

Adrian Mallabo

Damnation Books, LLC.
P.O. Box 3931
Santa Rosa, CA 95402-9998
www.damnationbooks.com

The First Two
by Adrian Mallabo

Digital ISBN: 978-1-61572-905-0
Print ISBN: 978-1-61572-906-7

Cover art by: Ash Arceneaux
Edited by: Juanita Kees

Copyright 2013 Adrian Mallabo

Printed in the United States of America
Worldwide Electronic & Digital Rights
Worldwide English Language Print Rights

I'd like to dedicate this book to all those that have helped me along this path. Thank you for your guidance and your support, and thank you for your endless patience when mine has run out.

I'd like to acknowledge my mentors, Malcolm and Danielle, and I'd like to thank my future bride, Andrea, for being my rock through the good times and the bad.

Prologue

"Goddamit, Gillian Run!"

Jack came to a halt, his eyes full of desperation. Gillian stopped and looked back at him, and her eyes widened with understanding. Jack shook his head as he took a step away from her.

They'd had a long run surviving in this rotten world, but now that luck had to be repaid. It was unfair, he'd only wanted to make her life normal again, and to keep her and his son alive. He knew what he had to do. He had to find the strength to stop looking at those beautiful eyes.

"Gillian, *please*," he begged, his words coming out in ragged gasps.

A loud crash drew his attention back to the street they'd just fled, and he peered through the dust to find its source. The road was covered with rusted old vehicles, broken glass, and the decaying bodies of the living dead who now walked the earth as ravenous beasts. The restless bodies of those who'd once been human, plowed their way through the heaps of derelict cars—snarling, bleeding, hungry monsters. The undead oozed from the darkness of the night, drawn as always to the smell of flesh and blood.

A shriek came from Jack's young son beside Gillian. Clark's bravery crumbled at last at the sight of the hungry ghouls. Jack was proud that his son had lasted this long without breaking down. His son called out to him, tried to pull away from his mother's hand, but Gillian held him firm. Jack smiled at her, knowing that she would be strong enough to survive without him.

There were too many of the dead, and the streets were just too crowded with garbage to maneuver through with any ease. The enemy came from all sides. His knee injury was slowing them down. It wasn't fair they had to slow down just

Gillian nodded, her dirty face streaked with tears, and fled. Soon they were lost around the corner of a mangled bus that had landed on its side. Their footsteps disappeared amongst the sound of the hordes that now drew closer. Amidst the waves of doom lurching towards him, Jack smiled.

Jack turned to face the coming beasts and lifted the slender katana to his side. It seemed like such a long time ago now when he'd first pilfered this weapon from some old antique store miles away from here. He looked at the smooth blade and memories, both dark and bright, flooded into his mind like a thick tide. He'd found this relic during a time of desperation. It had served him well over these past few years, and when their guns had been emptied and discarded, this weapon kept those he cared about alive. Still, a large part of him wished that he had his hands on a loaded pistol right now.

"*Come on*, you bastards," he spoke defiantly over the rising moans.

The horrifying wails and groans of the dead fell upon him, clouding his hearing and driving the last recollections of his family away. The undead shuffled towards him wearing clothes that had lost their color and now hung from their mangled forms like tattered drapes. The air was rank with a stench he never would get used to. Their arms reached out as if the hundreds, and perhaps even thousands, wanted to give him the biggest collective bear hug in the world. It wouldn't be a kindly embrace, like one shared between lovers. This was the final embrace, the one that meant the end of him.

Jack, thinking of his family one last time, cried out and charged into the hungry mob.

Part one
The Charon Initiative

"You are my first. I hope you aren't the last."

Chapter One

Everything was red. The world was red, blanketed in a brilliant crimson hue.

The creature's thoughts focused only on the need to hunt, to feed. Sometimes flashes of this body's memories from its previous life surfaced, but the monster couldn't make sense or meaning from any of these strange thoughts. The undead thing felt no emotion other than rage.

It opened its veined eyes, stood from the dusty floor, and crawled out of the hiding place it had found beneath the ruins of a highway overpass. It perceived the clear blue sky as a sea of blood.

It was time to feed. It did not need to eat to live, but it still ate. It did not derive sustenance from what it found and devoured, but it was driven to slaughter all it could nonetheless.

The creature peeled its glazed eyes from the sky and commenced its trot down the long stretch of deserted highway. Forty-five minutes brought the creature to the heart of a shopping center. Its heavily labored steps carried it past the ruins of a burger joint and a fitness store before ending up in the middle of a parking lot belonging to what once was a popular bookstore.

It found no food. The area around the creature was desolate and silent save for the wind that made an audible whistling noise as it passed through the hulks of abandoned vehicles. Everything that had once been alive was now dust, and everything else was either covered in the same remains or consumed by rust.

Lazily, the creature's head lolled one way and then another. Before long, it understood that there was nothing to eat in this area.

The creature started to lurch towards the heart of the city when something out of place caught its vague attention—something so unnatural that even this stupid beast was forced to stop and take notice. A low moan escaped from its dry throat, and it took a shuffling step forward, its eyes focused on the small, bright red dot.

The dot shone against the faded silver paint of the passenger door of a late model sedan. It hovered there for a moment, then moved, and the creature was startled when the dot centered itself against its decaying chest. Another moan spewed from between its rot-caked lips, almost a question.

Suddenly a small portion of its chest exploded. Decayed remains flew in the air like scraps of dry leather. Slime and putrid puss flew from the wound. The creature groaned as the force of the blow sent it backwards to land firmly on its side.

The zombie stared up once more at the crimson sky. Without fear, it puzzled over the figures that moved into its view.

* * * *

"Are we sure about this one?"

"He's the most intact one we've seen so far," Jenny Kenyon commented.

"Well, except for the small hole in his chest," Danny Keene joked.

Sergeant Thomas Black ignored them and studied the downed monster. He almost thought it would be impossible to find a relatively intact creature out here. All the ones he'd encountered were missing vital pieces of themselves. Some were so decayed that not even the professor's so-called cure could help the poor lost souls.

This one was different. Other than its obvious undead characteristics, this zombie was whole. A single bullet through the sternum was enough to reach its spine, effectively neutralizing its mobility. Now all they had to do was cart this specimen back home.

"I've waited almost two months to fire that bullet," Thomas grumbled to himself.

"Nice shot by the way," Jenny said, admiring her sergeant's work.

"You lucky sonnovabitch." Danny kicked the creature on its back. "Do you realize how lucky you really are?"

"Leave it alone, Danny," Thomas warned.

"Sorry, boss."

"That's alright." Thomas couldn't help a small smirk from forming on the otherwise hardened features of his face. He reached a free hand to his earpiece and opened communications with the fourth member of his squad.

"Tennant, this is Black. Get the APC warmed up."

"Did you find one?" The surprise was clear through the small speaker. Even now, the sergeant wasn't used to a voice that sounded so young. Isaac Tennant was perhaps too young to be on a team like this, He was smart, quick on his feet during an emergency, and the best driver who'd ever sat in front of an APC's controls. Even though Isaac was still in his early twenties, he was a valued member of his squad.

"Yeah, we did." Thomas nodded to the team members standing beside him. "We're going home guys."

"Oh, I can't wait," Danny cheered.

Jenny smirked. "I can't wait to breathe some clean air after hanging out in this dump for so long."

"Enough, ladies," Thomas grumbled. "Secure the specimen while Tennant gets his act in gear so we can get out of here."

"Yes sir." They spoke as one.

Jenny removed a large pair of chain-linked steel gauntlets from her backpack. The thick and heavy contraptions were made to bind an undead's hands and restrict its movements. Danny set to work fixing together the assembly that would wrap around the creature's entire face, protecting all of them from its diseased jaws.

While the pair worked, Thomas strapped his rifle to his back and stared down at the beast. Danny was right about one thing. If the professor's serum actually worked, then this particular bastard was a lucky one. One in twelve billion zombies on earth and this one managed to snag the golden ticket for itself. Like his team and the rest of the surviving human population, Thomas hoped that this procedure would in fact work. It was a trying job; searching around for an undead that was still whole in order to try the serum on it.

Perhaps they had finally succeeded in their mission.

"How long do you suppose it's been out here like this, sir?" Jenny asked.

"I don't know, private."

"What *I* want to know," Danny grunted as he secured the beast's head. "Is how it's managed to keep itself together like this?"

"This one was a fighter," Thomas answered, and he knew he was right. "He managed to run away from the creatures before they could tear him apart. He did this even though he was already infected. He hid himself away as his body turned."

Thomas tried very hard to imagine the thing's face as it might have been when it was alive. He pictured a man hiding in the shadows, clutching a wound that was already festering with a virus that would soon kill him.

"What was he hiding from?" he wondered.

"That's easy," Danny added. He waved his arms around,

motioning to the horizon. "Them."

"Them," Thomas nodded slowly. "Or maybe he was trying to protect someone he cared about from what he was becoming."

Chapter Two

Everything was still crimson, but now there was a hint of another color that the creature couldn't define with its simple mind. Blue.

The creature floated in it. It hovered amidst a sea of something heavier than water but carrying a consistency close to that of blood. Shapes moved in and out of view, unfocused.

Through the murky depths came the outlines of people. They were talking, walking back and forth, and always watching the creature closely.

A sense of lustful hunger filled the monster. It tried to claw at the glass, but its bare fingernails couldn't tear through the clear, curved surface. The blue liquid filled its lungs. It tried to fight, to push itself against the surrounding prison, but the liquid was so thick that its movements were far slower than it would have been in open air.

A giant metal ring rose from the bottom of the cylinder housing the creature and moved up and down outside the glass. The inside of the ring emitted a golden light and steady warmth.

As the ring pulsated up and down along the cylinder, the creature studied the blurry images of those it wanted so badly to chew on. It wasn't afraid, and it didn't care what its food was doing to it. It just wanted to wrap its arms around those shapes and bite down.

Hard.

* * * *

The creature understood no sense of time. It floated and waited, and continued to claw at its prison. The blue liquid filled it body, the light ring continued to dance back and forth in timed intervals, and the human shapes watched.

Eventually the creature stopped trying to leave scratch marks on the glass. The desire to break free from this prison was lessened now. It grew tired of trying to reach what was obviously beyond its grasp.

* * * *

The creature continued to study the figures on the outside of the glass. It hung suspended in its glass prison peacefully and just watched.

The humans seemed excited about something. The creature still wished to feed on them, but it didn't want to so badly anymore. It realized suddenly that it wondered what those people were doing. It couldn't hear anything, but it studied the movements of their lips and knew they were somehow communicating with one another. It reminded the creature of how, when it was free, it would let out an occasional moan. Yes, the creature's food was somehow communicating with one another through the sounds that came from their mouths.

The creature was very interested in this, and it let out a few moans in its prison that none outside heard.

* * * *

The creature began to experience a strange sensation in its arms and chest. Its smoother skin began to itch.

* * * *

The creature began to perceive other colors. The thick liquid was bluer now. The red tinge that once dominated most of its eyesight was gone.

Through the looking glass it started to differentiate the separate hues that covered the landscape beyond the glass prison. Lights from several computer terminals flashed in front of it. The floor was shiny, made of metal, much like the ring that used to rise and fall around its prison. The ring was gone now, along with its pretty yellow light. It missed the warm feeling that it used to cast on its body.

* * * *

The creature's chest burned with a feeling that it couldn't comprehend. It struggled and thrashed its body within the small chamber, banging against the glass as hard as it could. The need to find some form of escape filled the creature.

Suddenly the water was churning violently, and the cylinder was being rotated to rest on its side.

Liquid rushed past the creature in a tidal wave that forced it out of the tube where it landed hard against the metal floor. The floor was pitted with hundreds of little holes that quickly drained the thick liquid away. It coughed up the blue fluid from its lungs onto the grated surface, and a feeling of relief filled the creature as it took its first few breaths.

The humans, now clearly defined to the creature, surrounded it. Their faces carried strange expressions that the creature still could not read. But the most astounding thing to enter this thing's mind was it no longer felt hunger towards them.

Instead it felt a powerful sense of fear towards those that surrounded it.

Chapter Three

For the first time since being turned, the creature slept. It dreamed of strange images that it couldn't make any sense of. There were smiling faces, a woman running along the grass of an open plain. There was the image of a wide ocean. Waves crashed against the sandy beach in a foamy assault that left the surface perfectly smooth. There was also something out on that water. Something solid and straight, floating far away from the beach. Figures on the floating shape—a boat—waved towards the creature.

In the dream the creature felt good. It felt like smiling.

* * * *

It woke up to find itself in a small, dimly-lit room. While lying atop a cushioned mattress, the creature surveyed its surroundings with calculated patience. A small table sat at the side of the tiny bed holding a single lamp.

Beyond the foot of the bed stood a locked door made of what looked like the same material as the grated floor. It felt another new emotion that it didn't like. It felt a sense of terror for the unknown, because it didn't know what was happening. It felt truly and utterly afraid.

* * * *

The lone figure in the locked room was aware of the passage of time. It didn't know how long it had been waiting in here, but it knew some time had passed. It knew it was being watched. Its eyes were stronger now, and it gazed out into the gloomy corners where the lamp's light could barely reach. The creature raised its attention to the ceiling. Tucked in the far corner was something that glistened just slightly against the pale light.

Standing for the first time since its emergence from the cylinder, it walked over to the corner, looked up, and found that the shiny thing was circular. The surface of it was dark, but it reminded the creature of an eye. The eye was encased in a black tube, where its stem disappeared into the surface of the room's sharp corner.

With its preternatural senses it detected no heat emanating from that strange eye, so it knew the thing was not alive. So why did it get the sense that it was being watched?

The monster took a step back, suddenly very afraid of that black eye. The corner of the bed caught the creature behind the knee, making it stumble backwards. It hit its head against the edge of the table with a sharp crack, and a loud cry burst from its lips as it crashed to the ground. Writhing on the floor, it caressed the back of its head, and then brought its hands in front of its face. It saw the blood on its fingertips.

The creature's instincts took hold, and it plunged its fingers into its mouth and sucked every bit of the blood it could. The coppery taste shocked its senses. A retching feeling turned its stomach, and it spit out the sickening flavor from its mouth. Confusion filled it. It no longer liked the taste of that slick liquid.

When the creature looked up at the glassy eye one last time, it wondered why it couldn't see the heat emanating from it any more.

After another minute passed, and the creature forgot that it had once been able to detect such things altogether.

* * * *

A sharp ring of steel woke the creature from his slumber. When he opened his eyes, he winced as a powerfully bright light spilled through the widening door to the room. Someone was coming in. He saw the silhouette of a person standing at the threshold of the open door, outlined by the light of the hallway beyond.

"Are you hungry, Adam?" the shadowy figure asked.

He didn't answer. He raised an arm to fend off the bright light, which was still too much for his sensitive eyes to take.

"When you look at me, do you still hunger for my flesh?" the voice continued.

"I think you should step back, professor," a deep voice—almost a growl—spoke up from somewhere behind the first figure. "You don't know if it's safe to go in there."

"I think Adam is safe enough to talk to today, Sergeant Black," the professor stated with confidence. "I've been waiting to meet with him for so long now."

"You should let me secure him first."

"If it makes you feel any better, I won't go in today. Tomorrow you can secure him. Today I will speak to him from this door. How does that sound to you?"

The sergeant's grunt was his only response.

Slowly, the creature's eyes became used to his brighter surroundings. He could make out the distinct lines of the professor's face now. It was the face of a very old man, with dark coppery skin and short black hair tinged with a little bit of white just behind the ears. He couldn't make sense of this man's words He knew there was no danger here. He wanted to ask this man why he'd been kept in this room He didn't know how to articulate such thoughts into understandable words.

"Can you understand what I'm saying? No, I guess you can't– not yet, at least. You still have a long way to go but I want you to know that, for you, everything is going to be alright now. I know this because I believe that we can save you. I don't know if we will ever repair your mind fully, but your body has already been cleansed from the disease."

The creature's eyes darted around the room, looking to the outline of the second man still standing back in the shadows, and then back to the calming face of the professor.

"I've developed a serum that I believe can stop this so-called zombie virus," the professor continued. "You are in a facility where I lead the Charon Initiative. With my serum, your body is repairing itself and becoming rid of the virus that's turned you into one of them. If we are lucky, enough of your past life will return so that we won't have to completely start from the beginning. But when you can fully understand my words I'll explain everything to you. I'll tell you everything about my discovery, and where you are. You are going to be better, Adam. You are my first. I hope that you aren't the last, because right now, you are our best hope."

The professor partially turned to leave. He hesitated, and then turned and smiled back at the creature.

"Sleep well, Adam. I hope you can understand enough to know that you are safe here. We're keeping you here for now because we want to ensure our safety...and yours."

The door closed shut, the locks engaged, and the room returned to its familiar gloom. Adam stared long and hard upon the face of the metal door, and his mind was filled with hundreds of questions he wished he could communicate.

* * * *

The next day a fearsome looking man entered and threw Adam a white fabric.

"Put it on," Thomas commanded with a growl.

Adam lifted the garment with confusion, and the sergeant groaned, wiped his face with one hand, and took a step towards him. He started to talk to Adam, trying to instruct him on what to do with the cloth, but Adam couldn't understand the words. Thomas began to mime movements that confused him at first, until an exhilarating moment of understanding dawned in his mind. It didn't take long for Adam to figure out how to put the white robe on.

Now that Adam was clothed, the sergeant secured his hands with the gauntlets that he remembered he'd worn before. To him, recalling these contraptions felt like a very distant memory. He didn't fight the stern-looking man while he was being chained and the professor entered. Thomas left the room with a final cautionary glance towards the professor, who nodded his consent.

The professor guided Adam to sit on the side of the bed. The sergeant returned again with a wooden chair and placed it behind the professor. Once more the large man exited, slowly shutting the door behind him. This time Adam didn't hear the locks engage. He figured that the sergeant left it that way in case he wanted to come back into the room in a hurry.

"Good morning, Adam," the old man began.

Adam noticed that the palms of his hands were starting to feel warm and sweaty.

"That's alright, my boy." The professor held up his hands in a manner to make himself less threatening. "That's alright. My name is Professor Florentine Mena. I'm here to help you. I know that you don't quite understand me yet, but I believe I can help you with that. You see, physically your brain is healed but much of your neural pathways have long since corroded with lack of use because you've been dead for who knows how long. I don't know how long you've been out there, living as one of them, but the memories of who you were may still be locked in there somewhere. We just have to work together to re-forge some of those bridges so you can start to relearn what it's like to live as one of us."

Florentine scratched the back of his head, trying to decide how best to continue.

"The first thing we're going to do is get you talking again. I mean, what's the point of me saying all this if you're never going to get it? I've decided that, for now, we're going to take things very slow. During the coming weeks I'm going to read to you from the books I've collected in my library."

Florentine's eyes lit up with excitement, and he smiled at Adam.

"Oh, you should see my library, Adam! I love books of all kinds, all genres, and from all places of the old world. Fiction, non-fiction, sci-fi, history, and almost anything else you can name. Well, anything you'll be able to name once you can talk again."

He breathed a heavy sigh, and for the first time, Adam noticed a strange object sitting on the other man's lap. The professor took the item, opened it and Adam's eyes narrowed as he observed that the inside was filled with sheets of a thin material. The sheets were covered in strange black markings that appeared familiar to him even though he couldn't yet place their meaning or purpose.

"What I have here is the *Bible*. I myself am not a believer but I do understand the meaning to what these stories are trying to convey. Also, I thought it would be best to start with one of man's earliest works; the book of Genesis in a literal sense."

Florentine began to read, and even though Adam didn't know what was happening, it wasn't long before he caught on. Through observation he determined that the other man was reciting the markings on the pages in front of him. Through his voice, he was trying to communicate. Adam sat with his back against the wall, and he studied that man's lips as the strange, familiar sounds came out of them. He wondered why the sounds seemed familiar to him.

Chapter Four

The days passed by quickly.

A new sensation hit Adam, like something clawing in the inside of his stomach. Luckily Florentine was there when Adam hunched over in his bed, groaning from the terrible pain. The professor quickly rose and walked towards the seemingly plain wall across from the bed. He pressed a palm against a recess on the smooth surface, and a soft electronic beep sounded just before a part of the wall pulled back slightly then slid aside, revealing another room beyond. In this room lights began to flicker to life.

"Your body's finally completing its regeneration, Adam."

Behind the wall, Mena revealed a nicely kept bathroom. Adam stared with confusion and wonder, and the professor laughed kindly at the younger man.

"Oh, I've been dreading having to reach this point in your development. Alright, let's get this over with so we can get some food in you."

* * * *

Afterwards, Adam was served the first meal he'd had since rejoining humankind. It was brought in by a young woman in white, who looked at him with terrified eyes. The sight of the food confused him, but the scent his nostrils caught in the air drew the fullness of his attention. His first meal consisted of steamed vegetables and rice, garnished with spicy herbs. After Florentine's first fumbling attempts to show him how to use a spoon and fork, he eventually gave up and relegated himself to watch as Adam scooped mouthfuls of the delicious meal with his hands into his greedy mouth.

Adam never noticed that his face beamed with a radiant smile while he ate his first meal before the professor.

* * * *

Eventually Florentine reached the last page of the *Bible* and closed the book. He returned the next day with another he called, *Inferno,* written by Dante Alighieri, a man born in Florence in ancient times. After that he brought in John Steinbeck's *Of Mice and Men*, Mary Shelley's *Frankenstein* and finally, Stephen King's, *The Stand*.

The days turned to weeks, and Adam sat throughout these readings and listened as the older man read to him. He kept trying to understand the words being spoken to him because he wanted desperately to know what this human was saying to him.

Florentine dove into his books and was happy with his captive audience. One book led to another and another, and Adam absorbed the works of Homer, Dumas, Dickens, King, Clarke, and Hemingway. The readings eventually incorporated music; something else which Adam found wholly and surprisingly enjoyable.

The professor brought in a small, transparent, palm sized device. The entire face lit up to show images which astounded the silent man. When Florentine touched the screen with his pointer finger the images would shift and change. Suddenly, a soft, clear melody began to play from the device. At first Adam let out a shocked cry. He backed himself away into a corner while kneeling on the bed, and he stared transfixed at the little machine. The music continued to play, the professor sat patiently, and as he continued to listen it slowly dawned upon him that he wasn't in any danger.

Slowly, Adam made his way back to the edge of the mattress. He sat, and he listened. He didn't know what it was, but as he opened his awareness to the music, his mind was filled with a calm feeling of contentment. The music made him feel good. The melody played on for him and seemed to fill him up completely inside. Whatever it was, he liked it, and he found himself closing his eyes as he started to absorb this new wonder.

Then a voice started to speak from the small device. At first this shocked him, and then he realized that the words were supposed to be there. Suddenly it made sense why the words fit in time with the music.

"It's Sinatra. One of my favorites."

Adam looked at the professor, who was smiling at him in turn. Florentine nodded and continued his reading; and his silent companion continued to give him his full attention as the song ended and continued with a new song called, *Fly Me to the Moon*.

* * * *

Adam stood in a deserted, ruined city. He was hunting, and wherever he looked the world was covered in crimson. Before him was a woman who was trying to flee from him. As she ran, she tripped on a loose chunk of pavement and landed hard, grazing the side of her face against a car's side mirror. She lay, trembling, weeping, and fighting to get back to her feet. Her ankle was twisted in an unnatural angle. The woman screamed.

He lurched forward, pushing his body as fast as it could go. He looked upon her and all he could think of was how much he wanted to bite her warm flesh.

The dream flashed forward, and he was kneeling on the ground, feasting. There wasn't much left of the woman's lower torso. In his hands he gripped slimy, slippery entrails. His mouth chewed greedily on meat his simple mind couldn't identify.

* * * *

Adam woke up, bolting upright, as a sickening feeling devoured his stomach. He rushed to the bathroom and stared at his reflection in the mirror and noticed how pale and sickly he looked. His brow was covered in sweat and there were tears in the corners of his eyes.

He was sure now that he was changing. Something had happened to him because now he could differentiate the difference between him as he was now, and the thing that had been hunting alone out there before. He saw his old self as a monster and he knew thought was true.

He was becoming human, and he was very close now to achieving that goal.

The images from his nightmare once more assaulted his thoughts; and he bent over the toilet to expel the contents of his stomach. Afterwards, he sat on the bathroom floor, with his face covered in the palms of his hands, and he wept as grief and guilt tore apart his newly re-made soul.

* * * *

The following morning he wasn't receptive of either the reading or the music. Florentine stopped in mid-sentence and placed his copy of Richard Matheson's *I Am Legend* back on his lap.

"What's wrong?" Florentine's concern was etched on his face.

Adam sat with his feet on the edge of the bed and his head between his knees. His eyes had been downcast for most of the morning.

Then, as if the silence were beginning to suffocate him, Adam started to cry silently. Within seconds the tears became wracking sobs, which left the professor at a loss.

He noticed the untouched tray of food at the foot of Adam's bed, and he thought that maybe he understood what was wrong. He closed the book, left it on the chair as he stood, and dared to embrace the grieving man in his arms.

"It's alright," he whispered. "It wasn't your fault. Everything's going to be better now, I promise."

Adam wept bitterly in the embrace of the only other human being he knew.

* * * *

Adam remained withdrawn for the next two weeks, but as Florentine read to him, he continued to listen. He also listened attentively at the music pouring forth from the little device.

"What's wrong with him, professor?" Thomas had asked one morning after shackling Adam's hands.

"Guilt, sergeant, for the thing's he'd done."

Thomas left it at that, and the sessions continued.

* * * *

Adam continued to dream but sometimes they were not all about the monstrous beast he was. Sometimes he would be greeted with images of a woman with long black hair, and a child who looked very familiar somehow. There were times when he would dream about a vast ocean and a boat sailing on its rippling surface. Other glimpses of a past life came to him, and he always woke troubled because he couldn't make sense of any of it.

Throughout the weeks he would find himself bent over the toilet, vomiting. Sometimes he would cry, and at other times he would stay up all night because he was so afraid of the idea of falling asleep and dreaming about the monster reflection of himself.

* * * *

Then, one day as he was listening to the professor read, he

experienced the worst headache ever. He tried not to show his discomfort He guessed that the professor could tell. The pain was like a fire burning just under his scalp.

Adam listened to the tune of *Moonlight Sonata* and focused all his attention on the professor and his confusing words.

"...they..." Adam suddenly picked up from the jumble.

He sat upright, his eyes wide in shock, but Florentine continued reading, having not noticed Adam's alarm. Adam, his head still burning, focused his full attention on the man.

Twenty minutes passed and still none of it made any more sense. Then Adam winced as a feeling similar to a needle poking into his brain assailed him.

Suddenly he caught on to something else the professor said. What was the word he thought he heard just now? Already he couldn't remember He knew he understood something more of what the other man was saying.

Another hot needle poked into his brain, and Adam fought hard to contain the hurt from showing on his face. The hurt turned and twisted in his head and he thought that the burning sensation would become so hot that his head would explode into a sudden burst of flame. The needles turned into sharpened blades, cutting not only his head, but his mind open. Throughout the silent torture he thought he could understand a few more of the professor's words.

"—called the out-wall that they had—"

Shock filled him. As fast as the stabbing pain started, the hurt was suddenly gone. It left his head throbbing and feeling like mush.

"There Anduin, going—"

Adam's eyes widened once more. Then it happened, and it came upon him like a wave gently rolling up the slope on a sandy beach. He didn't cry out; he just sat and listened as it all came to him, unhindered and wondrous.

"Now after Gandalf had ridden for some time the light of the day grew in the sky, and Pippin roused himself and looked up. To his left lay a sea of mist, rising to a bleak shadow in the East..."

The words—the blessed words—made sense to him now. Excitement rushed through him like fire, his temples throbbed, and he felt that he'd lost all control of his body. Unknowingly he mumbled something through his lips and like the sudden crack of a whip, everything was silent in the room except for the soft music playing nearby.

Florentine stared at Adam. "What did you say?"

Adam didn't know how to answer. In fact he didn't remember what it was he'd uttered. The professor let out a short chuckle. He bade Adam to repeat what he'd said with the kindest note of care. Like a cub crawling out of its cave and into the sunlight, Adam dared to reply.

"Please...keep reading."

The professor's face lit up with joy and Adam got the sense that he just made this man very proud.

"Of course, Adam. This is an excerpt from a great novel by J. R. R. Tolkien. It's called *Lord of the Rings*," he said, lifting the book once more. "Let's continue."

Chapter Five

Adam brooded silently for hours, He couldn't bring back anything else about his past. It was all lost to him, like large chunks of a painting ripped out forcefully from a canvas. There were nights when he'd weep over this because he somehow knew what he couldn't remember was worth grieving over. The sadness was like a gut instinct, and he knew he'd lost more than just the memories. The professor helped distract him from the pain, and soon Adam was left with books to read on his own. The professor had said he had a large library and that he could probably provide Adam with almost any subject he could ask for.

Adam chose world history and began devouring the words like a hungry...Adam cringed at the thought. *Better to leave it at that.*

As his self-awareness grew, so did his need to ask more questions. Once he asked how long he'd been out there as one of them, but the professor couldn't answer him.

Florentine explained that when the undead virus turned a person the body was set in a frozen state where it couldn't age. The body did not continue to reproduce cell division as it did when it was alive, nor did it shed dead cells for new. The body of a walking dead was a decayed thing that simply remained, animated, but not truly alive. Cannibalism was an unexplained aspect of the virus. The creature did not need to eat to survive; it didn't need to seek nourishment.

They just ate.

"You could have been out there for years," Florentine had said one afternoon. "You could have been...one of them since the beginning."

"And...when was that, professor?"

"Two hundred and forty-nine years ago, in the year 2112. That was when the first documented case occurred. At the time this *zombie virus* was treated as something of a joke or a tabloid hoax. It didn't take long however for the world to realize that this was not so."

"And my body...it's aging now, isn't it?"

Florentine nodded slowly. "Oh yes, Adam. Believe me when I

say you are human once more."

* * * *

The words comforted Adam for a time, but the truth of what he'd done—and the guilt that followed it—seeped back into his soul like black oil. What he couldn't remember continued to haunt him through the days, and so he read about the world as it had once been long ago, in hopes that he might somehow learn something about himself. He hoped that a simple fact, or a piece of information, would suddenly trigger the resurgence of more memories.

He had to believe that one day it would all come back to him. There was no escape from the nagging feeling that he'd left something very important to him behind somewhere out there. Suddenly it didn't seem very fair that he was in this room and safe from the things that roamed the long since dead world, a world that had not seen peace in almost two hundred and fifty years.

* * * *

"You said you weren't a religious man, so why did you decide to call me Adam?"

The professor stared at him with a sort of weird smirk on the corner of his lips.

Adam leaned back, unsure. "What's wrong?"

"I'm sorry," Florentine held up a hand. "I'm still trying to get used to you talking to me. It's strange. In only a few months you're talking–asking me all these questions–in a manner that suggests that you'd never lost the ability to talk."

"I guess I'll take that as a compliment," Adam smiled.

The chains binding his hands clattered together, drawing his attention and a deep frown upon both of their faces.

"I'm sorry again. I'll talk to Sergeant Black again about removing your restraints."

"I can understand why he wouldn't want you to be left alone in a room with me if I were unbound. I would probably feel the same way."

"Have you remembered anything else about yourself?" Florentine asked, obviously trying to change the touchy subject.

He shook his head. "Just random feelings, professor."

Florentine nodded, and looked away. He seemed to think for a moment, and then looked back to Adam with a smile on his face.

"I'm not a believer. I believe it's appropriate to call you Adam because you are the first."

"The first what?"

"You're the first person whose been subjected to the ZF-93 antivirus. It was a miracle that you were a success. The Charon Initiative I established has been in effect for many years now, developing the very process that has returned you to us. I don't know if it's too soon yet to hope, but I want to someday perfect this process so that I can bring them all back."

"Well it looks like you're off to a good start, sir," Adam grinned.

The professor noticed that Adam liked to smile a lot. He wondered if it was a mask for his inner pain, or was it a part of the person he used to be.

"It's not as simple as just administering it to all the undead we run into just because it worked on you." Florentine pointed at Adam's chest. "You were selected because your body was intact and in fairly good condition. The serum can't promote growth of parts that have been lost. I needed to find a subject who wasn't heavily damaged, and that was you."

"Lucky me."

"Yes, you are," he laughed. "There's also the matter of how ZF-93 will react when administered to another human body. Sure, you were able to return to us, but everyone's body is different. There are many complexities that number in the thousands that I couldn't possibly account for yet. Will a person's age, sex, or race change how they react to the serum? What if they are carrying a different disease on them? How would our *cure* work with this other disease? The last thing I want is for my cure to mutate inside a subject and become something worse than the plague that we've been trying so hard to destroy."

"I never even thought of any of that," Adam admitted, looking solemn.

"I'm sure there are a multitude of other factors that I haven't even thought of yet. I'm just glad that it worked on you. The fact that the first subject took to the cure so well is a very promising thing. I don't want to get my hopes up, but I have high hopes for this project."

* * * *

The following week, Adam finally decided to ask the professor something that he'd been afraid to ask until now. According to the bedside clock they'd provided for him it was close to midnight when he put down his copy of Daniel Keyes' *Flowers for Algernon*. The question had been gnawing at his mind, chewing away at his thoughts so much that he could no longer stand to read. There was something he wanted to see because he knew he needed to see it. How would he feel after he saw it? Devastated for sure, but at least he could finally face it and perhaps be able to move on with his life.

Florentine protested his request at first. Adam couldn't blame him. Maybe it was too soon, but when could there ever possibly be a good time for something like this?

The professor left immediately without another word. The door shut and locked, and Adam waited for over an hour before it opened again. This time it was the sergeant who entered holding a large rifle that put him instantly on edge. Adam shrank backwards on the bed, feeling the sheets pull with him as he drew away from the frightening man. With his hands shackled he could do little to defend himself if Sergeant Black suddenly chose to attack him.

But the sergeant didn't attack him. Instead he stood within the threshold and gave Adam a worried look. It was a look that was so strange to see upon the grizzled man's hardened face that it took away just a little bit of Adam's fears. He understood that the professor must have told the sergeant about his request.

"You don't need the gun, Sergeant Black," Adam spoke, surprising even himself with his forwardness.

The other man, however, obviously had other plans for his weapon and did not stir.

A pretty woman, with her blonde hair tied back in a low bun and holding a thin rectangular device, waltzed in. She was dressed in a similar dark uniform as the sergeant's. Her eyes held Adam for a long stretch, her gaze distrustful.

She set the device on top of the table beside his bed and quickly backed away quickly from the bed just as Florentine entered.

"Thank you, Jenny," the professor said. "That will be all. I think Sergeant Black and his big gun will be enough protection for me today."

"Sir, you can't know that it's really safe to be in here with him." Jenny's eyes never left Adam.

"That will be all, Ms. Kenyon."

Jenny Kenyon nodded her head at the curt reply and left the room, closing the door behind her.

"And I don't want to hear any more complaints from you either, sergeant."

"Got it," came the sergeant's only reply.

"Good." Florentine turned to Adam, who was still huddling against the wall. "Now, Adam, are you sure about this?"

Adam relaxed now that the professor was near. "You asking again and again is only making this harder. I have to see."

"Then I won't ask anymore," Florentine nodded. He took his usual seat in front of the bed and flipped open the top cover of the rectangular object. A colorful display sprang forth upon the screen, revealing a desktop littered with carefully categorized and labeled folders.

The professor proceeded to navigate his way through the complicated maze and found the file that Adam himself had requested. Soon a video began to play upon the screen, and Adam watched with silent wonder and dread.

Chapter Six

"We're coming up onto the city limits right now, sergeant," said a young looking–perhaps too young–dark-skinned. The soldier sat in front of a wide console of what looked like the inside of a large vehicle. The camera's focus shook and the sound of a loud engine led Adam to believe that the vehicle was already in motion.

"Good work, Tennant," Sergeant Black replied. "Watch out for any roamers. I don't want to draw the attention of any large groups. We're only looking for one of 'em right now, someone that's hunting alone."

"Man, I am sick of this shit," a new voice said. "If I'd known it would take so long to find this asshole I would have logged in more vacation time this year."

"We don't get vacation time, Danny," the camera panned to focus on Jenny. "Just shut up for a minute so I can get some rest over here."

"Why is that, Sergeant?" The camera turned to Danny, a man who looked to be of Asian descent. "Aren't we the protectors of this last haven of mankind? We should be treated with a little more respect, or at least better pay."

"You are treated with respect, Lieutenant," Thomas growled. "And it isn't the last human city. Just the second last."

Danny groaned, shook his head, and diverted his attention outside the vehicle's small windows.

The camera was mounted somewhere on Thomas' person. Judging from the way the sergeant's shadows were seen against the inner bulkhead of the transport, Adam believed that the camera was located perhaps over his right shoulder.

After a few minutes of listening to the vehicle's tires grind on broken asphalt and loose rocks, Danny turned and gently backhanded Isaac across the shoulder.

"Hey, Tennant, how about when we get back you and me go score some ladies down in the Commons?"

Isaac burst out laughing, and a smirk grew on Jenny's lips.

"Don't go corrupting the rookie now!" Jenny exclaimed.

"I'm just kidding around," Danny, shrugged.

"You always do," Jenny shook her head as she regarded him humorously.

Danny grinned. "So what do you say, Tennant?"

"Man, don't ask me," Isaac laughed uneasily. "And don't bring me in the middle of your little fights with Jenny. I don't need the stress. Why don't you ask the sergeant?"

"Boss-man? Nah, his kind of party is too wild even for me."

"Damn right," Thomas replied in a gravely tone.

The other three laughed and the sergeant groaned tiredly.

The image flickered and shifted to a different point, later on in their journey. The camera was now mounted on Jenny's shoulder. The sergeant was standing closer to the vehicle's control console, staring out through the front window at something that wouldn't quite come into focus on the camera. The sun was blazing and bright beyond the view port. The inside of the large vehicle was completely silent except for the sergeant's short, even breaths. The tension in the cabin was palpable. Both Danny and Jenny stared out through the very same window with looks of deep concern etched on their faces.

"Do you see it?" Thomas asked.

"I'm not sure," Isaac said from where he still sat in front of the console. "It's hard to see through the dust clouds."

"It's there, rook. I know I saw the little bastard out there in the parking lot. He's hunting and he's alone."

"I see him," Danny spoke up. "Holy crap, you're right. There he is. He looks...well, not good...He's whole. Complete. You think we can use this one?"

"I'm thinking so," Thomas confirmed with an obvious note of excitement.

"You want to do it?" Jenny asked, her voice loud over the camera speaker. "Or should I?"

"I'll do it," Thomas said. "I have a bullet with that guy's name all over it."

"Always hogging the best parts of the job."

Thomas ignored Danny and moved away from the forward console. He made his way to the truck-mounted weapons rack, retrieved a rifle, and started to load it. Loud clicks issued from the sniper rifle as the sergeant worked fast with a tool he was obviously very familiar with. Excitement shone on his face.

"Uh...the creature is moving away," Isaac spoke up. "He's headed towards the bookstore parking lot. If it decides to go in there we might lose it completely."

"We aren't going to lose him," Thomas growled. "Danny and Jenny, load up. Form a perimeter around me once we exit the APC. Make sure the area is secure and free of any roamers. If you see one, call in first and don't fire. The last thing we need is a gunshot bringing down a whole horde of them on our position."

Danny grinned. "Like ringing a dinner bell."

The camera footage flickered once more, switching to the view of a wide parking lot. Interspersed throughout the vast expanse were derelict vehicles and rusted shopping carts from a nearby supermarket. The condition of the vehicles were either in a state of near collapse or reduced to rubble altogether. The stores themselves fared no better. Most of the roofing had caved in and there was almost no trace whatsoever of windows and glass. Foliage had begun its slow retaking of the land, although only a few dense patches of green grew through the cracks in the pavements and sidewalks.

Thomas moved fast but produced only a whispering sound of his footfalls as he raced across the remains of the old world.

The image shifted again and now it appeared that he was leaning against the side of a slanted pick-up truck's flatbed. The long, dark barrel of his sniper rifle came into view. Beyond that, Adam finally got his first view of the creature that Thomas and his crew had been pursuing.

The very sight of it stole Adam's breath, and a feeling of cold creeping fingers began to massage the back of his head. Terror couldn't clearly describe what Adam felt when he saw that thing. No words could have articulated best how a man should feel if he ever saw himself as Adam did now.

Thomas and Florentine studied Adam's expression and his body language. What they saw in the other man left them with no words they could offer that could possibly begin to ease this man's obvious torment. The sergeant eased his grip on his gun and lowered it. He hadn't expected this reaction from Adam.

What he saw was a man, not a monster, whose soul was tearing itself apart in front of his eyes. Adam wept, but his tears fell in silence. Somehow it was a worse sight to see than if the man had been wailing aloud. Thomas also began to realize that if the man in front of him could experience such emotions, then perhaps he'd wrong about him after all.

Adam was truly the first and only of his kind, because no man in all of history had ever seen himself the way that he did when he stared at that screen. Inside was pain so deep that it left his heart scalded and stripped completely bare.

He stared at the screen as if looking at his distorted, perverted reflection in a broken mirror. Dead but living, walking around with a body in shambles and decay. The look of that creature's face was unlike the face that he saw when he gazed at himself in front of the bathroom mirror. The face on the screen was recognizable but pale and stretched across the skull like sheets of dry leather. Its expression carried with it a vacant look that never changed.

A shot rang out, crackling through the device's speakers, and the creature jerked backwards from the force of the blow.

"God dammit," Thomas muttered, and Florentine hushed him.

Adam watched as three soldiers surrounded the twitching undead creature. Some of them began to make jokes at its expense. The camera zoomed in on the small hole in the center of its chest. A wound that neither bled nor healed.

The footage then moved forward to a more recent time. They were in a spacious laboratory. Consoles and screens shone in various sections while technicians in white coats went on in the background with their assigned duties. In the center, dominating the camera's attention, a tall glass cylinder hung suspended above the ground by a large robotic arm. Attached to the ceiling, the arm held the cylinder like a gigantic claw.

A familiar creature floated within the glass cylinder in a sea of blue liquid. The solution glowed faintly with its own luminescence.

Fascination dispelled a small fraction of Adam's grief while he watched that creature float in the gigantic tube. The thing's attention wavered between its surroundings and the scientists. It didn't seem to require air to survive. Sometimes it clawed and banged its thin hands against its prison, although its efforts were to no avail.

* * * *

The footage continued to play on before Adam, chronicling the subtle changes in the subject over the course of several weeks. The professor was seen on camera often, conversing with other scientists. Their talks grew animated every time the creature exhibited any sign of change. It was stunning to witness the changes in the creature's appearance as time passed.

Suddenly, the next clip showed the creature—now looking healthier—thrashing in the blue water. The robotic arm whined as gears and motors shifted the orientation of the capsule. The cylinder tipped over, dropping the creature on a silver grate where it vomited and gasped deeply for air, its body whole.

Adam watched himself through the eye of a very familiar corner camera of his room. His appearance more man now than one of the undead. And he watched for a while as the footage progressed through the days. Then it cut to a shot where the bathroom door was open. Light spilled from this doorway, illuminating a portion of the dim bedroom. He was standing in front of the mirror, crying as he studied his reflection upon its smooth surface.

Adam asked the professor to stop the playback, and then he stood and walked away from the two men to disappear into the bathroom, closing the door behind him.

Chapter Seven

"I need to get out of here," he asked the professor.

It had been three days since Adam had viewed the surveillance tapes of his capture and treatment. Florentine, surprisingly, didn't decline him. So Adam was prepared to finally leave his dark room and rejoin humanity. From the look on Sergeant Black's face, he only guessed that there would be a heated argument between him and the professor later.

The next day Adam was given a new suit to wear. He allowed himself an extra-long shower, and it didn't take him long to figure out how to get into these clothes. In front of the small bathroom mirror he studied himself and was pleased with his reflection.

Later, dressed and having carefully combed his dark brown hair, he met the professor in the bedroom. Florentine gave Adam a pair of dark shoes and instructed him how to put them on.

Florentine smiled proudly when they were finished. "Today you walk out of here free. I'm glad that you didn't take long to get over what you saw."

"I had to see it," Adam nodded. "Besides, I'm over that now, and there's no point dwelling on it, is there? I have to admit that if I'm kept here for much longer, I might actually go a little crazy."

"That doesn't sound reassuring," Thomas spoke up from where he leaned against the closed door. There was a smirk on his face that allowed Adam to relax somewhat.

Adam didn't say anything back to him, but his eyes did dart to the shackles the man held loosely in his right hand. He looked up with a silent question.

"The professor and I compromised," Thomas said. "You aren't leaving this room unless I have you secured."

Adam wanted to make a snide remark about how the sour sergeant would be the last person he'd consider devouring, but decided to keep his mouth shut for now. No sense in ruining his one chance to prove to everyone that he was changed; that he was one of them. Warmth crawled against his skin, and he loathed the fact that he had to prove himself at all.

"Aren't you afraid to go out there?" the professor asked.

"He should be," Thomas scoffed. "They'll eat you alive out there before they give him a chance." His neck went red. "Sorry, I didn't mean it like that."

"I am afraid," Adam answered. "I'm terrified of what's out there, but I have to go. I can't live like this forever."

Thomas bound Adam's hands in the heavy gloves. To Adam, the weight felt like nothing compared to the exhilarating flutter in his stomach. With his head held up, and his fears reigned in, he waited as the door was opened before him. Warm light flooded through, temporarily blinding, but welcoming him kindly back into the new world.

* * * *

Adam, Florentine, and Thomas wove their way through a maze of seemingly endless hallways. Three others joined the entourage and he recognized them from the video as being members of Thomas' squad. They were all armed, and they looked at him with expressions of uncertainty and fear.

The halls were wide and filled with a common sterile look of Berber carpets and white walls. Soft light from above illuminated their surroundings as they passed by many more closed doors and windows. Most of the windows showed him dark offices and other labs. Some of the windows were larger than others, and some were hidden by closed shutters. He wondered where all of the other scientists were, and figured that perhaps the sergeant had evacuated the rest of the facility just for this day.

"I don't like this one bit," Thomas said to the professor as they both walked ahead of Adam. "This sideshow of yours is going to cause a riot."

Florentine shot Thomas a look. "I informed the mayor and the council. They will all be there when we arrive. We have to show them what we've accomplished. I don't care if you don't fully believe yet, but Adam is human. He is one of us."

The sergeant took a quick look behind him and eyed Adam with a conflicted look that was both suspicious and confused.

The hallway ended at a pair of doors that slid open as the professor pressed his palm against a panel protruding from the nearby wall. What they entered was a much larger chamber with a tiled floor and tall walls painted a deep yet soothing purple. An empty crescent shaped reception desk sat in the middle of the spacious area.

Adam looked around, for the first time a little nervous. "Where is everyone?"

Florentine smiled and motioned him across the room to the far wall, where another door sat quietly. He looked to Adam, and then pressed him palm against the panel. The portal slid open with a low rush of air and Adam beheld this world's society for the first time.

Adam staggered back at the sight. A crowd had already gathered beyond the wide glass walls of the front of the building. Word had spread quickly of the professor's big reveal, and they had gathered into a large throng that reminded Adam of a mob. He was astounded to see so many people.

The portal had opened up to a great courtyard in the center of an intersection of roads, surrounded by buildings of all sizes. Nestled in its middle of the courtyard was a tall and wide circular fountain with a very distinct statue rising above the pool of water. It was a sculpture of an old man holding a young boy's hand, and they seemed to be walking towards a yet unknown destination. Behind them trailed a large German Shepherd, its tongue hanging out, and its eyes fixed upon the backs of its owners.

Adam looked up at the cloudy blue sky that hung above them for the first time since his return to the human race. He recalled the last time he'd seen the sky its color being much redder. The sight of it now stole his breath with wonder.

"Welcome to New Edmonton," Florentine proclaimed with great pride.

Adam swallowed. "Incredible."

"Oh yes, my friend. You're standing amongst one of the last outposts of mankind."

Adam did not look away from the sky. "But how? How did you build all this?"

"It was a terrible undertaking, but I can't take the credit for it. My great grandfather and his peers were a few of its founders. During the beginnings of its reconstruction, my parents were still children."

He turned to face Adam fully

"Mankind wasn't as weak and unprepared as many thought. Some of us were organized. My family had a lot of political influence in the old world. One of my ancestors had been a general in the army in the old world. My great grandfather, his descendant, was one of the first to propose the idea of building over the ruins of downtown Edmonton. So many died, but somehow we managed, and here we are.

"Over the years word got out about this city, and as more survivors arrived, its expansion grew faster and easier. We are still adding more sections even to this day. We've established our own economy, political structure, and organized a sufficient military force to protect us from the infected. Sergeant Black commands a small team called Sparrow Company. There are many others patrolling these streets hourly, and scouting in the world beyond this city's protective walls."

Adam stared at the professor. "I don't believe it," he said.

"That's what most everyone says when they see this place for the first time," the young driver from the video, Isaac Tennant, added as he stepped closer. "It's how I reacted when I got here a few years ago."

"Professor," Black growled, drawing everyone's attention to what he was looking at.

Adam and the professor, as if having completely forgotten about the assembled mob, took full notice of them now. Their faces all carried looks of concern and fear. It drove a dagger of ice into Adam's heart, instilling him with a sense of fear that he couldn't ignore.

Months before Sergeant Black had shot down the creature who would become the first subject, Florentine's project had been announced to the public. At first, New Edmonton's leaders debated on whether or not it was wise to inform the people; however, in the end it was decided that the people's morale was so low that it was worth lifting up their spirits with the hope and possibilities the Charon Initiative project could bring.

Now, a hint of fear began to grow amongst those assembled. It would only take a single mistake to end the lives they had here. That one mistake could be the end of everything they'd worked so hard to build. People began to shift uneasily as their stares melted from curious to hostile.

Adam sorted through the heated conversations, and sweat began to collect on the skin of his brow. A lot of what he heard was laced with fear and dread. Adam could sympathize with their feelings. But what could he possibly do to hurt these people? He was no more a danger to them than their own neighbors might be. These soldiers were more dangerous with their guns and weapons.

It wasn't fair.

Florentine had his arms up, speaking, He could barely be heard over the growing clangor of the crowd. When the large mass of the crowd began to push forward, the soldiers fought to keep the rabble back, barking at them to ease off. The situation was quickly getting out of hand and the professor had no clue how to stop it. Perhaps even he had miscalculated how the citizens of New Edmonton would react towards his reveal.

A chorus of curses and accusations assaulted Adam as the crowd pressed forward.

"I'm not letting him near my family, my kids!" a woman shouted.

"What if he turns back?"

"He doesn't look cured..."

"If he's safe, then why the armed escort?"

"Murderer!"

"Get him out of here!"

The accusations stunned Adam. He never asked for any of this; he never wished to be turned into a monster in the first place. The onslaught brought on a slew of questions about himself. Who the hell was he anyways? Did he even have a family, and if so, where were they now? Were they even still alive? Another terrible thought slithered into the back of his mind: Had he eventually turned upon those that he'd loved and murdered them?

"Please," he tried to make himself be heard. "I don't want to hurt anyone."

They couldn't hear him. Perhaps they didn't want to hear him.

Sergeant Black observed the shackled man with a dark expression. Over the last few months he'd watched this creature change, crawl out from what it once had been, and fought to regain as much of his humanity as he could. He fought hard, and Black saw that now. The sergeant groaned and took a step towards the gathered crowd.

"Everyone, shut the *fuck up*!" his voice rose to an incredible volume. His deep-toned shout suddenly quieted everyone in one swoop. "You bunch of assholes! Turning on each other like animals! You're no better than those things outside!"

He broke away from his squad's formation and moved his massive bulk to front of Adam. Without pause he freed Adam from his bonds. Some of the crowd gasped, and as the sergeant tossed the heavy metal gauntlets angrily to the walkway, the throng waited anxiously to see what was going to happen next. The sergeant saw it in their eyes that some of them actually expected Adam to suddenly go on a rampage.

But that didn't happen. Instead, Adam massaged his cold

wrists and regarded the sergeant with shocked eyes.

"Sergeant, I…"

"Don't mention it," Thomas growled. "I've watched you change over a long period of time now, but I'm a very stubborn man. The professor was right; his serum is a miracle cure."

Thomas' eyes squinted as if the words were hard for even him to get out. "I'm sorry, Adam. I should have given you more of a chance."

Tears slowly rolled down Adam's face. He couldn't help himself, and he didn't care how it made him look in front of all these others. He was so moved that even a person like the sergeant, who had mistrusted him since the beginning, would now decide to put some faith in him and in the professor's project.

"I don't want to hurt anyone. I never did."

The sergeant turned to the professor, who was smiling at him in return with radiant pride.

"You were right, old man," Thomas sighed. "We can be saved, and it's all because of you."

We can be saved the sergeant had said. That was all the people needed to really hear. They looked from the sergeant back to Adam with renewed interest, and awed respect. The sergeant was their protector, the one who went outside. If he said that this man was their salvation, even with the slight chance of success, it was enough to grasp to. It wouldn't be a stretch to imagine that Professor Florentine Mena had hoped for something like this from the very beginning, that he could trust Black to do the right thing.

The first success born from the experiments of the Charon Initiative had arrived, and it changed the face of civilization forever. Now there was just a little more to hope for in this new world.

Part Two
Adam And Sparrow Company

"I think we found our second subject, folks. I think this is her."

Chapter Eight

All across his field of vision, Adam took in the great breadth of the grassy open plains. Untouched by the hands of man for many years, the vast stretch of land continued on seemingly without end. This was something he didn't expect to see outside of New Edmonton. Before actually seeing the land outside his dark room, he'd assumed that the world would be covered in nothing but dry, decayed landscapes of death. Instead what he saw before him was more beautiful than anything that had been described in any of the books he'd read. This was something else, something wondrous and grand, and he wanted to stand out here for the rest of the afternoon and just take it all in.

It was very different from the way he'd seen the world only a short time ago. Flickering images and scattered memories as his life as one of *them* lingered in his thoughts like unwanted guests. One of the most prominent aspects of his old life was that he'd seen the world through a red lens that painted the world in shades of crimson. Now he saw the earth as it truly was, painted in rich colors and sights that sent a tremor through his heart.

Sadness clung onto his soul because of what had happened to him. He suspected that the pain would always be there, but now there was something more. He was given a new chance at life, and even though his past was still a mystery to him, he would stop at nothing to hang onto this life. The promise of happiness flickered in his heart like a small but strong flame. He nurtured this feeling of hope, held tight to it, but hid it from the others all the same.

The people he was with were his saviors, He still didn't know them very well. He wanted to reach out to them, to form connections with real, living people, but right now he was still wary of any contact. He supposed that one day he would become used to opening himself up to others, but for now he wanted to keep it all locked away inside.

Rolling hills dotted the landscape, and a warm wind blew across the azure grasslands covering it. The emerald sea wavered back and forth, moving in all directions, as if possessed of a life of its own. He saw the edges of a wide forest in the great distance.

The air was silent except for the faint sound of the winds against his ears.

The sun shone down upon Adam, making him sweat underneath this dark combat uniform. He didn't mind this feeling because it made him feel alive. The weight of his Sharpe-73 Assault Rifle was a welcome weight against his left shoulder. A soft, cool breeze brushed against his bare face, gently ruffling through his short cut spiky brown hair.

Somewhere out there the dead continued to hunt, roaming those very same beautiful lands, mindlessly destroying whatever living thing they happened upon. Adam wondered if any animals still existed out there, or if mankind was now truly alone—save for the dead.

The contrast between what he was seeing and knowing that there was so much darkness in this world baffled him.

When would the dead come out to greet him? Were they somewhere out there, hiding in the tall grass, watching him and his allies as they gnashed their gums hungrily? Mindless creatures didn't plan, so he knew they weren't out there hiding like a wiser creature would. He couldn't help feeling exposed, that he was in fact being watched by something. A cold shiver ran through his arms, up his shoulders, and across the base of his neck. Once again, he was glad for the warm touch of the overhead sun.

His mind began to wander to the dreams he'd been having for the past few weeks. In his sleep he sometimes envisioned the same woman, with her dark hair blowing in the wind. She was always accompanied by a young boy, who looked to be around seven years old. Sometimes their faces were dirty, covered in soot and ash, and he watched them as they ran through the streets populated with ruined vehicles and...

Adam brushed his hand across his face. As always, when he thought of these dreams his chest would begin to ache. Something inside of him hurt, something that reached out to those two figures in his mind, making him feel depths of sorrow he couldn't explain. He began to wonder if these dreams were a window into the past that still eluded him. Were the woman and the child important to him, and if so, what had happened to them? Adam wished he knew the answer.

During his talks with the professor, the both of them had tried to figure out ways to pierce the cloudy veil that still shrouded his past life. So far nothing they'd tried had been able to help. Florentine was still confident that Adam's regenerated brain would one day be able to restore the rest of his memories. Just as Adam's speech had returned to him, Florentine believed that the memories would one day reveal themselves to him. Adam, however, was growing less optimistic and patient and as the weeks passed he grew less hopeful.

"Private, we're ready to move out," the sergeant called to Adam from behind.

Adam turned to face Sergeant Thomas Black, his new commander, and the leader of Sparrow Company. The man's grizzled face regarded him with the stern look of a true veteran officer. There was also respect in those eyes, and something else darker that Adam couldn't read.

Adam soon discovered that, although he was a human being once more, it was almost impossible to find a place for himself in New Edmonton's society. For a while he had held a job in the professor's library–one that was larger than Adam could have imagined–He soon discovered that hiding himself behind shelves of old books wasn't a place he felt he belonged. The citizens of New Edmonton looked to him for inspiration and hope, but there were still those that looked upon him with suspicion and fear. Adam couldn't fault them for this, but it also meant that he was becoming more and more ostracized from those that should be his equals.

There had been days he'd spent a portion of his afternoons looking at the world atop one of the city's great walls. He'd watched as military APC's left and returned from through the wall's heavily secured gates. Sometimes, he had spotted Thomas' group returning from another mission and he'd felt a strong desire to go out into that world and do something meaningful with his new life.

The more he read through the professor's history books, the more he desired his own adventures and to be free of the heavy, concrete walls. At first the thought of facing one of the undead on the outside terrified him, but that feeling soon subsided the more he watched the brave soldiers going beyond the wall, sent on whatever missions they'd been assigned.

A request to the professor, and a short meeting with Thomas was all that was required to grant Adam a position in Sparrow Company. Now, here he was a defender of one of the last havens of mankind; he'd finally found a place he felt he could really belong. Thomas was taking a big chance in allowing Adam onto his team, but the world was short on people willing to join the army, and the sergeant trusted Florentine and had decided to let the first subject try.

Life amongst the company wasn't as neat and rosy as he'd hoped, however. Jenny and Isaac had taken a liking to him shortly after his reveal to the citizens of New Edmonton. Thomas treated him with respect, but there was still a vast gulf between them that would take longer to shorten.

Danny was an entirely different matter altogether. The man shared a lot of the fears that many in New Edmonton felt towards Adam and his supposed full recovery. Danny's mistrust towards Adam was plain and open for all to see, and he did not seem willing to give him a chance. There was no friendship between the two save for a mutual respect shared between fellow soldiers in war.

Thomas' eyes shot fully open, and he raised his rifle to point its sight somewhere above Adam's right shoulder. The rifle's muzzle flashed once as a sharp crack ripped through the air. Something flew close past Adam's left ear, zipping by with blinding speed and leaving him momentarily stunned. A groan lifted up into the air, and something heavy collapsed upon the grassy earth.

Adam spun to face the fresh kill behind him. He took a moment longer than the sergeant to ready his gun, still learning how to use the weapon, but within seconds he was looking through the powerful lens of his scope towards the felled target. A large mound of flesh and decay lay face down in the dirt. The creature, a man who had been an overweight individual during the time of his death, lay unmoving. A gaping bloody wound marred the back of its head, marking where the single round had made its exit.

Adam looked up from the still corpse as two creatures, one female and the other male, shuffled over the fallen body and trod toward them.

Adam fought to steady his aim, sucked in a breath, and then pulled the trigger. The silencer masked most of the gunshot noise, and the round flew past without hitting either of the two targets. Adam hissed under his breath and fired another round. The chest of the male zombie exploded in a shower of fleshy gore and crashed onto its back upon the grass. Beside him, Thomas fired another shot that instantly took down the female on the left. Once more his aim proved far better than Adam's as half of the woman's face was shredded by the bullet before she fell onto the ground.

"Not bad," Thomas managed to make the compliment sound threatening as he walked past Adam.

They both secured their rifles as they walked towards the

bodies. Behind them Jenny and Danny both flew out the open hatch of the APC, guns at the ready.

"Are you alright, sir?" Jenny called out.

"Everything's under control," he barked as he raised a hand over his head to wave her off.

The four members of Sparrow Company gathered around the corpses. The rotting stench of the undead rose up and assaulted Adam's senses. It was the first time he'd been up close and personal with one, let alone three of them together. The warm sun above lit the gnarled and horrid faces of the dead, twisting them into grotesque masks that barely resembled the human beings they once were. It was a stark and disturbing contrast to see such terrible savagery under the light of day, surrounded by grasslands he recently thought of as beautiful.

"Good work," Thomas looked up at him.

Adam replied with a halfhearted smile. It was the first time he'd ever killed anything in this life—at least since he'd become human again. Even though these creatures were no longer considered human beings, an uneasy feeling settled in the pit of his stomach. Regardless of what it now was, he had killed it, and it left him feeling unsettled. He swallowed down the bile that rose in his throat.

"How many did you get?" Jenny asked excitedly.

"Just this guy," he pointed to the thing he now realized had long ago lost both of its arms.

"You couldn't get him in the head?" Danny scoffed.

"Leave him alone," Jenny responded. "This was his first time."

"Enough," the sergeant said angrily, and then glanced back at his newest recruit. "Like I said, good job."

"Thanks, Black," Adam replied with half a heart.

"Well, can we use any of 'em?" Danny shrugged.

"None of these three look like a viable subject," Jenny answered, before gesturing to each one of the corpses. "This one's missing both arms, this girl's missing half of her face, and the fat guy..."

"We'd have a hell of a time squeezing him in the professor's glass tube," Danny chuckled.

Jenny laughed as well, and even the sergeant's grizzled face hinted with a ghost of a smile. Only Adam remained silent, worried he would draw any more of Danny's contempt.

"In any case," the sergeant began after clearing his throat. "The professor asked us to find him a live specimen."

"Live, sir?" Danny's left eyebrow arched upwards. He shot Adam a dark look.

"You know what I mean," Thomas growled. "The professor believes that the subjects need to be..."

"Animated," Adam offered.

"Yeah, the professor needs *animated* bodies to use in his experiments. I don't understand the specifics of why, but for now he refuses to use the procedure on a cold corpse."

"That settles it, then," Danny interjected. He glanced over at Adam and scowled; however, after a moment his heated emotions seemed to subside somewhat and his glare relaxed a little. "Good work on your first kill, new guy."

And with that he turned and began to walk back towards the APC. Thomas and Jenny followed while Adam remained behind.

He looked down into the face of the creature he'd killed. The body was discolored and the skin bubbled and portions were missing in places, showing strips of missing hair and ripped muscles. The man's jaws were locked open, revealing black and decayed gums that had lost almost half of their teeth, leaving blackened protrusions that stuck out at odd angles that Adam imagined was even now coated in the mysterious virus that had almost wiped mankind from the face of the earth. How many people had these venomous teeth devoured?

Adam shuddered at the thought, and when he looked into the middle-aged man's cold, glazed eyes he reminded himself that not long ago he had been just like this thing.

How many people had he unknowingly killed?

The hand, which held the grip of his rifle, shook and his heart began to hammer madly beneath his heaving chest. The cold fingers of creeping madness circled around Adam's heart. There was no doubt in his mind that he had killed and fed upon other human beings. The thought of crouching over the fresh corpse of a man or woman slithered into his thoughts like a poisonous snake. He imagined himself opening his jaws and exposing his rotted teeth before plunging them into another hunk of warm, stringy flesh.

He imagined the pure, rage-filled joy that filled his stomach along with the blood and flesh of his kill.

He jerked his head up, realizing the others would soon wonder what was taking him so long to follow them back to the APC. Adam pulled himself away from the precipice of madness, and he breathed in heavy gulps of air to calm himself. Slowly his trembling hands began to steady, and he composed himself in a way that he hoped would hide his sudden panic attack from the others.

Adam stared down at the lifeless zombie one last time. He wondered if he would ever escape this terrible guilt. With a heavy sigh, he peeled his gaze from the corpse's face and returned to the others.

Chapter Nine

When Adam woke in the APC a few hours later, he found that the sergeant had taken over for the driving. Isaac sat in his same seat, snoring lightly with one arm hanging over the side of the chair. Jenny was also fast asleep, with her head bowed forward. Danny surprised Adam a little as he held in one hand a copy of *The Coming of Conan* by Robert E. Howard. A small overhead light helped illuminate the pages in the shadows, which permeated the rest of the inner confines of the cabin.

Night had fallen outside, and it was near impossible to discern a single thing from the inky blackness blanketing the Albertan plains. The vehicle's low beam headlights pierced small slivers of the dark world ahead of them with white light. They were travelling on a highway road cracked and pitted from decades of no maintenance. The thin white lines on the highway had long since faded to pale remembrances of the old world. The APC rumbled and shook from the deep potholes and uneven cracks. It'd been the sharp bumps that had roused Adam from his sleep, and he was impressed that Isaac and Jenny were still able to sleep in this. Perhaps they were just used to this kind of life now. Adam couldn't help but feel a pall of sadness for them knowing that this life might just be the only one any of these people knew.

This was their life and now it was going to be his. Even now he did not regret his decision to join this company. He had chosen this path; for some reason he had longed for this loneliness, to be away from the city and the remnants of human civilization that dwelt within. Perhaps he'd wanted to face these creatures himself, on his own terms, and to stare into the faces of the things that he had once been. Maybe he hoped that somewhere out here he would find some answers to the things that still haunted him almost every night of his new life. Another part of him wanted to repay what the professor gave back to him by finding another usable subject.

"Have you ever been to Canmore?" Danny asked suddenly, although he didn't remove his eyes from the pages of his book. He flipped a page and continued reading while he waited for Adam's answer.

"I don't know," Adam answered. "Maybe I did...before."

Danny glanced up at him for an instant before returning to his careful study of the pages in front of him. In that brief look Adam thought that he'd caught a hint of regret, He couldn't be sure. Ever since he'd joined Sergeant Thomas Black's squad, the man in front of him had shown him little else but open hostility towards his presence.

"Yeah, I forgot that you don't have your memories," Danny muttered. It almost sounded like an apology, but it was very difficult for Adam to tell.

"Don't worry about it," he said as he lowered his gaze to the scratched up surface of the cabin's metal floor.

His thoughts momentarily drifted to the nightmares and dreams that chased after him in the night.

Jenny, having been roused from her sleep by their voices, smiled warmly at Adam.

"So, have any of you been to Canmore before?" Adam asked them.

"Been there a few times," Jenny answered. "Normally we don't go out that far on our missions, but this week we're going to give it another visit."

"Any reason why?"

"Other than our search for another subject, we have to check out a few things there concerning communication with one of our safe houses. Also, it's one of the safer places to visit. For some reason they don't seem to take to the cold very well. A few don't seem to mind, but for the most part they shy away from places with lower temperatures. It's part of the reason why the earliest survivors came north to Canada before founding New Edmonton and Himura Valley."

"I can't believe that there's another city besides New Edmonton," Adam said mostly to himself.

"Yeah," Jenny smiled. "It's good to know that the cities are linked by the Romero Bridge. If anything were to happen to either one of the cities, at least the civilians can travel across the bridge to safety on the other side.

Setting up the protective walls around the old downtown sector of Edmonton was a monumental task that had nearly taken five years to complete. The survivors and founders of this protective haven had then spent nearly a decade after completing the wall establishing their new way of life within these great walls.

Because much of the city's downtown area was built upon a large hillside, it was easier to establish this new civilization in a place where the undead would have a harder time reaching. In this case, the zombies didn't take too well with climbing steep slopes, while their meals rained down with rocks or bullets from above.

It was later, when the professor's ancestors had reinvented radio communication, that they were shocked to discover they were not the only new city to establish itself in the province of Alberta. After initial relations had been established, it was deemed that New Edmonton and the city to the far east, called Himura Valley, should be connected by a giant bridge, which would be raised above the level of the plains to protect its travelers from the creatures that might lurk below.

The Romero Bridge, strangely named after a long dead director of zombie movies, was designed to accommodate two tracks upon which could ride a system of trains that would make travelling between both cities easier and faster. This task alone had taken over twenty years to accomplish, but when the bridge had been finally deemed operational, it had solidified the friendship between the twin cities.

* * * *

When dawn arrived the next morning, Isaac was back in control of the APC.

They had come to a stop on the side of the highway, the front of the vehicle facing the remains of a very old, but very large two story farmhouse. In the distance were the trace remnants of a fence and beyond that the collapsed roof of an ancient barn. The house sat as still as the dead, silhouetted by the glow of the rising sun that painted the sky with swaths of oranges and reds. A lone wooden pole stood just beside the APC, and on the long grass Adam could discern a mailbox that had since fallen off from its place long ago.

The crew sat in silence for a while, watching the house, while the sergeant contemplated his next move.

"What are we doing here?" Adam decided to break the tense silence.

"We're making a little stop first," Danny said curtly.

"We passed by this house a few months ago," Jenny elaborated. "We didn't have time to stop here before."

"Okay," Adam raised his brows. "But why are we here?"

"It's our job to make sure if there's anyone in there that might need help," Thomas finally spoke from where he sat up front. "If there are any survivors, then we offer to take them with us to New Edmonton. If there are only undead, we kill them or take them back with us for the professor. We clear the home, and when we're done we burn it down to make sure nobody else strays in there by accident and find themselves trapped."

Adam nodded. "So what's the plan then?"

"Just full of questions, aren't you?" Danny said. "Let the boss think it through first."

"I already have," Thomas declared.

He turned to face the three waiting in the rear of the APC.

"Tennant will stay with the vehicle as usual."

Beside him, the young man let out a frustrated groan. Danny and Jenny shared a smile with one another, and Adam guessed that this decision had been made concerning the youngest member of their team on more than one occasion.

"Danny, I want you to hang back and protect the vehicle. Set up a patrol around the APC, and make damn sure nothing waltzes into the front door of that house after we've gone in."

"You got it," the man saluted with obvious pride, and perhaps a little relief.

"Adam and Jenny, you're both with me."

Isaac opened the side hatch of the vehicle, which slid aside with the help of its motorized hinges. He stepped out after Thomas, while Jenny followed behind him. More than once, Adam checked to make sure that he had a fresh magazine loaded in his rifle. His eyes scanned his surroundings with worry, and he made sure to pay careful attention to the waist-high grass that rose around the perimeter of the large home.

"The second floor looks surprisingly intact," Jenny said after a moment, "but I can't guarantee its stability."

"Can you handle it?" Thomas asked.

"Well, we do need to clear it all out before we burn it down, don't we?"

Thomas returned with a respectful nod at her direction.

Then the three of them shouldered their rifles and advanced towards the front of the old house. The floorboards of the short flight of steps creaked loudly, the screech of rusted nails grating in their ears and setting Adam on edge. The porch fared no better, and every groan and creak sent jolts of fright across Adam's skin.

Thomas took the lead, nodded to the two behind him, and

gave a swift front kick to the rickety front door. The door swung inwards and Thomas strode into the dimly-lit hallway beyond. Jenny and Adam followed.

Filtered light from dust-caked windows illuminated the foyer in a pale, yellow glow. Faded family photos hung in frames on the walls to either side. The picture quality had degraded so much that the faces of the figures portrayed had become indistinguishable. The images, with their faceless occupants, took on a ghostly, haunted quality. A family huddled together in one of them—two parents and a child—and a strange feeling crawled up against the length of Adam's spine. The almost featureless faces stared back at him, and Adam had to turn his gaze away.

The living room was filled with more photographs. Two chairs and a sofa sat against this room's walls, their surfaces covered in dust and their inside stuffing and springs spilling out from tears on all sides. Overturned furniture and broken vases littered the floor. Adam carefully watched his step as he passed over the broken remains of a child's wooden rocking horse. Jenny cleared the adjoining dining room before returning to the living room.

"Nice home," Jenny commented gravely.

"The stairs look solid enough," Thomas said. "Okay Jenny, proceed with caution. I'll take the rooms on the ground floor, and Adam, you can take the basement."

"Thanks, sergeant," Adam smirked at the man.

"Move it, newbie," Thomas grinned back at him.

They went about their separate ways, and Adam made his way to the door leading to the basement. To his dismay, the door stood partially open, the crack revealing to him only an inky darkness beyond. Adam flicked on the front mounted torch on his rifle and reached out to grasp the brass door knob slowly. The top of it was covered in a thick layer of dust. As he swung it open, the door let out a teeth jarring squeal that filled the hallway with its frightening cry. His rifle torch illuminated what Adam felt was an extremely small circle on the stairway leading down. He swung its light around for a bit, making sure that nothing waited for him on the lower floor below. Around the corner of the stairway, soft light hinted from somewhere below, just beyond his view.

The boards of the stairway strained under his weight. He wasn't a very heavy man—probably nearly half of the sergeant—and the way that the boards bent under his feet made him even more wary about the age and sturdiness of the place. Step by step, he made his way down into the basement, the darkness closing in and threatening to choke him. He halted on the bottom step, inhaling the musty air and looking around.

Boxes and old furniture waited for him below, sitting comfortably against the far walls. Two dirt-caked windows against the right wall let in some of the morning sunlight. Cobwebs hung from a forest of lamps gathered in the far corner. A crackled movie poster from an old western flick hung against one of the walls, facing the collapsed remains of a filthy looking pool table.

Adam stepped onto the concrete floor and immediately began to shower his surroundings with his torch light. There were pools of dried blood just beyond the foot of the stairs, old and caked, and leading to the more shadowy parts of the L-shaped basement to his right.

A cold prickly touch rushed up against the back of his neck and chilled the top of his scalp. His light trailed along the length of the dried blood and rose up to reveal more boxes and a small mountain of stacked tables and chairs. Other odds and ends stood beside that mountain; cast off items that had belonged to the small family that once lived in this place. Adam squinted his eyes and noticed something peculiar lying within that messy pile. As he listened to his companions searching rooms up above, Adam began to step towards what looked like a dried up hand rising from behind the tables and chairs.

It stood unmoving, as still as death, and as he rounded the corner he discovered what was indeed a long dead corpse wearing a white blouse and a dark skirt. Adam's spirits fell somewhat as he stared upon the dried up, eyeless face of the dead woman. He wondered if it was the mother that he had seen in the photos upstairs. This corpse's face had become so decayed that what she might have looked like in life was now left only to his imagination. She lay within the forgotten belongings of this household, and her eyeless sockets were cast downwards upon her chest. Dried dark stains covered her once pretty white blouse. Adam lowered his rifle and a crestfallen expression shrouded his features as he continued to gaze upon the lifeless corpse.

Adam heard heavy footsteps coming partway down the stairs and a large shadow obscured most of the light filtering down from above.

"The first floor's clear," the sergeant called down to him. "There's not much to check. Just the usual abandoned rooms, signs of previous family life. How are things looking down here?"

"I found a body," Adam replied.

"Dead?"

"Definitely. It looks like she died a long time ago."

Thomas was silent for a time before telling Adam that he could take his time to finish up before meeting them back upstairs. The man's heavy footsteps receded back up to the first floor, leaving Adam alone once more with the lifeless corpse. He took one more wary glance at the body and swung his light over to investigate the rest of the basement. It was exactly as he'd expected it to be. There was nothing left here but the memories of life from the old world, more than two hundred years ago.

Were there other places around the world where humans had made a safe haven for themselves? The professor had explained to him previously that one of the last remnants to survive the old world were its satellite systems, but because they had to pretty much build most of their equipment from scratch, it was a massive undertaking to even be able to regain communication with the orbiting remnants of the old world. Even then, they had received no word from anywhere else from the rest of the world. But that alone did not mean that there were no other cities out there. Perhaps they had simply been unable to reach the technological levels that New Edmonton and its sister city have yet.

Something shuffled behind Adam. Wooden chair legs scraped loudly against the concrete floor.

Adam's hackles rose, and he spun around as terror seized his heart and flooded him with horrifying images and fears. The torch light illuminated a familiar figure, one wearing a skirt and a bloodied blouse. He'd been wrong about the dead woman.

The corpse shuffled towards him with alarming speed, and though she had no eyes with which to see him, there was no doubt that the monster knew exactly where he was.

His scream froze in his throat. He raised his rifle but the undead creature was just too fast. He was pushed back as dry, dusty hands grabbed a hold of the shoulders of his uniform jacket. The strength in the creature was shocking, and it pushed against him until he tripped on something that was lying on the floor behind him.

The breath was stolen from his lungs as Adam's back slammed painfully against the cold and dirty floor. The object, which had tripped him from behind, pushed itself against the back of his ankles, shooting pain through his legs like warm fire as the creature threw its full weight against his body. The leathery skin on its cheeks split with sickening, audible crackling sounds as it opened its withered jaws. For a moment it was like he was staring down into a hollow darkness with no end.

He'd lost his rifle in the fall, and he grasped the dead woman by her bony shoulders as she tried to force her teeth on his neck. Her jaws were mere inches from his neckline and her gaping maw dripped with putrid fumes of decaying blood and rot.

Fighting with disorientation from the fall, and using every ounce of strength left in him, Adam pushed against the corpse hard and flung it away from him suddenly as if he had just tossed something that weighed little more than the weight of a thick book. The creature flailed comically for a brief moment in the air before she crashed down in a cloud of dust a few meters away from him. Adam sat still for a moment, shocked. He'd thrown her as if she weighed almost nothing—something that shouldn't have been possible.

Then the creature was moving again, trying desperately to bring itself back onto its feet. Adam snapped himself out of his shocked state and he crawled quickly over to the sliver of lamp light illuminating a part of the floor to his right. The creature was back on its feet and it lumbered after him with terrifying agility. Adam twisted himself on the floor as he took hold of his gun. Instinctively he aimed the barrel at the creature and pulled the trigger. The rapport of the silenced rounds echoed in the large basement. Five rounds tore into the monster, throwing it back as its chest exploded from the blasts. The creature landed about a meter away, but it was still active, and it flailed as it tried to get back to its feet once more.

Adam rose, and as he heard hurried footsteps racing down the basement steps, he finished the zombie off with two shots right into the front of her scalp. Dried hunks of brain matter flew outwards along with shattered pieces of scalp and bone. The thing finally stopped moving, and it lay still and at rest. Its head, and its dry contents, reminded him of a broken clay jar.

"Jesus," Jenny exclaimed as she and the sergeant joined Adam.

Adam breathed hard as his heart continued to race. He felt his body electrified with adrenaline. He bent over his knees as his vision swam in swirls of white and red.

The sergeant glared hotly at him as he moved his gaze from the corpse to the new recruit.

"I thought you said she was dead."

Adam shook his head, trying to settle his churning stomach. "I thought she was...I didn't know."

The sergeant's expression softened somewhat, and a look of relief melted away some of the hardness from his face.

"Are you alright?" he finally asked. "Did it bite or scratch you anywhere?"

Adam shook his head. His heart rate was finally slowing down, and he blinked a few times as he began to replay the events through his mind. How had he thrown the creature so easily from him? Where did that strength come from?

"Jenny, make one more sweep of the basement and make sure there's nothing else down here," the sergeant commanded. He motioned to Adam. "Adam, let's get you out of here."

* * * *

As he stood a few yards away from the home, Adam gazed silently as he watched it burn underneath the bright afternoon sunlight. Beside him stood his squad mates, and behind them waited the armored vehicle. The house's ancient foundations crumbled in minutes beneath the searing heat of the flames, and loud crashes filled the air as the old home collapsed beneath the billowing cloud of black smoke. The memories of those that had once occupied that home turned to ashes along with the corpse of a woman who might have been the mother in the photos he had seen. The nightmares that had fallen upon that nameless family were finally being put to rest, and Adam watched as the remnants of the family were being reduced to nothing more than ashes and dust.

His thoughts were filled with troubling questions about what had happened in the basement. The others, when they looked at him, assumed that he was quiet because of his harrowing experience with one of the undead. He was silent because of how he had been able to throw the corpse from off of him so easily. No human could have done what he did, and he began to wonder if the professor's cure was as successful as the man hoped that it was.

Adam remembered how strong the thing had been, even though its body was pretty much reduced to nothing more than leathery strips of flesh and atrophied muscle tissue. The zombie's strength had been astounding.

And so was his.

Chapter Ten

The death of the zombie woman, and how he managed to defeat it, continued to haunt Adam. The APC possessed the ability to communicate with the city of New Edmonton, He wanted to have a private talk with Florentine. Though he knew he would have to wait until they got back to the city before he could tell the professor what happened back at the old family home.

The vehicle continued to make its way towards Canmore, and the afternoon sun hung strong in the sky by the time the mountains began to rise and dominate much of the view ahead. The Rocky Mountains rose up high into the sky with white capped peaks and hillsides covered in loose rocks and sparse vegetation. Portions of the slopes were covered in dense patches of forest. The air held a slight chill that hinted of the harsh winters that occasionally covered these lands. No undead could be seen, but the forests surrounding the highway were sinister and dark. Anything could be hiding within those shadows. The eerie sight of the woods lent a haunted feeling to their surroundings, filling Adam's head with thoughts of monstrous corpses prowling through thick brush, aimlessly searching for something to eat.

"We'll be there soon," Isaac declared. "So, what's the plan boss?"

"We haven't been here for some time, but do you remember that hotel we stayed in last time?"

"Setting course for New Haven," Isaac grinned as he pressed his foot heavier on the gas.

The vehicle launched forward with greater speed and the view outside zoomed past. A smile grew on Danny's face as the cabin bumped and lurched forward. Adam grasped his fingers around the overhead handle bar tightly. They curved along winding roads and the view of the mountains grew more majestic as they gradually drew closer to them. The turns were sometimes frighteningly sharp, but Isaac handled the large vehicle like a natural, navigating the roads with surprising and impressive skill. It was like he'd been born to pilot the APC and nobody alive could drive it as well as he could.

The young man hooted aloud as they cleared a sharp left, just barely missing a large mound of boulders on their right. Isaac was in his element, enjoying this chance to cut loose for a little while out on the open road. Thomas didn't try to tell the man to slow down. Instead he grinned as his large form jostled in his seat following another sharp turn. Jenny, on the other hand, seemed to dislike the dangerous ride Held her complaints to herself.

* * * *

It wasn't long before the forest opened up around them, revealing a hilly landscape surrounded by a backdrop of looming mountains. Isaac gradually slowed the vehicle, gearing it down to a more comfortable speed. The highway rose up a steep hillside, which then split into three separate directions. Isaac took the exit and they were soon driving through a location the rusted, green highway sign indicated as *Three Sisters Drive*.

Adam held his breath as he viewed the city of Canmore for the first time. It lay far ahead and up the road, and even from their distance they saw that several structures still appeared intact, hovering above the desiccated ruins. Without anyone to be around to maintain the city, it naturally began to decay, slowly being retaken by the earth. Vines and overgrown brush left the confines of the forest and parks to creep in on the cracked city streets and lower lying rubble. A wide river flowed far to the right, and he saw a bridge leading up over that river and into the heart of the small city.

They drove slowly through silent neighborhoods where the lawns were overgrown pockets of wilderness, spilling out onto the sidewalks. The houses all around them were in varying states of disrepair, and none of the homes looked like they'd been occupied for centuries. Abandoned vehicles littered the streets, and Isaac had to carefully maneuver their large vehicle around these rusted hulks. The APC shook violently for a brief moment as they drove up on a sidewalk and over the grass, avoiding a rusted BMW and an overturned school bus that had collided years ago.

As they drove past the wreck, Adam saw a glimpse of a skull on the dashboard of the smashed car. He avoided looking into the darkened windows of the bus as they rolled past it; however, the thoughts about what might have occurred on that fateful day continued to form on the surface of his troubled thoughts. Had the plague already been in full effect when that bus driver had been transporting those poor children, or had they been on the road on what seemed like a normal day? What had caused the crash? The driver of the BMW might have been already infected when he'd left his home that morning, kissing his wife goodbye while wondering why his damn headache just wouldn't go away. Had he looked in his wife's eyes and seen the crimson veins surrounding the irises, making her look like she hadn't slept in days?

The very state of this neighborhood spoke of the chaos that had occurred here long ago. Frozen forever in time, it was a constant reminder of what had happened on the day the outbreak began to spread out of control. It weighed down on Adam's shoulders, crushing his chest as if held in a vice. He forced his eyes away from the bus, determined to move on.

As they continued to make their way through the outskirts of Canmore, the homes gave way to a road that rose up to a higher elevation. Soon they came upon another area filed with what had once been beautiful two story homes. They passed by a sign which read: *Welcome to New Haven.* All around them were more dilapidated houses, but these were far larger than any of the others he'd seen in the more domestic neighborhoods. Isaac parked the vehicle in front of a large two story dwelling.

"What is this place?" Adam asked.

"It was a resort for the wealthy way back in the old world," Jenny grinned.

Adam looked upon the home and gasped because the place was more of a mansion than some average house. The overgrown lawn was separated by a winding stone path, which led all the way up to the house's front doors. The doors themselves were very different than the usual rotting portals that he'd glimpsed in the ruins of the city. These doors were made of a dull looking metal, and seemed very much out of place with the rest of the structure. A small black panel was mounted against the wall on the right of the entryway and looked about the size of his palm. The windows on both levels were heavily barred on the outside, and metal shutters were closed shut just behind them. Adam was bewildered by the heavy security of this place. Even the outside of the home seemed relatively well kept, with its cream colored paint only hinting at a few decades of age.

"Welcome to your temporary home," Jenny said to Adam. "It's a safe house. The army has a few stationed in every city around New Edmonton. This is just one of three that we have kept and maintained in Canmore. So, what do you think?"

"I...I can't believe it."

"Well, you didn't really expect us to sleep in this small tank for the whole trip, did you?"

"To tell you the truth, I did," Adam smiled and nodded towards the large home. "I think this will do just fine."

They exited the vehicle together, accompanied this time with Isaac, who locked the armored door behind them. At first it was strange for Adam to see a rifle in the hands of a man who still looked so young, He suspected that Isaac knew how to handle the weapon as well as anyone else in the company. Isaac noticed Adam's stare, and he lifted the barrel of his rifle skyward and flicked the safety off on the weapon with a loud click. He nodded to Adam with a smirk.

Together they quickly made their way towards the home; all the while training their gun barrels around them to makes sure that the area was clear. Upon Thomas' signal, Jenny advanced ahead of the group and arrived at the steel doors first. A colorful digital interface flickered to life on the small dark panel Adam had noticed earlier. It seemed to react to Jenny's close proximity, switching itself on as soon as she stood in front of the panel. She keyed in a series of codes and a sharp click was heard beyond the reinforced doors. She pressed one final key, and suddenly the twin doors began to slide open at an agonizing crawl.

"I always hate how slow these damn things open," Danny complained.

Jenny smirked. "Do you have any idea how heavy each one of these doors really is?"

"Will you both shut up and keep a look-out?" Isaac growled.

"Kid, you are starting to sound more and more like the sergeant every day," Danny grinned.

When the portal was fully opened, Thomas signaled them into the house. The interior was heavily shrouded in darkness. Not a speck of light could filter through the metal shutters that closed off the windows of this place. They all flicked on their lamps as they filed into the main hallway. Another panel began to glow on the wall inside the hall. Jenny keyed in more commands and the door began to close shut behind them. As the powerful locks engaged, the interior lights of the home sprang to life, blinding Adam momentarily with its sudden and unexpected glare.

When his vision cleared, Adam discovered a cozy looking hallway, dusty beige carpeting, and walls that were completely bare of the family portraits and paintings that should have decorated its surface. Directly to his left was an opening leading into a large living room. Ahead of him was a wide staircase leading up to the second floor, and behind that appeared to be an entrance to a wide kitchen.

"I don't believe it," Adam gasped. Then he felt a little embarrassed as he realized that he must have said this line quite a bit now.

"Tennant and Danny, you take the second floor," Thomas ordered. "Jenny, you get the first. Adam, you and I clear the basement. Now, for the love of God, if you see a corpse, please make sure it's fucking dead this time."

The others, including Adam, chuckled before they split up to their assigned tasks. Even though the home was heavily secured, he understood the need to ensure that the area was free of any of the roaming dead.

Just in case.

* * * *

The home ran off powerful solar batteries located in the basement. These batteries were recharged constantly by the energy harnessed from the sun. The solar panels, Adam had been told, were located on the roof of the home, and were constantly monitored by automated systems controlled by the computers found in the basement. When he'd initially gone down there with the sergeant, he'd been stunned by what he'd found. Large white computer towers hummed softly against a wood paneled wall as a single monitor glowed within the gloom of the faintly lit room. The computers were used to monitor not only the condition of the solar panels, but to also monitor security around the perimeter of the home. Reports were sent back to New Edmonton on a timely basis, which the higher ups of the army would file away in whatever forgotten folders they kept in their own secure systems.

After a complete sweep had been performed of the enormous house, Isaac had come down to the basement and began to type away on the keyboard, doing whatever it was he was supposed to do to make sure that everything was operating as it should. Adam was impressed with how quickly the young man worked.

Thomas took Adam up to the second floor, where he was assigned a room for himself. When he was finally left on his own, Adam observed the simple-looking accommodations and felt a pang of sadness creep back into his soul. Here he was, once again alone in a room that was both strange to him and very foreign. The walls, like the hallway downstairs, were bare, devoid of any personality or that simple human touch to give it some character. A three drawer dresser sat beside a shuttered square window, and a queen sized bed rested in the center of the large room, covered in a dark purple sheet. Adam wondered who had last made that bed before leaving this safe house; if that person was even still alive to this day.

He walked up slowly to the bed and patted one of the white pillows with the palm of his hand. A cloud of dust rose up from the pillow making him sneeze. This place had been left alone for quite some time, long enough for a healthy layer of dust to settle on just about everything in this home.

Beyond the foot of the bed stood a set of white closet doors. Carefully, Adam crept to the closet, making sure that the safety was off on his rifle. Even though his team had cleared the house, a pervading fear remained within Adam, making him worry about what might still be hiding in the darker confines of this home. It was a primal fear that all creatures felt when they looked into the shadows, wondering what might lurk in the places that their eyes couldn't see.

In haste, he threw both doors open with one hand. Beyond was nothing but an empty rack and hollow square cabinets. No zombies waited to jump out at him, gnashing their teeth as they threw their decayed arms around his shoulders. No bogeymen, or psychotic murderers with machetes or chainsaws tried to chop him to bits. The silence was almost deafening. The result of his brief terror was almost anti-climactic.

Adam forced himself to relax as he lowered the barrel of his rifle. He was jumping at shadows, and the tension he felt stemmed from his recent incident with the horror he'd encountered in a basement miles away from here. A footstep landed on the carpet behind him. Adam spun and lifted his gun, only to come face to face with Jenny, who had raised her open hands in fright. Her eyes were wide, and for a moment Adam was too stunned to move.

"Jesus Christ!" she called out as she quickly lowered her hands. "Adam, are you alright?"

"Sorry about that," he apologized as he lowered his gun. He was surprised to find that he was out of breath, his heart hammering beneath his breast as if he had just run a marathon.

"What's got you so spooked?"

Adam hesitated, mouth open. "Everything," he commented

truthfully.

Embarrassed, and suddenly feeling very weary, Adam lay his rifle down on the bedside table and sat down on the comforter. This time he ignored the cloud of dust that wafted from the bed. His mind was a million miles away, and he was barely aware that Jenny was still there in the room with him. Concerned, she walked over and took a seat on the bed beside him. Adam stared numbly at the blank wall by the door, and in his thoughts there lingered the image of the dark haired woman and the young boy from his dreams.

Once again he wondered who they were, why he dreamt of them from time to time, and questioned himself constantly whether or not they had even been real. Maybe he was going slowly crazy, as he'd suspected from time to time. Perhaps the process that had brought him back hadn't revitalized enough of the man he once was. Maybe in death he'd lost a vital part of his soul, something that couldn't be brought back by drugs or the will of one very smart and ambitious professor. Could it be that there were some things that died with you that you couldn't ever retrieve even if you were brought back from the dead?

"Adam, tell me what's wrong," Jenny asked gently. "Whatever it is that's bothering you, we're all here to help."

Danny's scowling face flitted across his thoughts, and Adam wondered if what she'd said was really true. The man had always harbored some unspoken grudge towards him, even after he'd been accepted into Sparrow Company. Adam doubted that the man would go out of his way to lend him a supporting shoulder.

Adam shrugged. "I'm not sure what's wrong. Maybe I haven't given myself enough time to process my new life in your world."

"When is it enough time? Adam, nobody's ever experienced what you've had to go through. You're the first of your kind, and nobody that's ever lived can really sympathize with what you're going through. But we're here to help you when you need us, and we will always be there for you."

"Thanks, Jen," he smiled sideways at her. "It's just that I'm wondering if I moved too fast in trying to find a purpose in my life. Maybe I shouldn't be here with you guys. Maybe I wasn't ready to leave the city."

"You've earned your place with us, and that's not just me saying that to try and make you feel better. Look, you're absolutely right. You probably aren't ready, but you're trying the best you can to make sense of a life that doesn't really make any sense at all.

You're coping in the only way you can, and so far you've handled yourself amazingly. You have no idea how strong you really are. I've seen it in the way you've approached this new life."

She placed a finger under his chin and drew his face so that he stared only at the sincerity in her gaze. It was the first time that he'd noticed how green her eyes really were, how the emerald tinge created a ring around her iris and grew lighter as it spread outwards.

"I am proud to have you in our team," she continued. "I've only known you for such a short while, but I think you're probably one of the bravest people I've ever met. There are so many others that would have crumbled under the weight of your circumstances. That's why I'm happy to have you with us. If, and when, we find this second subject, it's right that you should be there to guide this person on his or her new life. Because the fact is, I doubt a lot of people would be able to remain as strong as you have been, and this person will probably need your help."

Adam wasn't quite sure what to say, but as he processed her words in his head, Jenny got up and made her way towards the bedroom door. She turned around one last time before leaving and glanced at him with a warm smile on her face. The look stirred something inside of Adam, and for the first time since his resurrection he felt an honest and strong attraction towards this woman. Adam looked away before she could catch the embarrassed look on his face.

"I hear that Isaac's pretty much completed updating the software in the computers. If you need to get a hold of someone back in New Edmonton, I think you can ask him to connect you."

She knew there was only one other person he would possibly call at the city. Yet the invitation was there, and Adam felt that it was time that he should take it.

Jenny left, leaving him alone with his thoughts once more. The lingering attraction he'd felt for her remained in the forefront of his mind, and for reasons he couldn't explain, he felt a strong guilt over it, as if he'd unknowingly betrayed someone else's trust.

* * * *

When Isaac quickly showed him how to contact the professor, he left Adam to have a little privacy in the basement. As the monitor's display showed the call was being connected, Adam sat back in the comfortable, padded leather chair and waited. He waited until the call automatically timed out and was disconnected. He tried again, dialing the professor's number into the keyboard, but once again there was no answer on the other end of the line. After three more subsequent tries, Adam decided to give up.

There were a hundred and one possible reasons why the professor hadn't picked up the call. Perhaps he was simply out late, working in the Charon Initiative facility. Maybe the man had fallen asleep and simply hadn't heard the calls. Whatever the reasons were, a troubling feeling settled in the pit of Adam's stomach.

His distress followed him for the rest of the night, even when he'd returned to his room and tried to find some rest.

Chapter Eleven

Canmore was spread out all around him. The desolation and remnants of the long past apocalypse remained in the relics of the old vehicles that littered the road and in the haunted buildings that stood like empty husks. A cold breeze blew against the street, stirring the loose dirt and garbage.

Adam shivered under his thick uniform. They had started their patrol of the city early when the sun had barely even breached the horizon. He hadn't been able to get much sleep last night, He felt energized regardless. Here he was, in the center of a dead city, and anywhere the dead could be waiting. The fear of death kept him alert, kept his senses sharp, and he steadied his hands on his rifle. Beside him stood his companions, and a few blocks away, Tennant sat in the forward console of the APC, monitoring them from the vehicle's cameras.

The streets were covered in mounds of dirt that reminded him of sand dunes in a desert. Hints of the concrete roadway showed that it was in a terrible state of disrepair. It would have been impossible to drive a car, or even a truck, through this city without the risk of getting stuck. Luckily, the APC wasn't your usual commercial vehicle, and he had little doubt that the heavily armored machine could plow through quite a bit before having to come to a stop before some impassible obstruction.

The winds blew once more, sending a fresh scent of clean air down from the distant mountains. Despite the ruins all around, at least the air was still as pure as it always had been. Had it smelled different during the early days of the outbreak? Adam imagined the air smelling like rot, permeating the air with a foul stench that reached across the entire country. How terrible it must have been for those living in those first years, trying to survive in a world where they were hopelessly outnumbered by the walking dead.

A sharp pain suddenly shot through his head, and Adam groaned as he doubled over and nearly dropped his weapon. He felt nauseated, and for a brief moment he felt as if he were standing someplace else entirely. Suddenly Sparrow Company was gone, He wasn't alone. She was there once more, the woman with the dark hair. And in his hand he carried a very curious weapon. It was the handle of a Japanese sword...

"Adam, snap out of it!" he heard the sergeant bark from what sounded like miles and miles away.

Thomas and Jenny were at his sides, while Danny surveyed the area around them for any lurkers. He wiped sweat from his brow as he took in several deep breaths. The last time he'd felt anything like this sensation was a long time ago, when he'd first remembered how to speak. This, however, was far more intense, and if what he'd experienced was in fact a sliver of his memories coming back to him, then he realized there was hope after all. He hadn't realized he was smiling until he began to chuckle softly to himself. The images and sensations he'd felt were so real, and to be back here with his companions once more in this cold place was a jarring shift for him to process.

"The man's losing it," Danny grumbled mostly to himself.

"I'm alright," Adam assured them.

He explained to them what had just happened to him. The sergeant's face was unreadable but a wide smile spread across Jenny's lips. She told him it could be a taken as a good sign that his memories were slowly coming back to him. After he reassured them that he was better, they continued on their search through the seemingly deserted city. While he walked beside his friends, he was more than aware that they were all stealing occasional glances at him.

He wanted to sit down and think on what had happened further, He'd have to wait until later tonight when they were back at the safe house. Adam also couldn't wait to tell the professor about what had happened. Hopefully he would be successful this time on getting ahold of the old man.

Sparrow Company made its way down Ninth Street, heading towards Seventh Avenue. They passed by a Library & Arts Centre, whose front doors had been shattered long ago. Dark stains marred the concrete pathway leading up towards the front entrance. The stains suggested that someone had been attacked here not too long ago. Adam grieved for whatever poor soul had met their end in that spot.

When they made their way by a small tourism information center, Adam came to a sudden halt. For a second he thought he'd heard the sounds of light footsteps in the air following from somewhere behind them.

He turned and surveyed the empty sidewalk and didn't see a

hint of what could have made that sound. However, he was sure that it had been the sounds of footsteps. The air was silent, and he wondered if he'd just imagined it all. A part of his mind, the cautious part, told him that he'd heard something, but the street was empty. A lurker didn't have the intelligence to stop and hide if it thought its prey suddenly detected it. An undead creature wouldn't bother trying to sneak up on its prey. It would stumble forward, perhaps moaning aloud, as it moved as fast as its decomposed legs could take it. It wouldn't try to hide.

Also, what he'd heard hadn't been the sluggish scrape of feet being partially dragged along the ground. They had been carefully placed footsteps, almost as if someone was following him and didn't want to be noticed.

The others had stopped and joined him. Danny's expression showed that he was growing frustrated with Adam's interruptions. Thomas asked him what was wrong, and Adam explained what it was he thought he'd heard.

"Oh come on," Danny sighed, exasperated. "Are we going to stop at every block because you get spooked by something?"

Thomas looked around, and then settled his stare on Adam. "We have to be sure," he said after a moment.

They went back the way they'd come, travelling up the street slowly, carefully searching the area around them. After a few minutes Adam admitted that maybe he'd been wrong after all. Thomas assured him that it was alright to be cautious, that he'd made the right call. Danny's sour look told him that the man thought otherwise. Adam ignored the scowl and followed closely behind the sergeant as the larger man continued to lead them on their patrol.

* * * *

The rest of the day was thankfully uneventful. The sun was still high on the horizon by the time they'd made dinner and sat together around a large table in the dining room. Isaac's talents weren't saved for only driving the APC around, and with Jenny's help, he'd prepared for them a delicious meal of fish and vegetables. All of it had been brought along with them in the APC, and they had enough stores left for another few days in Canmore and the journey back home. They ate and laughed together around the table, and Adam was pleasantly surprised to discover that the sergeant did possess a funny bone beneath his gruff exterior. The man laughed and shared jokes with the rest, and for a while Adam really felt like he belonged.

Shortly after, Adam was back in the basement, sitting in front of the computer monitor, waiting and hoping to talk with the professor. As he waited he tried to organize in his mind what he wanted to say. When the screen flickered, and the professor's face came on, everything that Adam had run through his mind blew away, as easily as a scrap of paper might out an open window.

"Adam," an earnest smile spread out across the professor's face. "I'm so glad that it's you. I must admit, I'm a little surprised to see that you're calling me."

"Probably better than being greeted with the sergeant's face, I hope," Adam grinned as he rubbed the thin layer of stubble that grew on his chin.

"Indeed it is. How are thing's there with the company?"

"Better than I'd hoped," he answered honestly. "I still feel a little bit out of place here...but it feels right that I'm out here with them."

A sad look crossed the professor eyes as he gazed at Adam through the old computer screen.

"I'm sorry. I can't help myself. It's hard to explain, but it's difficult for me to see you out there, away from the city. You've...grown to be like a son to me, and I guess I'm just a little bit worried about you."

Adam was stunned, completely taken aback by what the professor had just said.

"It's true, and I hope that you can understand this old man, worrying that you are out there with those creatures running around. Are you well? Are you and Sparrow Company safe?"

"I promise that we're fine, professor. We're staying at New Haven in some safe house. I never knew the army had places like these. I've been told they're spread out throughout the country. It's a very nice place, even if it's a little barren."

"I think I understand," the professor nodded. "I am glad to hear from you. I saw that someone tried calling earlier from this location. Was that you?"

Adam nodded.

"I'm sorry I missed it. I was out, back at the Charon Initiative. I was just working on my numbers, going over the project with the other researchers."

"I'm not surprised. Professor, there's something that I have to tell you about...well, it's more of asking you about something... something that happened to me while I was out here. It's...

complicated, and I still don't understand it myself. I hoped maybe you could shed some light into it."

The professor's face grew concerned, so Adam explained to him what occurred back in the basement with the dead woman. He told the professor about what had occurred, about how he threw the undead woman off of him with ease. He told him about how he tossed her into the air with little effort and how she crashed on the floor a short distance away. The professor breathed a sigh of relief, and he obviously expected that Adam had some more dire or disastrous news to tell him.

Florentine cleared his throat. "It could just have been adrenaline. Maybe you were just so frightened at the time that you were able to throw the...creature off you like that. There are an infinite number of cases where extreme levels of stress, generated from some terrible crisis, could cause an individual to suddenly do something that they would otherwise have thought impossible of them. People that have near death experiences have reported occurrences where they rip off doors to get out of burning cars...or so I've read from the archives."

"Maybe," Adam said doubtfully. "This just felt like something else."

"When you get back we'll run you through a few tests, to see if there's anything abnormal. Have you experienced anything else strange?"

"None at all, just that. Thanks, professor."

"Of course. Look, I'm sure that everything with you physically is fine. But if there is anything else, please let me know as soon as you can."

Adam thanked him, and they spoke with one another for a little while of the current news in New Edmonton and of the things that Adam had seen so far while he was with Sparrow Company. After they said their good-byes to one another, Adam sat for a while in front of a darkened screen, thinking to himself about the explanation the professor gave him. The computers' fans hummed nearby, but the sound of it became a lazy drone that was pushed to the far back of his mind. What bothered him was that the sudden burst of strength hadn't felt like it had been caused due to some sudden moment of extreme stress.

Adam had been so absorbed in his thoughts that he hadn't heard the figure approaching from behind him. He jumped when he felt the hand on his shoulder, only to sigh with relief when he saw it was Isaac who snuck up on him.

"Sorry about that," the young man grinned. "Man, you are really out of it today, aren't you? I didn't even try to scare you."

"Yeah, I've been pretty distracted," he laughed as he rose from the chair to relinquish it to the other man.

"Anything I can help you with?"

"Not unless you have anything that can cure this headache."

Isaac laughed and pointed at the staircase behind his shoulder with his thumb.

"There's some medicine in the kitchen, in the cupboard just above the sink. It's not the marketed crap from the old world, so you don't have to worry of it being expired. The professor helped brew it though, so I'm guessing it's a lot stronger anyways. Go ahead and help yourself. But stick to just two a night, unless you're really that tired and don't mind passing out and sleeping on the kitchen floor."

"Sounds good, maybe I'll grab four."

They both chuckled as they exchanged places. Adam watched as the young man began typing away at the keyboard like it was second nature. Isaac's hand's glided across the keys, and the sounds of his typing sounded almost lyrical.

"So, is everything okay so far?" Adam inquired.

"Everything but one of the safe houses in the east."

Adam frowned, and Isaac glanced at him.

"Safe House Four, on Eagle's Run Road; it's been off the grid for a while now. I haven't been able to connect with its computers since we've come here. Sometimes things like this happen. Computers can fail from time to time. The ones we use in the safe houses are especially old. Anyways, tomorrow we're going to make a stop there so I can see if I can reboot its systems."

"I'm sure you'll muddle your way through," Adam joked. "Hey, do you mind if I ask you something else?"

"Of course. What's up?"

Isaac stopped what he was doing and swung around to face him. Adam found a lone chair near the far wall and dragged it closer to the computer desk so that he could sit in front of the man. He sat and stared at Isaac for a moment. Then he stared down in the open palms of his hands. He felt a little uneasy bringing this up, but it had been worrying in the back of his mind for quite some time now.

"What's up with Danny?" he finally asked.

Isaac lifted his head and laughed, and his body relaxed as he sunk back a little in his comfortable chair.

"Oh, is that all? Adam, you had me a little worried there."

"Sorry. I just wanted to know if you knew anything. The man seems...upset with me all the time, and I don't know what I did to deserve it."

"You didn't do anything to upset him," Isaac looked back and smiled. "Look, Adam. He's...well, Danny doesn't do well at first with people he doesn't know. I mean, he jokes around a lot but the truth is that he isn't really that much of a people person. It takes him a while to get used to anyone. I'm sure that he'll warm up to you eventually."

"It feels like a lot more than that," Adam bit the bottom of his lip.

Isaac's face fell, and he looked at Adam for a while with a troubled gaze. To Adam, it was obvious there was something more behind why Danny seemed so hostile towards Adam most of the time.

"It's about his wife," Isaac began.

"He has a wife?" Adam exclaimed.

"Hey, keep it down," Isaac gestured with his hands for Adam to quiet down. "Yes. Well, more like had a wife. This was years before he ever joined our crew, years before he even came to New Edmonton. Her name was Amanda. Now, we don't know much about his life before New Edmonton, He did tell us about her one night, when he was really drunk."

"I'm guessing that you've never met her."

"No," he shook his head, his face painted with sadness. "He lost her the night before he'd finally made it to the city. They'd been staying in an abandoned home together, and he'd made sure that the house and the basement were empty. The problem was that he didn't account for the shed in the back yard. She was asleep when it happened. Danny was up on first watch, sitting in the living room. He didn't hear the creature come in through the back, and he was completely unaware of it when it shuffled down the hall towards the bedroom. He only realized that they were under attack when he started to hear Amanda's screams. Then..."

"It's okay, I think I know what happened after that," Adam said quickly, looking away.

"He talks about her sometimes." Isaac sighed. "There are nights when I'd be hanging out with Danny and he'd bring her up. Most of the time he'd smile and tell me good things about her, things like her snoring or how she'd loved sunflowers. He told me that she was a beautiful woman. She must have been something special."

"He hates me because I was one of them," Adam guessed.

"He doesn't hate you, Adam. He knows that you never chose to become one of them. Give him some time. I'm sure he'll come around eventually."

* * * *

When Adam returned to his room, he lay in bed for a long time and thought about what Isaac had told him.

Eventually, when he finally succumbed to blessed sleep, he dreamed of that dark-haired woman and the young boy that was always at her side. He called out to them in his dream, but they didn't seem to hear him. They were standing on the beach together, but she was far away from him along the shoreline. He was screaming at her because of the things that emerged from the trees behind her, up along the length of the beach. Neither she nor the boy heard them coming. Adam cried out to them, ran towards them as fast as he could, He already knew he would be too late.

* * * *

Sparrow Company started early once more in the next morning. They were back across the river, in the heart of the dead city. Adam heard the rumbling first before any of the others and what he heard were the roars of loud engines. His blood ran cold as a rusted old yellow Hummer came barreling down Fourth Street. It was still a block and a half away, but it came upon them in seconds. Adam glimpsed another vehicle behind the first; a gigantic, heavy-duty pickup truck that spouted black smoke from its rear exhaust. He now saw that there were people in the back of the pickup, wearing masks and goggles that hid their faces—and they were all armed.

"What the fuck?" Danny shouted.

"Move dammit!" the sergeant barked.

The Hummer plowed between them, separating the group in two. Adam and Thomas leapt back and rolled against the sandy street as the large vehicle roared past. Clouds of dust blocked his view of the others. The Hummer skidded to a halt a half a block past them, and the truck fishtailed and came to a screeching stop at the east end of the road. The two vehicles had just effectively blocked any hope of escape for Sparrow Company. On either side were abandoned shops, which were all boarded up with nailed planks of wood. Horror filled Adam as he realized that these people had planned to attack the moment the company had entered this street. There was no escape for them since they couldn't get past the vehicles or enter any of the blocked buildings. Whoever these people were had been lying in wait, biding their time as Sparrow Company walked into this trap.

The doors of the Hummer flew open, and Thomas and Adam raced to duck behind cover between the hulking remains of two derelict cars as rapid gunfire spattered out and slammed into the rusted metal around them.

The rounds slammed and ricocheted all around him, and Adam's world was engulfed in the chaotic noise of gunfire and shouting. He was frozen in terror, huddling between the ruined vehicles, clutching his rifle tight against his body. The air whizzed with the sounds of flying bullets. He wondered where these people, after two hundred years of the end of the world, had collected so many rounds. Where did they get the fuel for their vehicles?

Somewhere in the distance he heard Jenny scream. Danny was shouting from somewhere that sounded like a hundred miles away. The man was returning fire, and when Adam dared to peek over the hood of the Honda, he saw one of the men standing in the flat bed of the truck suddenly collapse and fall dead on the road.

"Adam, get your head together and fire back!" the sergeant yelled at him.

Thomas aimed and fired, pelting his enemies with carefully aimed shots. A man screamed from somewhere near the Hummer, followed by the sound of a body hitting the street. Adam gathered his courage and fired back at the Hummer, then spun and let a rain of bullets fly towards the truck. His vision became tinged with red. He was hardly aware that he was shouting out loud, screaming at the top of his lungs as he fired madly at the enemy. One flew back from the rear of the truck, landing not to far away on the dusty street. A momentary feeling of overwhelming guilt washed over him, and then it was gone, replaced by the powerful desire to survive.

He could still hear Jenny crying out, and as the dust finally began to settle, he saw three men dragging her towards the truck. Danny continued to scream as he fired at those shooting at him, He didn't dare to try and shoot at the people dragging Jenny. Black's radio squawked, but Isaac's voice could barely be heard over the thunder of all the gunfire.

One of the men struck Jenny across the face with a haymaker, and her body suddenly went slack in the men's arms. A feeling of pure hatred replaced Adam's fright, and he almost bolted up from his cover to try and rescue her before the sergeant–sensing his intent–grabbed a hold on his arm and forced him to remain in his position behind the cars. Adam glared heatedly at the sergeant, saw the look of terror in the older man's eyes, and understood that going after her now would be suicide.

Tires squealed on loose gravel and cracked pavement as the truck peeled away down the road. Barked orders cried out, and the remaining attackers leapt into the rumbling Hummer before taking off after the first vehicle. Adam ripped his arm away from the sergeant's and rose from his cover. He ran after the retreating vehicle, firing madly at its rear as he shouted into the cold air. Guns were trained on him from the back seat of the Hummer, and bullets smacked flatly into the ground around his feet. For a moment he didn't care that any of those shots could have easily ended his life. Danny rose from behind cover as well and began to fire round after round into the back of the armored machine.

None of the shots slowed the vehicle down, and with the retreating sound of loud engines, their attackers soon fled around a sharp corner and out of their view.

Adam and Danny stood in the otherwise desolate street together, with sinking feelings of dread plunging deep into the hollow confines of their stomachs. One of their own had been taken from them, and terrible thoughts of why they'd taken Jenny added fuel to their mounting horror.

Chapter Twelve

Adam's heart pulsed quickly, and he wasn't sure if it was because of what was going on or something else entirely.

Isaac drove the APC into the street, skidding to a speeding halt in front of him. The remaining members of Sparrow Company filed into the vehicle without a word, and Isaac slammed his foot down hard on the gas as he followed down the general direction of their escaping attackers. Thomas told him to make a left down the road in which they'd disappeared. Other than a vague idea of where they'd gone, no one was sure where to look. If the trail grew cold now, there was little chance that the company could track down the vehicles. The streets were littered with garbage and debris of all sorts, making it difficult for Isaac to maneuver the large vehicle. On several occasions, the APC shook violently as the armored tank scraped or slammed against the sides of abandoned vehicles.

Danny was in the back, frantically reloading his rifle. Adam offered to take the sergeant's and reload it. Thomas nodded in thanks and handed it over. Its barrel was still warm from the firefight they'd just had only a few minutes ago. Adam almost lost his footing as the vehicle jostled violently, and he saved himself by reaching out and grasping the overhead support bars.

Then Adam had an idea of where the kidnappers might have gone to.

"The safe house," he blurted. "Isaac, what about the safe house you were trying to get in contact with?"

Isaac seemed to understand immediately, and smiled when he glanced back at the company's newest member.

"That's a good idea," he exclaimed. "I'd bet my next month's pay that they're staying there."

The sergeant seemed to understand as well, and nodded in approval.

"I want you to drive this thing until its frame buckles," Thomas urged. "Do you understand me, private?"

Isaac answer was the sudden lurch of the APC as it shot forward with even greater speed. The cabin vibrated, and a low droning hum filled the air as the powerful engine of the vehicle was pushed to its limits and beyond. The city's abandoned buildings seemed to zoom past in a blur, and once more Adam was astonished by how well the young man could handle the large vehicle around large debris and over such ruined streets.

* * * *

On Eagle's Run Road, the safe house came into view amidst a rural area covered in spacious areas of overgrown grass. Adam knew it was Safe House Four, because of the familiar vehicles that were parked in front of the two story home's large garage. Excitement flooded through his veins as he finished reloading his rifle and readied himself to leap out of the vehicle's side door as soon as he was ordered. Isaac took the APC off road and onto the fields of grass, driving the thing through the emerald landscape towards the distant and well-kept dwelling ahead of them. They hit the dirt path leading up to the garage, and continued on until Isaac brought the APC to a sudden, jarring stop right at the foot of the stairs leading to the front balcony of the home.

The armored roof of the APC would provide some cover from those wanting to shoot at them from the windows of the second floor. Adam saw that the steel door was locked shut, and that the windows on the first floor were closed off by the now familiar metal shutters.

"If they've been able to gain access to the house, then there's a big chance that they've changed all the codes," Isaac said after a moment.

"Thanks, private," Thomas acknowledged. "I think we've got a way around that."

He turned and gestured to Danny, who went to retrieve something from the back of the APC. When the three were ready, they gathered around the APC's starboard hatch.

"After Lieutenant Keene takes care of the front door, we clear the first floor. Kill anything that moves besides Jenny. I don't know what these fuckers think they're doing and I don't care. If there are any of the undead, and they try to bite you, shoot them twice just to be sure; if they're alive and try to shoot you, be sure to make these bastards feel the hurt before they meet their makers."

The sergeant's speech roused something strange inside of Adam. The vengeful need to take revenge on these people was almost a good feeling, and he couldn't help but acknowledge this primitive urge to both protect someone they cared about and to utterly destroy their enemies.

"Heavily armored base, unknown numbers, violent locals with infinite ammo, the undead waiting somewhere to eat us, and one of our own in trouble," Danny listed it out, counting them on the fingers of his right hand. "You really know how to throw a party, boss."

"Shut the hell up and get ready to do some work, lieutenant," the sergeant growled.

The hatch slid open, and as soon as they were outside, they were under attack by a hail of live fire from above. Most of the rounds ricocheted off the thick hull of the APC. Thomas and his team made it up onto the front porch unscathed, and from above they heard the frantic shouts from those on the second floor.

"Hold onto this for me, would ya?" Danny said as he tossed a strange small object at Adam.

Adam caught it and then looked down to study the small cylindrical metal device with a blue button mounted on one end. The object was no longer than the width of his palm, and he guessed that he wasn't supposed to push the button until he was ordered to.

Danny pulled a small silver container from his side pocket. With this he began to spray a light green foam all along the wall surrounding the large metal door. Then, after tossing the can behind him, he placed two small black circular objects into the thick foam, one on each side of the door. When Danny gave them the thumbs up, Thomas ordered them to move away from the door. They took their positions, each one crouching a few meters away. Thomas gave the order, and Adam pressed firmly on the trigger of the small device in his hand.

For a moment it was as if the world around them had suddenly gone to hell. The loud explosion shook the foundations of the house violently, and a bright flash momentarily blinded their eyes. The team ducked low as a hail of loose debris shot out and high up into the air. Adam's hearing was filled with a painful ringing noise, and he suddenly felt so disoriented that he was tempted to puke his guts out onto the porch. The patio itself threatened to tear itself apart from the terrible rocking explosion.

When the debris began to settle, Thomas and his team moved into the now gaping hole that had once been the front door only seconds ago. More gunfire rang out, and as Adam dove through a thick cloud of lingering smoke, white flashes burst out in front of him, hinting at the firefight that was occurring just ahead. He followed close behind Danny and Thomas, and as soon as he found an opening, Adam dove into it.

He found himself in an empty living room with an open doorway leading to another area of the house in front of him. A shadow fell across the wall in the other room, and before he knew it, a large bearded man burst into the living room, holding a small pistol in each hand. They both stopped and stared, neither having expected to run into each other so suddenly.

Adam was the first to collect himself, and he raised his rifle and gunned the man down with three shots. The man's blood splattered against the wall with shocking power, painting the surface in splotches of thick crimson. The bearded man crashed against the wall shortly after, slipping on his own blood and sliding down to the floor and toppling dead on his side.

He pressed himself against the wall, with his back facing towards the door. He glanced quickly over the edge and saw that the kitchen beyond was empty. Gunshots continued to ring out from somewhere else in the house. For a second Adam swore that he heard Danny laughing from far away, hollering as he probably took down another target of his own. Thomas he heard nothing from. Any one of the fired rounds could be his. Adam suspected that the man was a more professional kind of soldier, keeping completely silent as he wove his way across the battlefield, dealing death as swiftly as a scythe cutting its way across an open field.

Adam's mind reeled as he imagined the possibilities of their plight through the house. How many where there in this house? Where the hell were they keeping Jenny? Was she still alive?

He thought he heard a commotion coming from downstairs, but before he entered the kitchen, he heard the sound of footsteps behind him. Two strangers—one a man, and the other a woman—rushed into the living room and raised their rifles at him. Adam spun, spraying the area with shots. He felt a bullet fly past his ear, perhaps only a couple of inches away, and his heart jumped up in his throat as he continued to fire.

The woman careened backwards first, spraying blood and gore from fresh wounds on her forehead and left arm, her rifle clattering to the tiles. The man screamed as he ducked behind a sofa and fired.

Adam felt a round graze his left shoulder. Pain shot through him, He continued to fire. The powerful rounds ejected from his weapon tore through the couch and the stranger's meager attempt at shielding. The man cried out as the bullets ripped through the old fabric and entered his body. The man was riddled with blind shots and finally died when one exited through the center of his forehead.

"Adam, where the hell are you?" he heard Danny call out.

He ignored the man's call and raced through the kitchen and made his way to the door leading to the basement. He would have laughed had the situation been drastically different. What was with him and basements lately? Was his fate to be forever tied to such places? It would have been funny if it weren't for the chaos that was going on around him. For now he had to focus on his objective, which was to find Jenny and make sure she was safe. That was first and foremost in his mind. The second was to get the hell out of this place.

With one hand, Adam quickly swung the basement door wide. His trained the hot barrel of his rifle along the flight of steps leading down into the underground. Luckily nobody came to meet him as he made his way swiftly down the steps. Each wooden plank creaked and cried out like the wailing cries of banshees. Each one made him cringe involuntarily beneath his thick uniform.

Struggling sounds issued below, followed by the sound of fists smacking soundly on flesh. Adam's hackles rose at the noise, and his anger rose as he reached the bottom of the steps. What he was greeted with was a long hallway housing eight shut doors. The sounds of struggling came from somewhere to his left. Adam wasted no time and drove his foot into the face of the closest door. The wooden frame shattered underneath his kick, and large chucks of wood flew into what was otherwise an empty chamber.

Adam decided to ignore how easily it was for him to utterly destroy the door with one strike. For now he had other things to focus all his attention on.

He plunged his heavy boot into the second locked door, and the frame shattered in more or less the same way. It was almost too easy.

The room beyond was also empty of people, but a single bed sat in the far corner. Its mattress was very old and very dirty. It was in a horrible state of disrepair, and sharp springs poked out through the top surface of the mattress in several places. His spirits sunk at the sight of the dried bloodstains that covered much of the bed. Rusted handcuffs hung loosely against all four bedposts. Deep, jagged gouges had been worn into the surfaces of these wooden posts, signs of struggle from whoever had been bound to these chains before.

He growled under his breath, and he had to force himself to look away from the room and the unspoken savagery that hinted from within. He made his way quickly to the third door, but as he raised his leg to kick it down, the door suddenly swung open right in front of him. He raised his rifle, and for the second time in this one week, he found himself training the sight of his gun at a very familiar face.

A dark bruise marred the cheek on the left side of Jenny's face. A trail of blood flowed from her nose, and she looked extremely tired. When she saw who it was that stood outside the door, her face lit up into a brilliant smile. In her hands she held a pistol. Behind her were the bloodied and dead bodies of the two people who'd probably tried shackling her in the handcuffs in the room's single bed. Adam could only imagine what these people had intended to do with their new captive. Relief flooded through him and washed away the ice that had begun to collect in his veins with the realization that she seemed mostly unhurt.

She called his name as she wrapped her arms around him in a powerful embrace. He spared an arm to hug her back. It seemed that her full weight was being supported by him, and he felt the frantic hammering of her heart beneath her breast. It made his breathing quicken, more so than the earlier struggle.

"We have to get out of here," he said as he pulled himself away from her.

Her eyes switched to a look of urgency.

"When they brought me down here, one of the other doors was open. I saw something in there. I don't know if I saw what I think I saw, but it's...sick."

Confused, Adam turned to look at the closed door that she gestured towards. It was a few meters further down the hall, and on the opposite side of the room that had been meant to be Jenny's permanent prison.

"I don't know what these people were doing to her. But what I saw...Adam, what's wrong with these people?"

She was almost hysterical, and he didn't know what to say to her.

Adam suddenly realized that the commotion upstairs had gone silent some time ago. The house was bathed in a strange, almost unnatural pall of silence. Adam and Jenny stood in front of one another, her arms resting gently against his as if she were still too afraid to allow herself to lose contact with him. Heavy, hurried footsteps rushed down the stairs, and Danny and Thomas emerged from around the corner. Black's face was etched in its usual stony impression, but Danny looked at Jenny with a look of pure relief. He glanced at Adam for a moment and nodded. Danny let his weapon hang loosely on its sling as he rushed forward and embraced the frightened woman. Adam backed away and looked up at the sergeant, who nodded at him respectfully. Adam returned the gesture, but his thoughts were more focused on the door that Jenny had pointed out to him just now.

Thomas followed the direction of his gaze and walked closely behind him as Adam made for the door. He tested the dark bronze knob and wasn't overly surprised to discover that it was locked. Adam shared a look with the sergeant and sighed when he returned his focus on the ominous door. Instead of driving his foot with haste into the frame, Adam gave the door a slightly lighter kick. The lock broke with an audible, loud snap. Thomas gave him a strange look.

"I've been working out a bit," Adam commented off-handedly.

Then he opened the door and looked at what lay on the filthy bed beyond.

"Jesus Christ," was all the Sergeant said.

Chapter Thirteen

A single nude figure lay bound to the bed.

It wasn't just a woman who lay there, shackled by her wrists and ankles to bedposts that had obviously seen better days. The creature looked at him through the tangled bangs of her long black hair. In her gaze was nothing but the look of pure desire and pure hunger. From Adam's angle it looked like a few of the sharp bedsprings had pierced into the creature's desiccated flesh. Deep cuts and scars marred her face and body. The undead skin on her wrists and ankles were horribly torn, chewed into by the rusted handcuffs that bound her in place.

A strange silence fell amongst all those assembled in the basement. For a long time the members of Sparrow Company looked upon this prisoner, this undead creature, and nobody could utter a single word. It was no wonder that Jenny was so distraught over what lay behind this room's door. What the hell had these people, these monsters, done to this thing?

The creature gazed at them all, and in a horrifying way, it licked its lips with a tongue that looked like it hadn't been wet for a hundred years. It chilled him to the bone, and made him feel somehow dirtied and violated inside. Then the creature broke the strange, uneasy silence, and it thrashed within its bonds madly while its restraints made fresh wounds upon its flesh. The sounds of its fury were like a mixture of some wild cat and an angry, spoiled child. It gnashed its teeth in the air, and its lips curled and formed the most sinister and unsettling smile any of them had ever seen.

Thomas' radio squawked to life and Isaac's voice came through, sounding very worried.

"Guys, we've got dead heads inbound. They're coming out from the city, and they're about five hundred meters away."

"How many of them are there?" the sergeant asked.

"Lots, sir," the voice grew increasingly concerned. "Did you guys find, Jenny?"

"Yes we did, and she's alright."

"Thank God."

"We'll be up soon, Tennant. Get the APC warmed up."

"Already on it, sir. Uh...what's that sound I hear in the background?"

The group looked at the restrained creature together, unsure of what to do.

"Just another lurker," Thomas answered off-handedly.

"Oh...okay. Well, please don't take too long. Some of these guys are pretty fast."

"We need to move," the sergeant said. "Danny, help Jenny back to the APC. Adam..."

"I think we found our second subject, folks," Adam said as he continued to stare at the rabid monster. Despite her horrid features, her body was whole. Plus, there was something about her, something that lingered in her eyes that drew Adam. The color of her hair reminded him of the woman from his dreams, He knew this wasn't that same person. He felt glad about that, and even though he didn't know who the woman in his dreams was, at least it wasn't her that had been put through the terrible things that this creature must have been experienced. "I think this is her."

"We might not have time," Thomas said.

Adam stared at the other locked doors that remained unexplored, and he knew what he had to do.

"Sergeant, can you head back to the APC and bring the restraints? I need to check the rest of the floor to make sure we don't leave anyone behind."

Thomas stared down the hall, understood, and nodded.

"Be careful, rookie. I'll be back."

The sergeant escorted the others upstairs, leaving Adam to deal with the thrashing thing in front of him. The creature seemed even more furious now that three juicy morsels left its view. The undead monster redirected its full attention on Adam's face, and what he saw in those eyes was simple, insatiable greed. He knew what it wanted from him, and he saw that this particular monster was a very strong one. Despite the desiccation that covered its entire body, it pulled and wrenched powerfully on its unyielding bonds.

He glanced down at the other closed doors and knew what he had to do. Steeling himself, he held his rifle poised in front of him as he began to search the remaining prison cells. To his relief they were all empty, and only one of them mirrored the few that he'd seen so far. He wondered how long ago these people had broken into this safe house. It couldn't have been too long ago since they'd established this place as their new home. He had little doubt that what they intended was to one day fill all of these rooms with dirty beds and bloodied mattresses. Perhaps within a year from now this basement would have been filled with the chorus and sounds of anguished wails and the weeping hearts of damaged souls. Their victims, it seemed, weren't limited for only the living.

Thomas came running downstairs carrying the accoutrements, which Adam recognized very well. Adam undid one handcuff as the sergeant quickly fastened the zombie's hand in one of the steel gauntlets. Then they did the same to the other. They fixed the armored head piece around the zombie's head. During the entire procedure she snapped at the air with her teeth, straining her neck in a frightening way towards each one of them. Thomas held her shoulders down against the filthy mattress, using his powerful strength and his weight to try and hold her in place as the finished binding her shackles.

"Goddamit, she's strong," the sergeant complained.

Adam unholstered his sidearm and pointed its barrel in the center of the mad creature's rib cage. He stared at her one last time through her metal headpiece and gazed deeply into her horrifying eyes. They were dark green, but they shone in the gloom of the basement despite the low level of light. He knew what he had to do. It was similar to what the others had done to him on the day that Sparrow Company had found their first subject.

"I'm going to help you," he whispered to the beast. "I promise."

"Adam, do it!"

The gunshot rang throughout the whole house. It made the residence sound hollow, devoid of life except for the two of them.

* * * *

Thomas and Adam brought the incapacitated creature out of the house and loaded it in the APC as the lieutenant continued to take down more and more of the hungry monsters.

With her spine shattered, the undead creature they loaded into the APC could only glance at her captors. Her mouth opened and closed shut with loud clicks as her rotted teeth smacked together. Her eyes held that same hunger which unnerved Adam, and they seemed to focus on him and him alone.

Danny fired repeatedly at the advancing undead. The creatures were still several meters away, but they were quickly surrounding the vehicle, and Danny was having trouble keeping them at bay.

The festering masses of the undead shocked Adam with their numbers. Where had they come from? How had so many come together here, and why? They moved together without any order or reason, other than to shamble along towards them until they could drive their teeth into some warm flesh. A few of them walked with their arms partially raised before them, almost like in the old movies Adam had viewed back in New Edmonton. Others pulled themselves along the grass and dirt, their useless lower extremities being dragged along behind them through the muck, ripping away chunks of decaying flesh and bone against the rough earth until some ended in mere stubs. They were all in various states of decomposition. Some still retained some of its human appearance, while others appeared nearly like walking skeletons with only a thin layer of cracked and peeling skin holding the bones together. Adam glanced at one whose slimy eyeball hung loosely from out of its socket, and shuddered.

Adam helped Thomas secure the specimen in the specially prepared bed located in the rear compartment of the vehicle. Strong metal arches held the creature in place in case it somehow regained the ability to move.

That was when they all heard an unfamiliar gunshot from outside. That was when Adam and Thomas shared a look as they each realized that Danny was still outside. Jenny cried out.

"You stay in your seat!" Thomas yelled at her.

He moved outside first and he fired at someone Adam couldn't see from where he was standing. When he followed after the sergeant, Adam found another dead body lying face-down on the porch—someone from the safe house they'd missed. A deep pool of blood began to form around the dead man's head, and he could clearly see the open wound in the back of the corpse's scalp.

The sergeant was down on one knee, holding Danny in his arms. Their rifles lay beside one another in the grass, forgotten. Danny's eyes were closed, and a dark stain began to spread across the man's uniform, originating from a dark hole in the middle of his gut. Black called out the man's name, but Danny didn't answer. Thomas held the still form in his arms, the urgency and fear in his hardened eyes clear.

Adam shot down a couple of zombies just over three meters away. They were very close, and they didn't have a lot of time to vacate the area.

A burning sensation began to tickle the back of his mind, and he winced as pain shot through him from somewhere behind his eyeballs. He moved forward and forced himself to focus through the strange fog that slowly began to cloud his thoughts. With his help, Thomas carried the downed soldier into the vehicle. As the APC's hatch closed behind them, Adam saw that Danny left behind a trail of crimson along the floor.

"Get us out of here!" Thomas ordered, and the APC shot forward and away from the swarming undead.

Before long the horde would reach the open Safe House Four. Inside they would find the fresh corpses of all those that Sparrow Company had slain, and tonight they would feast to their dead hearts' delight. Adam shivered at the thought and opened his mouth wide as the burning sensation turned to the feeling of hot pokers being plunged into the back of his skull. He collapsed on his side against the steel wall. The sergeant was on both knees now, trying to tend to Danny's still bleeding wound. Jenny was at his side, bringing with her a first aid kit. Her face was a picture of desperation, a canvas of worry. Danny obviously meant more to her than she cared to admit to anyone, maybe even including herself.

Adam watched everything through a haze of crimson as he fought with the pain that rushed through his mind like a red tidal wave. In the back, the specimen let out an audible moan that filled the cabin. It was a horrible noise that sounded like the creature was locked in torment, unable to escape despite how much it desperately wished to. Thomas and Jenny fumbled through the medical kit, but it was obvious that they weren't sure what they were doing.

The pain subsided in his skull and Adam moved towards them, shoving them aside as he grabbed the kit from them. At first they looked astonished, and even furious, as they turned to regard their newest recruit. Then they stared in awe as Adam began to sift through the bag, pulling out gauze pads and other items before setting to work on their unconscious friend. Even Adam couldn't understand why he suddenly felt the powerful need to do these things. As he ripped open the man's uniform, he stared into the terrible wound and somehow instinctively knew what it was he was looking at and what he could do to try and save him.

"The bullet's still in there," Adam spoke. "Sergeant, I can't work with the APC bumping around like this. We need to get back to the safe house—our safe house—as soon as possible."

"Adam, what's going on?" the man asked, perplexed.

"Just do it! The bullet's still in there, and if I don't get it out now, Danny is going to die."

Thomas didn't argue, and he turned to give Isaac the go ahead to return to the safe house.

* * * *

Somewhere far behind them, the monsters went into a feeding frenzy on the warm flesh they found inside the rural home. A few looked up at the retreating vehicle and the dust trail it left behind. At first a few followed after the APC. Soon more were drawn by the flock, and before long there were hundreds heading towards the direction the APC fled.

* * * *

Adam was done. Danny lay on the dining room table, sleeping but stabilized despite the bullet wound in his stomach. Adam had managed to stop the bleeding and finished stitching the wound with the needle and thread he'd found in the first aid kit. He stared at the stitches, which were done like how a professional would have. He stared at his own hands. Danny's blood coated the surface of his skin, but his hands didn't tremble one bit. He was still confused as to what he'd just done and how he'd done it, He felt relaxed despite it all. He'd known what he was doing, yet he still couldn't explain why.

A misshapen slug lay in a white porcelain bowl near Danny's sleeping form. Adam was able to locate and remove the bullet in minutes. It wasn't a difficult task. Other instruments lay beside the bowl, covered in more of the man's blood. Layers of gauze were wrapped around Danny's slim waistline. A dark stain was slowly forming on the white fabric, just above the wound.

He turned around and stared at the other members of the company. Isaac, Jennifer and Thomas all stared at him as if he'd just sprouted horns from out of his forehead.

"I think..." his voice cracked, and he collected himself before trying again. "I think...I might have been a doctor in my first life."

Chapter Fourteen

They came during the night, surrounding the safe house from all sides. The creatures had followed them after all, just as Thomas had feared. They pounded their hands lazily against the walls of the home. The reverberations of their feeble attacks filled the inside of the home with their terrifying sounds. Some of them were stronger than the others, and their strikes sounded like loud booms. The metal shutters and the heavily reinforced doors might be able to hold them off indefinitely, but the rest of the house was still made of some very old materials. Eventually the undead would get in somehow and even if that was months from now, Sparrow Company only had enough supplies to last them a few more days.

From the second story window of his room, Adam looked down at the horde, who stared at him in return with their undead, frenzied eyes. Hundreds of arms were raised towards him, groping aimlessly in the air. The sounds of their moaning calls filled his room and rang through the inner contours of his soul. He shivered as he looked down at them all and cringed at their sheer numbers. The stench of their rotted flesh filled his nostrils and made his eyes water, bringing up hot bile in his throat.

The APC lay less just a few meters in front of the safe house's front door. The undead paid the vehicle no heed. They were cut off from the APC, which had been their only real chance of escape. Inside the vehicle was the second subject, lying strapped in a bed. Adam wondered if the female creature called out from within, perhaps sensing the presence of her kind.

They didn't have enough bullets. They were surrounded by hundreds of the living dead. Danny lay wounded downstairs, and Adam still didn't know for certain if the man would survive through the night. He was confident of the man's survival, but because he didn't understand fully where this confidence originated from, he couldn't be completely sure.

Adam listed their numerous problems in his mind and thought of solutions of how to get him and his team out of this place. Then, with a flash of inspiration that came from nowhere, he knew what to do.

* * * *

"You're insane, you know that right?" Tennant frowned at him. They stood in front of Adam's open bedroom window. Down below the undead swarmed, arms raised up towards them as if in prayer. Sickly bile trickled down the side of a dead woman's mouth. Black ichor oozed from the ears of the teen beside her. The rotting stench wafted up towards them, almost making Adam gag. Thomas stared at Adam with an unreadable expression. The sergeant had approved of the plan but wasn't totally confident in its success.

"You're crazy."

"There are too many of the dead that it would be risky to try and file through the front door and start shooting at them all to try and get to the vehicle," Adam said. He looked at Thomas. "The front door of the mansion opens at a snail's pace, and they'd be on us before we were even through."

Jenny looked at him with watery eyes. Adam smiled reassuringly and placed a hand on her shoulder.

"Danny needs a proper medical facility if he's going to make it. We need to try."

"You could shatter both your legs when you drop down there," Thomas said. "Then where would that leave you? You'd be unable to get back to your feet, and they'd be on you in seconds."

"I can make it," Adam said. "Trust me."

"Do you remember the code for the door?" Isaac asked him.

Adam pointed to the side of his temple and smiled.

"Alright, Adam," Isaac expression looked solemn. "I trust you."

Adam stared down once more at the swarming undead and swallowed a lump in his throat. The gravity of what he was about to do began to sink in, and a part of him hesitated before he turned to face the sergeant one last time.

"You ready for this?" Thomas grinned.

"Nope," Adam replied.

He lifted the bedside lamp in his hand and held tossed it out the window. The lamp was covered in the same explosive compound that had been used to blow open the door of Safe House Four. A single, black detonator lay embedded in the opaque substance, and as it fell towards the masses below he lifted the thin metal trigger in his other hand. The makeshift bomb was swallowed by the horde. Only a few of the creatures bothered to look down at the strange object that had fallen amongst them.

Adam pressed his thumb down on the trigger firmly.

The explosion rocked the entire house. Adam and the others hid behind the window as the world outside was momentarily engulfed in fire and a mighty roar. Clumps of dirt and bits of dead flesh were cast so high that it flew through the open window, pelting the soldiers with the vile debris. Isaac shook off the remains of a hand that was missing most of its fingers. Adam brushed off bits of teeth and a lower jawbone from the back of his shoulder. When the sound of the blast subsided, pained moans began to rise up into the air.

Quickly, Adam raced to the window and looked outside. The side of the APC was partially blackened by the explosion, but otherwise the thick hull had withstood the blast. The area where the bomb had been dropped was completely clear of the undead. A wide ring, surrounding the small crater directly below him, had been cleared of the zombies. The creatures that did survive beyond the rim of the blast had mostly been knocked off their feet. Many of them had already begun to lift themselves up, although they struggled awkwardly with the effort.

Without another word, Adam leapt out the window.

He descended with alarming speed, dropping to the ground below. A waft of hot air whooshed up at his face, and he could smell the sickly char of burnt skin and hair. He landed hard on the blasted earth, bending down in a crouch as he tried to lessen the impact of his downward momentum with his hands and legs. Pain lanced up his shins and his heart leapt up into his throat as his full weight settled. Miraculously he was unharmed, and he let out the breath he'd been holding.

A lurker, whose legs had been obliterated by the bomb, clawed at the soil to get to him. Adam rose and gave the creature a swift kick to its face. The thing's skull crushed easily with wet crackling sounds and went completely still in front of him. The shards of shattered bones had flown to the back of its head, shredding what was left of its brain.

Shots rang from above as Thomas and Isaac began to fire on the monstrous things that rose and came after him. Adam bolted, racing for the closed hatch of the APC. Another of the undead leapt at him with surprising agility and grabbed a hold of his left arm. He cried out as he spun and shot the thing right in the face. Adam averted his face, only to feel the cold muck that exploded outwards from its skull slap him on his cheek and ear. Hastily he wiped off the gore with his sleeve and shot two more that advanced towards him. Silenced gunfire ripped through the air as bodies dropped all around him. Adam continued on and at last arrived at the side of the large vehicle.

The panel glowed in response to the proximity of his body, and he keyed in the appropriate codes that Isaac gave him. The hatch slid aside with a low hiss. Adam leapt in, and he slapped a hand on the inner panel to close the door. Just as the door was coming to a close, half a dozen decaying arms reached inside, blocking the hatch from closing itself all the way. The groans of the dead followed him into the cabin, and the creatures reached out and clawed the air, trying desperately to grab a hold of warm flesh. On the table in the rear, the second subject breathed out loud with a sighing sound that almost sounded like relief. She—it—looked at him with eyes that appeared delighted that he'd returned to her. Adam shuddered and turned his attention away from her strange eyes.

Then he fired into the outstretched arms, puncturing flesh with powerful rounds that ripped limbs and bones apart. At last the arms pulled back, and the hatch was able to close all the way and lock. He was left alone with the strange whines coming from the captured second subject. Adam ignored the sounds coming from the horrifying thing as he made his way to the APC's forward console.

Isaac gave him a rudimentary breakdown on how to drive the APC. They only had a few minutes to discuss it, and Adam hoped to God that he hadn't forgotten anything too important. He sat in front of the console, experimentally wiggled his fingers and turned the ignition. Relief flooded through Adam as the engine roared to life. The console was lit with a hundred lights, and as the engine purred he grasped the wheel and slammed his foot down on the accelerator.

The two soldiers watched from the second story window and when the vehicle came to life below, they both cheered and high-fived one another. Somehow Adam had done it. Thomas wasn't sure how Adam had survived the jump down from the window, but right now the important thing was that they had a way out of here.

"Let's move," Thomas barked.

They ran out the room and flew down the stairs, where Jenny was waiting beside the still unconscious Danny.

"Get ready to move," Thomas shouted.

The living room wall caved inward with a loud crash. The APC forced its way through the home and rolled along the now ruined carpet as it came to a stop a few centimeters in front of Sparrow Company. They heard the hatch slide open. Thomas and Jenny quickly lifted Danny on the cot that they'd fashioned for him earlier. Isaac waited by the door, rifle at the ready, while they loaded the injured man into the vehicle.

The dead swarmed into the home, shuffling through the fresh opening in the wall. Isaac shot down five of them before he leapt in through the portal after the others. As the hatch sealed itself shut, Isaac quickly moved to the front and relieved Adam of his chair. He reversed the vehicle out of the hole and felt the satisfying crunch of bodies being turned to mush beneath the oversized tires of the large behemoth. As they quickly sped away from the infested neighborhood, they cheered Adam and laughed together as they escaped what would have been their certain deaths.

"Great work," Thomas commented.

Jenny gave him a strong embrace and whispered her thanks into Adam's ear.

Light-headed, feeling the adrenaline continue to rush through his body, Adam sank on one of the chairs and breathed a heavy sigh of relief. Somewhere behind them the zombies cried out in anger and frustration. None of that mattered to Adam and the members of Sparrow Company. They'd all gotten out of the pits of hell alive, and they were bringing home another person who would hopefully be saved by the professor's serum.

"I'm beat," Adam mouthed as he closed his eyes and slept.

Part Three
The Professor's Student

"Charon was a God of the Underworld, who ferried the souls of the dead across the Styx. I aim to ferry the dead back."

Chapter Fifteen

Over the next few weeks, the professor and the scientists of the Charon Initiative, had confirmed what Adam grew to suspect. The ZF-93 antivirus left him with a few unexpected side effects. He was sent through hundreds of physical tests, but the results were all the same. He'd become strong—stronger than any human should be. And he hadn't yet reached his full potential. Although his memories yet eluded him, his intellect had advanced beyond what anyone had expected. Statistically speaking, Adam was a genius, and perhaps at the same level as the professor. His grasp of theoretical physics, chemistry and the technology the Charon Initiative used became less intimidating and daunting to him over time. His skills with medicine developed further over the weeks and there was little doubt now that in his past life Adam must have been a doctor of some sort.

A doctor...it was something hard for him to believe, however he was filled with a sense of swelling pride, knowing that his past self had chosen such a noble profession. He wondered if he'd worked in a hospital in the old world, though that would imply that he was over two hundred years old. Perhaps he had died more recently and had learned how to heal the sick and injured while surviving a world ruled by the undead.

He feared that it would become a question that would endure for the rest of his days. He thought of this as he stared into the smooth curved glass surface in front of him.

Suspended above the steel grated surface of the floor by giant robotic arms, the eerily familiar glass tube was filled with the blue liquid known as ZF-93. The tube, which seemed almost like a highly advanced coffin to Adam's eyes, hovered in front of him, housing within it its precious cargo. The female subject they'd acquired several weeks ago on their mission to the second safe house stared down at Adam from where she floated with her feet at his chest level. Her rows of yellow teeth were visible through her torn and desiccated lips, and her eyes looks down at him with feral hunger. Her palms pockmarked with sores and gruesome trails of torn muscle fibers, were pressed against the inside of the glass surface. Her fingernails raked against the impenetrable glass, clawing ceaselessly in the forever need to find and rend human flesh. She floated in her bluish prison like an angel of death, her dark hair floating in the viscous liquid in a hauntingly beautiful way.

The subject suddenly slammed its shoulder against the inside of its prison. The surprisingly powerful blow shook the tube slightly even against the mechanized arms that were supposed to hold it perfectly in place. Adam lifted his rifle, worried that the creature might somehow break through the glass, but the surface held, and the thing continued to look down at him with seething hunger burning in its eyes. He shivered.

He jumped when a hand landed softly on his shoulder. He spun and found the professor standing there behind him, looking at him with a kind smile on his face.

"Are you all right?" he asked. "You seem a little jumpy."

"I don't know what's wrong with me," Adam lowered the rifle and scratched the back of his head. "I'll be alright, I promise."

"We're about to start today's trials. If you'd like to stay and watch, you're more than welcome to," Florentine offered.

Adam hesitated, pondering the prospect and nodded.

* * * *

Adam stood side by side with the professor and behind them dozens of men and women in white lab coats worked on their computers, prepping the day's tests and trials. Amongst the researches, he and the professor stood out clearly. Today the older man wore a brown tweed suit and a curious looking blue bow tie. Adam was dressed in his usual military attire and was the only one in the room carrying a weapon of any sort. He glanced over at the professor as the man looked on towards the floating dead woman and wondered if the old man carried a gun on him somewhere hidden on his person. Adam smiled and believed that the professor had some means of defending himself somewhere on him. He didn't seem the type to be foolish enough to believe that he was completely safe, even with that thing secured in its glass prison.

Beyond closed door of the large laboratory stood a total of eight guards, four of which were his teammates from Sparrow Company. The chamber was a half circle in shape and its walls were painted with a bright sterile white color scheme. The hum of the dozens of computers filled the air along with the sound of keyboards tapping rhythmically behind him. The room was divided in four levels, separate tiers that began at the entrance and descending gradually towards the capsule at the head of the room. A short flight of steps split down the center of these tiers.

Over the past few weeks, Adam had gotten to know a few of the researchers working behind him and the professor. There was George, an elderly looking man that the group had come to call *Uncle Sam* because of the similarities between his facial hair and that of the historical figure. Stan and Redfield enjoyed playing at least one game of poker during their lunch hours, and sometimes they would even try to deal Adam in and teach him the nuances of the game.

Adam had also grown to suspect that Stan had a strong attraction to the young woman named Lori, who stood to his left, just outside the red line, scribbling madly into a thick notebook she carried. Adam heard the whispers of Kenneth as he shared a lewd joke with Imogene behind their terminals. Jesse and Emma, who were actually newly-weds, focused on preparing the final preparations for the procedure.

Although Adam didn't have to turn around and look, he suspected that Campbell, sitting close to the married couple, was doing his usual best to sneak a few peeks at Emma's cleavage or backside. Victor, a middle aged man who always seemed to carry a disheveled look, raked his fingers through his head of wild hair and took another sip of his steaming mug of coffee.

These were the senior members of the Charon Initiative. All of them had their strengths and weaknesses, dreams and vices, but they were all people who helped to bring him back to life. Over the course of many months, Adam grew to know a little bit of each and every one of them, and though he wasn't close to all of them, he knew he would lay down his life for any one of them if the need ever arose. Now, here they were all, assembled once more and focused on continuing their work to save the last of the human race.

"Are we almost ready to begin, Mister Wagner?" the professor asked George.

"Just about, professor," George replied.

A few minutes later, machinery came to life with loud humming sounds as the robotic arms brought the glass capsule forward a few feet. Then, a silver ring descended from the ceiling, and with the help of more artificial arms, it began to move up and down the length of the tube. Bright yellow light poured forth from the inner surface of this ring, bathing the contents of the capsule in its powerful glow. The subject regarded the light with confusion as it moved back and forth along the length of its body.

Adam recalled a little bit about the process he was put through, and he remembered this light well. Like him, the second subject was most likely at a complete loss as to what the strange light was doing.

Adam had ascertained that the light was pouring UV radiation into the tube, in an attempt to stimulate the ZF-93 solution as well as the dead skin cells of the zombie. Because a zombie's veins lacked the ability to pump blood through its system, complete submersion of the creature was required in a large quantity of ZF-93. The UV light acted as a sort of catalyst for the serum.

As the metal ring continued to rise and fall in front of them, Florentine turned his head slightly to regard his first subject. The look on the old man's face was tired and worn. It seemed that he wasn't sleeping well again, and it probably had a lot to do with the creature in front of them.

"You've been visiting this facility quite a bit these past few weeks," he said to Adam. "I understand why you wish to be here, but you don't have to be present during every single session. You could get some rest. Go out a little. Maybe experience the city a bit."

"I want to be here as much as I can," Adam curled his lip into half a smile. "I am a little tired, but you look worse than me."

"The worries of an old man," the professor explained with a wave of his hand.

"You're worried about your children."

Florentine looked a little surprised. "Is that how you see the two of you?" he asked.

This time the smile that grew on Adam's lips was full and true. "I do consider you like a father, professor."

The professor held a look of swelling pride that bordered on tears. When he spoke once more it was with a hint of trepidation, as if he was a little uncomfortable to speak as such in front of the other scientists and researchers.

"I consider you like a son to me," he said as he did before when Adam had been in Canmore. "Thank you."

Had the situation not been so awkward, Adam might have embraced the old man. Instead he just smiled and nodded to the old man, knowing that there was no real need to express any further how he felt for the professor. Florentine knew how Adam felt, and that was all that really needed to be said for now.

"I will be away next week," Adam said. "We're being deployed outside the city to some place called Calgary."

"Well, take care of yourself," the professor replied. "It's a very dangerous world out there. I trust in Sparrow Company and I know that you're among good people. Plus," the professor continued, jabbing Adam once in the shoulder with his finger. "You have your unexplainable strength and intellect to help you out now."

"Do you know where it came from?" Adam asked.

"I have several theories. Perhaps it was something left behind from your experience as an undead. The walking dead are known to have the uncanny strength to tear through secured doors and rip their victims limb from limb. Maybe you retained whatever strange strength they gain after they die and come back as one of them. There is also another theory, but one that I'm basing on nothing more than fanciful conjecture."

"And what's that, professor?"

"Do you know what started this war? Do you know how the living dead first came to be?"

"Of course not," Adam frowned. "From what I know, nobody alive knows how they came to be."

"You have heard the theories though?"

Adam smirked, thinking of some of the more ridiculous ones that came to his mind then. Most believed that pollution and chemical testing had caused the end of the world over two hundred years ago. There were theories that the virus had originated from an asteroid that had come from a faraway galaxy, only to crash into the earth after its millennia long journey through the cosmos. Some believed that an ancient disease known as *mad cow* had mutated into it. And perhaps the most amusing and preposterous theory that Adam had heard of was that the zombie virus was demonic in nature, originating from devilish creatures from another dimension.

"Oh, I've heard theories," Adam grinned.

"There is one that I'm particularly interested in. It's about the idea that, in the old world, the military powers had each been experimenting with drugs to create a 'being' they dubbed a super soldier. Perhaps one of these countries had succeeded in developing a way to enhance a man's intellect and strength. It could be that this same process gave way to some more unforeseeable developments, particularly the plague that brought the dead back to life. It could explain their strength and yours."

"It's also crazy," Adam commented.

"True," the professor burst out in laughter. "But it is an amusing thought. Well, at least I think so. Who knows really how this all began. All that I'm concerned with at the moment is reversing the damage caused by this virus. So much was destroyed in those early days, and so very little survives today. For now, we have to keep looking forward, to do as much as we can to save those of us that are left."

Adam glanced towards the creature in its glass prison. It was looking at him fully now and he shuddered under its lustful gaze.

"It's more than that, I think," Adam said. "Because of what you're doing here, maybe we can turn them all back."

Chapter Sixteen

For the moment she had no name. For now the scientists simply referred to her as Subject Two.

Subject Two floated in her glass prison and observed the world beyond the small confines of her own. The world, as she perceived it, was awash with powerful shades of crimson. That color had changed somewhat over the past few weeks, and as the procedure continued, her undead eyes began to process other shades and colors. The liquid that she floated in began to take on a different quality, and her simple brain couldn't process what it was or why it had changed at all.

Another sensation that had returned to her was the sense of touch. The inside surface of the curved glass felt smooth to her touch, and as she scraped away at it with her cracked and brown fingernails, she felt the sensation of warmth flowing through her body as the strange light oscillated back and forth outside of the cylinder.

Before this, all she had felt was the endless hunger that gnawed deep inside of her. Unlike most of her kind, Subject Two could remember bits and pieces of what had happened up to about three months before. She remembered stalking the quiet city in search of something to chew on. It didn't matter what it was she ate. For all the creature cared, a deer or the carcass of a dead bird would do.

At times she would even try to consume the leaves and branches found in the forests. Eating such things only sated a mere fraction of her hunger, and no matter how much she shoveled into her mouth, it was never nearly enough. What she desired the most was human flesh. What she looked forward to the most were the wet bits that resided within their bodies. Unlike most of her undead brethren, she took a miniscule amount of pleasure from biting into squishy organs, or the dark marrow that could be found inside the bones.

With some relish, she recalled an incident that occurred shortly before her capture. She had been chasing after a couple who'd gotten lost from the rest of their group. Through the desolate streets of Canmore, she followed them into a darkened sporting goods store. She was faster than most of the other undead, and unlike the vast majority of them, her body was still whole and strong.

That was why it was easy for Subject Two to follow after the young couple as they fled into the dilapidated structure. There, she'd managed to corner them, and it was there that she had taken a hold of the woman and began to feast. The man had been screaming, and trying his best to pull her off of his friend.

But it was already too late, and with the zombie's teeth hungrily tearing at the flesh around the woman's neck, it was impossible for the man to try and save his girl. She was already infected, and within hours she would die and return shortly after as another of the living dead.

The man had beat on her head, still trying to get her off of the woman. His efforts had enraged Subject Two, and the creature had lashed out, grabbing one of the man's arms and driving her teeth deep into his hairy flesh. There wasn't much left that either could do now that they'd been bitten. Within minutes, the struggles of the two humans had ceased, and the hungry monster knelt between their bodies, feasting ravenously on the warm and wet meat.

As she floated in the blue liquid, Subject Two looked upon the creatures dressed in white and hungered. It had been quite a while since she'd fed, and she looked upon these humans with a maddening desire to break out of this prison and eat.

Her attention focused constantly on one particular human, one dressed in dark clothes. Occasionally he'd be accompanied by an older man, but what Subject Two focused on more was the man in the dark clothes. When she looked at him she hungered for his flesh and organs, but there was also something else about him that would draw her to gaze constantly at him. He was different. When she looked at Adam, she knew he'd once been something like her. She wanted to tear him apart, starting at his stomach, in hopes of discovering what was so different about him when compared to the other humans.

The metal ring passed over her once more, bathing her in its radiant light and its soothing warmth. Subject Two had changed enough now that she could appreciate the subtle sensation of the lights warm touch against her slowly regenerating skin. The touch of the blue liquid was slick against the subject's flesh, and even it noticed that it was banging its fists less and less on the glass.

Subject Two flicked its tongue out, tasting the strange water, making both the old man and the object of her interest flinch.

* * * *

Time passed for the Charon Initiative and for a while Adam wasn't around to observe the ZF-93 trials.

The creature didn't know that Adam had been deployed out of the city on duty, but it began to feel a sense of loneliness from his absence. It couldn't understand why it would even begin to feel this way but it did, and it felt that it longed to gaze upon this strange man once more. It desired the flesh of the living less, and when it looked at the old man and his scientists, it felt that it wasn't as hungry as it had been before.

Sure, it would still tear into the humans and feast like a rabid dog, but it no longer felt the red hot rage that had driven its madness months before. The memories of its life as a living corpse began to fade and it floated in the liquid often in a trance. The scientists were baffled by this behavior.

The only one who had an inkling of this truth was the old man. The professor watched the creature's strange, docile behavior, comparing it to the behavior of his first subject and suspected that the second subject was already beginning to question its reason for being.

More time passed until one day, it began to thrash madly in its glass prison. Its lungs had finally developed to the point where they began to seek the nourishment found only in oxygen. The second subject flailed madly, beating its fists against the glass with powerful blows. It was drowning and it didn't even know it.

One of the scientists quickly inputted a series of commands into a keyboard and the robotic arms activated and shifted the capsule to a horizontal position. A loud pop filled that air. It was followed by a sharp hiss, and as the top of the capsule flew off from the rest of the object, a tidal wave of blue liquid rushed forth and splashed loudly on the metal grate covering much of the floor below. The creature slid out, and as it landed hard on the metal grate it lay still like a lifeless doll.

Fear shot through the professor like a lightning bolt. The other scientists scrambled forward to help, and then they all paused and remembered that it wasn't that long ago that Subject Two had been a ravenous monster, willing to use any of them for a lunchtime snack. They all knew the woman's lungs were flooded with the blue fluid, but none of them were willing to come any closer than a few feet towards her. The professor, shaking his head in disappointment at the others, moved forward.

Before he could go down to his knees next to this cold body, Adam was there, gently pushing the old man aside and moving ahead of the others. Adam knelt on the cold and wet metal grate on the floor. There was no hesitation in his movements when he turned the woman over onto her back and began to administer CPR.

Minutes passed and as Adam continued to work furiously at the still form, the others watched in awe and silence. None of them wanted such a rare specimen to die, especially not after all the hard work they'd put in to helping bring her back.

The subject's chest heaved as it vomited blue liquid from its lungs. Adam backed away, panting and sweating, but with a look of stark relief on his face as the subject began to cough. It breathed in great gulps of air, and the professor relaxed a little and removed the hand he never realized had been pressed hard on his chest the entire time. The woman coughed up more fluid and when she opened her eyes, she was completely blinded by the bright lights of the room. The light was stronger out here than it had been inside the capsule and her eyes slammed shut as she winced in discomfort and pain.

The soldiers entered the room at this point and the members of Sparrow Company joined by Adam's side and watched as the second subject breathed in air for the first time in her new life in this strange and dangerous world.

* * * *

"My God," Thomas spoke. "It worked."

"You mean, it worked again," Danny said as he looked down at the struggling body.

"Tell me you're not checking her out," Jenny groaned.

"Hey, I've been in a hospital bed for a long time here," Danny protested. "All I got to look at were old doctors and even older looking nurses the whole time."

"You do remember me visiting you a few times, don't you?" Jenny frowned.

Danny nodded, grinning. "Yes. It was just about the only thing that kept me going, seeing your face every now and then."

Jenny was silent but the slight reddening of her face wasn't lost to any of the people present in the room. The only one who didn't seem to notice was Danny himself, who obviously hadn't intended the comment to elicit such a reaction from his female comrade. Isaac glanced at Danny, rolled his eyes at his friend's ignorance and groaned.

"We need to get her to a secure room, professor," Thomas growled.

"Yes, yes. Of course, sergeant," Florentine shook himself out of his deep thoughts. "Will you and your company assist her to Adam's old room? Redfield, will you and Lori find something for the young woman to wear?"

The two scientists retreated to do as they were asked. Adam hadn't said a word since helping resuscitate the woman. He still knelt beside her, his pants soaking in the blue solution of the professor's cure.

Silently he looked at the face of this seemingly young woman and what he saw in her face and dark hair reminded him of the woman from his dreams. He knew this wasn't her, but still the connection had already been made and he swore a silent oath to himself that he would do everything he could to protect this girl and guide her in her first steps in this new life.

"We need to give her a name," the professor announced. "Adam, since it was you that found her, I believe it would only be appropriate that you be the one to choose a name for her."

"Me?" Adam balked as he finally looked up for the first time in almost ten minutes.

Even though he knew he was far from alone in this room, he was still surprised to see so many gathered around him and the second subject. For a moment he was speechless and when he focused on the professor's eyes he saw that there was no way of changing his mind on the matter.

"Please don't tell me you're going to call her *Eve* or something," Danny sighed loudly.

The truth was that the idea hadn't even occurred to Adam, although now it did make sense. No, he didn't feel that calling the second subject Eve was right. Perhaps it was a little too obvious. When he glanced at Danny, he suddenly knew what he would call this new person.

"Amanda," he suddenly spoke almost in a whisper.

When he announced it for the first time, he glanced at Danny and found that his expression was completely unreadable. He'd expected something, anything that might indicate either surprise or anger towards Adam. Adam didn't intend to upset Danny. He wanted to honor the woman that had meant so much to this brave and lonely soldier. There were shocked expressions all around, including from those in the company. Obviously there were quite a few who'd heard of Danny and his lost wife.

Even the professor looked momentarily at a loss. Then he regained his composure and smiled down at Adam with a firm nod.

"Amanda is a perfect name," he said.

* * * *

Amanda sat alone in the dark atop the small room's single bed. She ran her fingers along the rough fabric of the shirt and pants that the others gave her. She looked up and noticed another one of the dark eyes staring down at her from he room's corner.

When the door ahead of her suddenly unlocked loudly, she jumped. Creeping terror ran along the length of her curiously smooth arms and up the back of her slender neck. When the old man entered, followed by the young man who interested her so much before, she relaxed a little. The old man smiled at her kindly as he stepped closer to her.

"Good morning, Amanda," he spoke. "I hope...well, I guess it's a little pointless for me to speak at all with you right now, but one day I hope you will understand what I'm saying. You, Amanda, are a very unique individual. Adam here's the only other person in this world like you. There's so much to explain, but we'll get to it eventually. I know you can't understand me, but I hope you know you are safe here."

Amanda stared back at him, then glanced over the man's shoulder towards Adam. He stood by the open door with a warm smile on his face. Amanda felt like smiling back at him, but felt that it might be taken in a wrong way somehow.

"Where should we start?" The professor clapped his hands together. "Well, I suppose that I should introduce myself first. I am Professor Florentine Mena, and I run a group known as the Charon Initiative. Our goal is to help those that wander the world outside these walls, those that we call the living dead."

"It's nice...to meet you, Florentine," Amanda suddenly spoke. "And you too, Adam."

The looks on both of the men's faces was that of utter shock. Amanda grimaced, unsure of what she'd done wrong.

Chapter Seventeen

The dreams started immediately on her first night in this new world. The same nightmare followed her through many of her lonely nights.

Amanda dreamt of death, but it wasn't death of murder she had been accustomed to as one of the undead. No, these were images of slaughter and violence so profound that in her sleep, she wept bitterly. She pictured herself in front of a tall mirror. The face that stared back at her was that of a child's. Long black bangs covered much of her face, but the dark strands failed to hide the purple welts that marred her sad features.

She was in a small room, and she heard shouting voices outside her closed and locked door. It was a man's voice, followed by a firm slapping sound and a young boy's pained cry.

In her room, Amanda trembled violently. Outside, the boy's vicious beating continued. The sounds of knuckles pounding on meat made her cringe with every blow. Amanda didn't know where she was, and she had no clue why her mind even conjured up such a horrible nightmare. All that she knew was she was so terrified that she couldn't move.

The boy's wails turned to frail whimpers.

Amanda continued to stare at her reflection. Warm tears continued to flow from her reddened eyes.

She knew these were images from her past. In her dream she cried, but she also knew this man was her father. The boy, her brother, was being beaten, but she knew eventually all of this would end. Somewhere further in the future she saw the bodies of both her father and her brother, as they lay on the ground surrounded by the shuffling forms of terrifying things better left to human imaginations and nightmares.

* * * *

"I don't understand, Professor. How can she already know how to talk?"

"Adam, everyone's mind is different." Florentine rubbed his

eyes, sighing. "No single person on this world is truly like another. The fact that she is already able to speak suggests a few theories to me. I believe that her brain was not as damaged as yours may have been. When she died, there might have still been enough blood flow or oxygen in her brain to keep enough of her mind together before the virus finally turned her. There are theories that also suggest that the time between a person's death and when they rise again can determine the amount of damage that occurs to that person's brain. There's a possibility that she just turned faster than you did."

"Or, maybe, she's special."

"That could also be true," The professor paused, looking hard at Adam. "Are you doing alright?"

Adam nodded quickly. "Yes. Sorry. I'm just a little tired I guess."

"How is everyone from the Company?"

"They're doing well. I couldn't ask for a better group of people."

"Are you making friends with them?"

"Actually, I'm starting to feel like I really belong with them."

"That's good to hear."

* * * *

Silence followed for a long moment. As she lay in her bed, slowing waking up, Amanda kept her eyes closed and listened. How long had they been in the room with her? She hoped that she hadn't cried out during her sleep. The dry tears under her eyes suggested that she'd been crying recently. She wondered if Adam and the professor knew.

* * * *

"I hear that you're starting up a new facility in New Edmonton's sister city, in...Himura Valley?" Adam inquired after a moment.

"That's right. I'm sending Imogene and a few others to help set up the new Charon facility. Kenneth will be leading the project there. Their military has already begun to send out parties in search of viable test subjects."

"I can't believe it, professor. It's finally starting to happen, isn't it?"

"Oh yes, Adam, and I couldn't be more proud. It's a miracle that the project has moved ahead so smoothly during this testing phase. We now have two individuals who stand as living proof that we can finally beat this ancient plague. Also, how is Danny holding up these days?"

"His wounds have healed. It's a good thing we got him back here quickly. It helped to treat him in a proper facility."

"That's good to know, but I wasn't really referring to that."

"Oh..."

"Why did you name her after Danny's dead wife, Amanda?"

Amanda's ears perked up as she strained to listen to Adam's reply.

"He...Dan...he lost so much. I know that I've lost people important to me, professor. I don't know who they are or where they fit in my past life, but they were very important to whomever I was before. I just...it wasn't like I wanted to hurt him. I wanted to call her Amanda so that his wife's name would be remembered as the second of the first two people who was cured by your serum, created by the man who saved the world."

"Adam, I..."

"It's true, professor. I know that you didn't start this initiative of yours to satisfy some personal need of self-gratification. You did it to help people, and you have. What you helped create is something that I believe is the cure for the plague. You, Professor Florentine Mena, saved mankind. You're a hero, and nobody even acknowledges you for it."

It was then, while the professor was at a loss for words, that Amanda sneezed. She groaned as she shook the last remnants of sleep from her head and she slowly rose up to a sitting position with her back resting against the headboard. Her whole body was still sore and the professor explained that was her muscles simply trying to rebuild what the procedure had started and left for nature to finish.

Amanda rubbed the sleep from her eyes and regarded her two visitors with a tired smile. The professor grinned as he took a seat in one of the two chairs next to her bed. Adam hesitated and their eyes locked for a brief moment. She couldn't understand the strange look that dwelled in those brown eyes, but a strange sense of warmth began to fill her belly. He glanced down towards the floor, breaking his stare and then moved to sit in the chair near the foot of the bed.

"Good morning, Amanda," Florentine greeted her.

"Hey," Adam managed to grin.

"How was your sleep?" the professor asked.

"Good," she lied, conscious of the fact that she knew how to do so. "Uh...I haven't remembered anything yet."

"Are you still dreaming of yourself as a little girl?"

Amanda frowned as she looked down at her knees. She suddenly realized that her hands gripped the blanket in tight fists. The skin on her palms sweated and her breathing came short and quick.

"Amanda, did you have another nightmare?" the professor pressed.

She nodded slowly and both men sighed.

"Yes," she finally spoke after a while. "I'm sorry, professor. I just don't like to think about it."

"We don't have to discuss it," Adam leaned closer and she smiled back at him.

"Of course not," the professor looked slightly crestfallen. "But have you learned anything new about your past?"

She shook her head and glanced at Adam once more. She knew most of his past was also a mystery to him. She also understood that he'd recalled a few key bits that hinted at the man he might have been. Amanda wondered what kind of woman she'd been in her past life, but unlike Adam, this mystery gnawed at her psyche during every waking moment. Adam, on the other hand, had either grown used to living with the mystery of his past, or he hid it very well.

"We have some good news for you," Adam tried to change the subject. The grin on his face was earnest, hinting at his excitement.

She frowned, guarded. "What's that?"

"Well, Amanda," the professor began. "We were wondering if you'd like to finally get out of here and see the new world."

* * * *

Five months passed quickly for everyone in New Edmonton. Life in the city continued on except now a sense of excitement permeated its way throughout its populous. With the reveal of Amanda to the world, belief grew in the possible success of the professor's cure. Many began to truly accept that it could be done, that one day in their lives the long fought battle for survival would finally come to an end.

Was it possible? Was there really a chance that they could one day leave the protective walls of their city and journey out into the world to rebuild? The thought of an existence without the constant fear of being murdered and devoured had become a long dreamt fantasy for every person living in the twin cities of New Edmonton and Himura Valley.

As Adam sat in the back of the darkened theatre with Amanda and the rest of the Sparrow Company, he thought about the possibility of peace on earth. He looked to his right where Amanda sat, her eyes glued to the movie playing out before her on the large screen ahead. He studied the slender features of her neckline and how gracefully her long black hair cascaded down her back. Sensing his stare, Amanda glanced at him and winked before returning her attention back to the movie. Embarrassed, Adam quickly jerked away, intent on looking at anything Her.

On Amanda's right sat Jenny and beside her, the sergeant, Isaac and Danny. The two of them laughed with one another softly as they shared some private joke.

The theatre was packed from row to row with people. Apparently it always was, being that it was perhaps one of only two remaining movie theatres in the world. The establishment played old movies on its screens, films found down in the archives, or recovered from scouting missions outside of New Edmonton.

In fact it had become somewhat of a side mission on any of their excursions outside the city walls. On one of his more recent adventures with Sparrow Company, Danny had discovered a treasure trove of old films in one of the various basements in an outlying neighborhood. One of those movies was playing in this theatre at the moment. It was an old movie about a serial killer and a female FBI agent tasked to stop him. Stumped in her investigation, she is sent by her mentor to seek help from a brilliant insane doctor currently locked up behind a strange prison with a glass wall facing the hallway.

For Adam, it was strange to see the world as it might have existed hundreds of years ago. The images perplexed him, making him wonder at how strange it must have been for the people on the screen to live in a world very much unlike his.

Danny and Isaac seemed to be particularly pleased with the movie. Thomas' facial expression was a blank caricature carved into stone, but that was nothing new. Jenny seemed to be enjoying it as well, and Amanda...He caught himself staring at her again and quickly shot his eyes back up towards the screen.

* * * *

Afterwards, they met up together outside the theater's front doors. It was getting late into the night, but even now two lines leading into the already packed theatre stretched out down the length of the sidewalk all the way to the end of the block. The winter air blew with a chill whisper across Adam's face, making him shiver under his brown coat. Amanda trembled slightly as well as she plunged her hands in the warmth of her own armpits. His friends were perfectly at ease even out in the cold weather. Adam suspected that they'd spent many nights out in frigid weather such as this.

"Well, thanks for the invite guys," Thomas said.

"Have a good night, sir," Danny said as Thomas left his companions and slowly melted into the shadows of the night without another word.

"He usually cuts out early," Jenny explained to Adam and Amanda. "He's not a very social man, but you've probably guessed that already."

"Shocking," Amanda laughed.

"Yeah, that's our sergeant," Danny commented. "I wouldn't go anywhere outside the city walls without him watching my back though."

The rest of the company nodded in mutual agreement.

For a few minutes they laughed and talked about their favorite moments and joked about some of the more intriguing and surprising plot points of the film. Adam once more felt at ease with the rest of the company, and he was starting to really feel like he belonged here with them.

Amanda glanced up at Adam's self-assuring smiled, and she inched a little closer to him. He didn't notice her as she admired him quietly, stealing glances at him from time to time.

When the group decided to part ways for the night, Isaac turned to face Adam.

"I almost forgot again." He slapped his palm on his forehead. "Congratulations on your promotion, Lieutenant Adam Whatever-your-name-is."

"You too, First Lieutenant Isaac Tennant," Adam laughed.

They each gave each other a mock salute and shook hands before Isaac retreated down the sidewalk.

Alone now with Amanda, Adam offered to walk her back to the apartment.

"Oh, such a generous man," she quipped. "Considering that we both live in the same complex and on the same floor."

"I am still walking you there," he pointed out. "The effort is still there, so technically I'm not wrong."

She laughed as she playfully punched his arm. He didn't doubt that she meant for it to be a light tap, Her punch surprisingly hurt him a little. Amanda didn't seem to notice and Adam decided to keep this to himself. He wondered if Amanda was aware of the changes within her and he wondered why she was developing faster that he had. For the time being, he and the professor decided to observe her for now, before delving with her on this subject.

"How's it been, working with the professor?" he asked, deciding to try and divert his thoughts onto other matters.

"Slow at first, but it's very exciting. There's so much to learn, and sometimes I feel like a complete moron when I'm surrounded by all those other scientists and doctors."

"Well, whoever you were in the past must have been a really smart woman. The professor mentioned that you've already begun to grasp some of the more complex mathematics involved with the ZF-93 serum."

A saddened expression clouded her expression. The look seemed wrong somehow, like it didn't belong on a face as beautiful as hers.

"I'm sorry," he apologized. "I'm also still trying to find out who I was."

"At least you figured out that you were a doctor," Amanda brightened up a little. "I mean, that's pretty damn significant, if you ask me. You should be the one working with the professor and his team. Not me."

"I might have been a doctor," he said, holding up one finger. "I'm not a hundred percent sure of it yet."

"Well, it doesn't matter to me," she smiled one of her warm smiles that made his insides feel like static. "I like you just the way you are."

Embarrassed, he said little else as they made their way through the snowy sidewalk. When they arrived at the apartment, Adam and Amanda stood apart and faced one another at the threshold of her apartment door. He worked through his head feverishly, sifting through his thoughts, trying to find something to say to fill the suddenly strange silence that descended between them. He suddenly felt like an idiot.

He still couldn't believe that it had been only a few months ago when he had found this woman and brought her home with him. At the time she was one of those creatures living beyond the walls of New Edmonton, she was one of the monsters that continued to roam the earth without purpose or reason. Now, she was developing in a seemingly faster rate than Adam had, and he was glad for it. Adam remained in the military, while Amanda had taken the surprising decision to join the Charon Initiative. After only a few weeks, she had already begun to grasp the work they were doing there. Adam smiled to himself and thought about how one day he might be bringing another subject back to the city for her, so that she could do her part in turning the thing back into a human being.

"We're like those couples in the movies," she teased him.

"It is pretty cheesy, isn't it?" Adam rubbed the back of his head with a sweaty hand. "Wait, did you just call us a couple?"

Without warning, Amanda leapt forward and kissed him full on the lips. Stunned, he simply stood there, wide-eyed, staring at her closed eyelids. His shock melted away quickly, and he wrapped his arms around her waist and kissed her back.

After a while they separated and Adam stared at her in disbelief.

"Too much?" she asked, gently biting her lower lip.

"Nope," he replied, an ear-to-ear grin splitting his face.

"Good night, Adam," she smiled as she began to slowly close the door on him.

"Wait a minute," he balked. He swallowed. "So are we dating now, or what?"

"Good night," she said in a teasing and playful way as she closed the door.

The door clicked shut in Adam's face and for a long while he just stood there with a shocked expression on his face. His surprise melted away and was soon replaced by an overwhelming feeling of pure joy.

"I'll call you," he joked.

He kept smiling to himself as he made his way down the hall to his own apartment. Since his rebirth, he'd never felt so good.

* * * *

Amanda kept a little secret from the others. She downplayed how terrible her dreams truly were and how often she would experience them.

They came to her periodically and when she'd wished Adam a good night and closed her door a dreadful feeling began to fill her. She took her time to get undressed, took even longer to find the nerve to get into the shower. When she was in there, she let the hot water soak her back and the top of her head for almost an hour as she kept her eyes closed and tried desperately to clear her troubled thoughts. Time slowed down to an agonizing crawl. Eventually she made her way to her bed, snuggled herself into her thick covers and made sure that the bed sheet was pressed tightly all around her.

It wasn't the darkness of the room that she feared. Rather it was what was to come when she closed her eyes and let the lull of sleep eventually take her.

* * * *

Amanda sat in the furthest corner in some unknown basement, and she watched as a shadowy figure dragged men and women down a flight of stairs where they always met some terrible and horrendous end beyond the foot of the creaky old stairs. The face of this killer was obscured by the inky darkness that seemed to cloak the figure in a shadowy drape. Amanda knew instinctively that the person torturing these people was not one of the undead.

This...monster...was human.

The killer never appeared to take notice of her as she sat huddled by herself in the corner of the cellar. Amanda, however, knew this person was fully aware of her presence, but for some reason always chose to leave her alone.

Perhaps the killer wanted Amanda to witness his atrocities. Maybe he took some enjoyment from slaughtering innocents in front of his single captive audience.

In the corner of the basement, hidden in the gloom of darkness, she watched with tear-filled eyes as the killer arrived once more with a new victim in tow.

He announced his arrival with the loud bang of the cellar door, slamming it against the opposite wall. Amanda heard the muffled cries of a woman whose mouth sounded like it was gagged with a thick binding of cloth. Her thrashing movements slammed repeatedly against the floorboards upstairs, and yellow light spilled through from the open cellar door, illuminating only a small section of the stairs that led down to her level.

Amanda watched and stifled a scream as she saw in that light, the now familiar shadow of the killer. He stood there at the head of the stairs for a long moment, dragging out both her and his new victim's terror. The killer began to descend the steps, each one creaking loudly, sounding like they could snap beneath their weight at any moment. The stranger made his way down slowly, taking each step with care and malicious pleasure. He—or she—fully understood the terror that each step injected into this bound and helpless victim. And who was she in this dream, other than an observer, completely unable to help?

The killer stopped at the foot of the stairs and looked upon the weeping woman with empty eyes. Not a trace of remorse lingered in those damaged eyes—eyes that had seen so much, too much, and still desired to witness more.

* * * *

Amanda woke up with a start and sat bolt upright in bed, gasping desperately as she fought frantically to escape from the terrible dream. Her skin from her forehead down to her stomach was covered in warm sweat. She felt her heart hammering madly in her chest. She placed a palm there as the tightness began to send ripples of pain through her. Her heart felt as if it was going to explode inside of her. As she struggled to gain some control over her heavy breathing, she grappled with the lingering dream that continued to haunt her mind.

Alone in her room, Amanda wept into the palms of her hands.

Chapter Eighteen

Adam took the rear position as the team exited the vehicle and made their way through the front doors of the two story building and up the two flights of stairs. As usual, Isaac waited behind, monitoring both the communications and the life signs of the team on his monitors.

Sparrow Company responded to a frantic distress call received from a location on 101st street. This was the first time Adam got to experience a case such as this and, as the company sped towards the location in the APC, he wondered what he would find.

It felt strange for him to carry his rifle within the city walls. He exhaled calm breaths as he kept an adequate distance behind Jenny. His pulse began to race and he felt excitement and fear growing inside of him as they made their way along the crimson carpet of the second floor. A few of the apartment doors on this level stood slightly open, and frightened eyes peered through the crack of the door, watching as these soldiers invaded the safety of their home.

The caller, a woman named Dana Blake, met them halfway to their destination. Adam observed she was wearing a pink bath-robe tied tightly around her waist. Her curly brown hair looked like it had been brushed in a hurry.

"Which apartment is she in, Ms. Blake?" the sergeant asked her in an unusual comforting tone. The words of comfort, com-bined with his sheer size and threatening appearance was a star-tling comparison, and Adam noted the moment of apprehension in Ms. Blake's eyes.

"She's in apartment nineteen," she said, pointing down the hall with a trembling hand.

Adam looked down the hall to the shut door. Warm sunlight spilled through the square window in the far wall, illuminating the slight swirls of dust dancing in the air.

"When I heard the noises, I knew I had to call it in right away," Ms. Blake continued with a little bit more confidence in her voice. "She's usually up earlier than my husband, to let her cats out so they can wander. I wondered if there was something wrong when

I didn't see her or her cats yesterday. I went to check this morning when I heard the noise."

"You did exactly the right thing, Ms. Blake," Thomas commended her. "Now let us take over from here. Please wait in your apartment and lock your doors until we're done. Does anyone else in the apartment live with her?"

"No," she shook her head. "She lives alone with her three cats. She's got no other family."

"Okay. Please get to your apartment and let us take care of this."

The woman nodded her thanks and rushed off to her home. The door swung shut behind her, followed by the soft click of the turned lock.

"That goes for everyone else," Danny spoke up with a voice that filled the hall. "Please lock your doors and wait in your homes until we're done here."

"You'd think they'd be tired of seeing this kind of thing," Jenny whispered beside Adam.

They formed a half-circle around the door leading into apartment number nineteen. Thomas gave everyone a firm look and nodded. The sergeant reached out and tested the door knob. Adam's pulse quickened. The knob turned only a few inches, apparently locked.

The sergeant pointed towards Jenny, who nodded and moved to stand directly in front of the door. She raised her right foot up into front of her and drove her heel into the face of the door. The door swung open violently, slamming against the wall inside. Faint light from within spilled out into the hall. The apartment was completely quiet beyond the door.

They all filed in as they'd been trained to do, as they'd done so a thousand times before. Even Adam, who was still relatively new to all this, moved into the kitchen immediately, and cleared the area in less than a few seconds. The air was still, as if undisturbed for a very long time.

Unlike his apartment, this one was filled with all manner of objects and personal belongings. A few framed photographs sat on a raised area behind the sink. They were all group portraits, taken of different people in various places within New Edmonton. Some of these places were locations Adam recognized. In all of the photos was an elderly woman standing with the others. Her skin was coppery and heavily wrinkled with age. The smile on her face was warm and welcoming and, when Adam stared at them sadly, a strong sense of loneliness and maybe even envy began to nag at his heart.

A loud crash issued from somewhere else in the apartment and Adam heard Jenny let out a loud cry right before the bursts of muffled gunfire that followed. Adam shouldered his rifle and rushed through the rooms to find the rest of the group already gathered inside the single bedroom. Lying on the floor, at the foot of the bed, was the body of the woman he'd seen in the photographs.

Adam almost didn't recognize her face without its smile. Instead her mouth hung slightly open, glazed eyes staring up at the ceiling in frozen disbelief. Her blouse was torn where the bullets had penetrated, but not a single drop oozed from the fresh wounds.

They all looked down with solemn expressions at the old woman's corpse. For a while nobody knew what to say.

"It looks like Ms. Blake was right," Jenny spoke with a voice that seemed to have lost some of its strength. "Danny found her cats in the living room. They're dead too."

The lack of blood told the group the whole story. This woman had died in her sleep, alone in this apartment. She rose once more post-mortem, only this time she woke up undead.

The distress calls had been growing in number for a while now. With the constant growth of New Edmonton's population came more and more deaths. Most of the time it was the elderly passing from old age, and at other times they were either accidents or murders.

The truth was that every person in the world was infected. Both the living and the dead carried the virus in their blood. In the living it remained dormant until the life of that person expired, allowing the virus to take over what remained. A bite from a fully turned zombie carried with it a more aggressive mutation of this strain, killing and then turning the victim by force. It was only a matter of *when* it would happen to them. Everyone in this awful world was already doomed, and they all knew it.

All of them except Adam and Amanda, who seemed not to carry a single trace of the virus. Whatever this virus was, it was airborne, yet the renewed bodies of the first two subjects seemed to be completely resilient to this sickness. It was this immunity that the professor hoped to use, to augment his cure so that it would also work on the living who carried it. It was only a matter of time before the professor was able to synthesize an improved retrovirus. The problem was how long it would take for that to happen.

In the meantime, the old would pass away and turn, just like this elderly woman had and groups like Sparrow Company would be sent out to put them down. It wasn't a glorious job to take. It was nothing like being out there, fighting to survive to find supplies or survivors to bring back. This was a different kind of horror, a more domestic one. In a way it was almost a more terrifying job to carry out. These ones hit a little closer to home, because it was so close to home—within the great walls surrounding New Edmonton, the dead could still rise.

Thomas put his fingers to his earpiece and radioed for Isaac to begin calling in a clean-up and disposal crew.

"They'll be here within twenty minutes," Danny offered.

"Adam?" Jenny asked. "Where are you going?"

Adam, on his way towards the apartment's front door, turned to regard the concerned look on his teammate's face.

"I need to get some air," he explained to her.

The sergeant threw him a nod to show he understood and Adam quickly made his way through the apartment and out into the hall. Despite their orders, the tenants on this floor had tentatively gathered outside their apartment doors, watching with keen eyes as he slowly moved to stand in the middle of the hall. He looked at all their faces, saw the worry in their eyes and he understood a little of how they must feel. They all knew when their time came they would rise again as one of the undead. As he gazed upon their tired faces, Adam began to feel a great swell of guilt because he was completely free and immune of this infection. The rest of these people weren't so lucky.

He wondered if Amanda felt the same when she looked into the faces of these people. Maybe this was a part of the reason she'd joined the Charon Initiative.

He noticed now that a few of the faces in front of him looked at him in anger. Everyone in New Edmonton knew who he was and he was no stranger to the fact that there were many who either still feared what he once was or loathed that he was immune to the virus of the living dead.

"Everyone, please get back into your rooms and shut your doors," Adam said aloud.

The sound of his voice, the hardened edge it carried, seemed to spook them. Even those faces which showed clear hostility were wiped blank and disappeared behind closed doors. The hallway quickly cleared and he heard the scurrying footsteps of those who had come up from the floor below recede into the lower levels.

Adam sighed and turned to face the window behind him. The warm sunlight that bathed him was a sharp contrast to the freezing winter outside. He looked down to the street below and saw the roof of the APC, parked in front of the apartment building's main doors.

A large crowd had begun to gather down below as well; dozens of figures dressed in warm coats and shivering as they stared at the building, waiting to see what might happen. Adam wondered if it was fear or interest that brought them out of their homes. Did they come to see a spectacle occur, or did they truly want to make sure that they could go back to their homes later knowing they were still safe? Adam hoped for the latter. He hated the thought that there might still be people out there fascinated by violence and death.

Amongst the crowd, he saw the faces of the elderly and understood that the look of terror in their faces was greatly due to them knowing their time was coming. There was no escape for any of them. The only salvation now lay in the cure that the professor was so desperately trying to perfect.

He heard the voices of his teammates inside the apartment as they discussed the possibilities of the professor's cure.

"Can't the professor use the cure he has now to bring this old lady back?" Danny asked the others.

Adam had already long since contemplated this idea and when Jenny spoke, her reply mirrored the conclusion he'd come up with a while ago.

"She died of natural causes, Dan. Her body gave up because it was her time."

Obviously, Danny and Jenny had thought of it as well. The question was how much were they allowed to tamper with the subject of life and death? If the ZF-93 could bring this woman back from the dead, did the Charon Initiative have the right to play God in such a way? This woman, whoever she'd been when she was alive, had died of natural causes. It had simply been her time and did any of them, even the professor, really have the right to bring her back to life?

But what if they *could* do it with the cure? Weren't they obligated to preserve life and give this woman another chance to live?

Adam himself was now living on borrowed time. Although the zombie virus may have been something unnatural, his time on this world ended when he had become one of the living dead. It was as simple as that, and yet here he stood with a rifle in his hands, living and breathing with the rest. What right did he have to live when so many were doomed to live the rest of their lives in fear?

Chapter Nineteen

The professor was impressed with how quickly Amanda learned and developed as an assistant in the lab. Her understanding of the basic science behind what they were doing developed steadily as the days passed in the Charon Initiative. There was no doubt in his mind now that ZF-93 had an additional side effect and he wondered what other changes might be lurking inside of both Adam and Amanda.

Science, Florentine had learned, was a system of balance and perfect order. You couldn't affect something without receiving some kind of repercussion. For example, by destroying the virus inside his subjects, he was able to bring them back to life. There was always a cause and an effect to all things; there were always consequences. He wondered with growing discomfort, what negative effects might his cure have done to Adam and Amanda, as they had yet to come to light.

He had to take stock in the fact that so far everything was going as planned. The fact that ZF-93 had worked at all, and as well as it had, was a miracle to be sure. Now he was starting on the next phase of his life-long project—to completely eradicate the virus from the bodies of both the living and the dead.

* * * *

The professor walked up the winding concrete walkway that led to his home. His family had lived in it for many generations now, situated in the western end of the city. The large mansion had a wide front yard kept by the few gardeners who worked there on occasion.

Many years before more had lived there with him, but his parents had long since passed away now. His older brother, part of the military, had lost his life over twenty years ago on a mission beyond the wall. A swarm had overtaken his squad and none had survived.

Before his brother, however, was a loss that stabbed deeper in Florentine's heart. Lindsay, his wife, had passed away from heart disease. She'd died when both she and Florentine were young. He was thirty-five at the time. She had just reached her thirtieth birthday.

She had passed quietly and he knew he would never forget the look of love in her eyes when he sat at her bedside, holding her hands in his as she breathed her last breaths. Lindsay had told him she wasn't suffering, He knew she had. Like him, Lindsay was stubborn and proud, and she had put on a brave face to save her husband pain as she kept her own to herself.

He'd wept bitterly when she'd passed. He refused to leave the room when a young lieutenant, a man named Thomas Black pleaded with him to do so. It had been Thomas' duty at the time to make sure that Lindsay didn't rise again as one of them.

Florentine rejected the notion of leaving his wife's bedside, He couldn't make himself watch as Thomas hesitatingly un-holstered his gun, attached the silencer and placed it on her forehead. The muffled shot would haunt Florentine for the rest of his days and sometimes he would still wake up in bed in the middle of the night, thinking he'd heard the shot in the same room. He'd turn quickly to face the area where his wife had lain in her final days, but of course she wouldn't be there.

On more than one occasion, Florentine wondered if his cure could somehow bring his wife back, but she'd been gone too long now. There would be little left of her body, buried in the cemetery not far from his home. Even if her body was able to be revived, he wouldn't allow himself to entertain the notion he could use science to force her back to life. It would be an immoral use of all he'd worked for. Her time had come and now she was at peace. Florentine refused to become this generation's Doctor Frankenstein. Lindsay was dead and buried long before he'd formed the Charon Initiative.

He entered the front doors of his empty home and let them close softly behind him. He took in a breath as he gazed around at the well-furnished lobby. Very few in this day and age lived in a home like his, but even with all of his possessions, Florentine felt penniless and alone. What good were the paintings, the small wooden pedestals holding rare vases and the fine carpet beneath his feet when there was nobody left to share them with? Florentine remembered what it was like to run around these halls and up the wide stairs in front of him when he and his brother, Robert, were children. The emptiness, the longing for those days long past, gnawed at his heart and made his expression go sallow and cold.

An oval mirror hung from the wall on his left and, when he looked upon his own reflection, he couldn't believe how old he looked. Where had all the years gone? After Lindsay's death, Florentine never remarried. Instead he began work on the serum which would one day bring Adam and Amanda back. For decades he'd spent his life toiling away in his laboratories. Now that his labours had begun to bear fruit, he'd finally taken a step back from it all to breathe and re-evaluate everything that had led him to this point in life. He stared for a long while at the deep wrinkles that made canyons across his face and never really understood how the years had passed by him...until now.

Florentine grew old. There would never again be children running through the halls of this home. No family gatherings, no Christmases spent together, no thanksgivings to share with friends and loved ones.

Finally, he realized he no longer wanted to be there. The weight of the memories and ghosts that existed in those rooms, in the drafty hallways were too much for him to bear. He hadn't bothered to dust the furniture. Clots of it hung from windowsills and on the picture frames housing faces that now gazed at him with soulless expressions. The truth was, Florentine didn't really notice until now how much neglect and disrepair had fallen upon his once vibrant home. He stared at his things, possessions he'd once cared for, and he felt a hollowness inside that made his hands shake.

He was saved from drowning in his thoughts by the ringing of his phone. He touched the screen and was surprised by a flood of fatherly pleasure as Amanda's face materialized on the small rectangular screen. When she spoke a jolt of pride ran through him, as it did every time she spoke with her soft voice, the perfect way she articulated her words. It was still somewhat jarring for him to accept that she'd developed and improved so fast. How did she even get her hands on a phone? He hadn't recalled setting her up with one.

"Professor Mena, I have some good news. I'm sorry to bother you, but you might want to make your way back to the facility."

"What is it, Amanda?" he asked, worry and concern edging itself into his tone.

"Tower Company is on their way back to the city and they have some good news. They claim that they have with them three viable subjects and they're going to head straight for the facility to transfer them into our custody."

"Thank you," he spoke in a calm manner that surprised him. "I'll be on my way shortly."

He ended the call and looked around the empty home one more time. It was time for him to get back to work once more. The wellspring of sadness inside him faded away as he accepted that this place was no longer his home. His work—his new haven—waited for him and he was more than happy to dive back into the maelstrom. He turned and left through the same doors he'd entered only moments ago and made his way back to the Charon Initiative.

* * * *

In the vast loading bay, located at the rear of the facility, Amanda and a large group of scientists waited and watched with great anticipation as the metal-shuttered door began to lift upwards. She hugged her arms beneath her chest as the chilled air spilled in from the outside. Before them, the APC began to slowly back into the bay. Other soldiers surrounded the large vehicle as it came to a sudden stop. The overhead motor came to life as the metal shutters descended and locked themselves securely in place.

One of the initiative's scientists, a woman named Lori, gently nudged Amanda's shoulder with hers.

"Are you going to be okay?" Lori asked with concern.

"Oh yeah," Amanda answered. "I'm just a little cold."

The white lab coat did little to protect her from the winter cold. She smiled across at her colleague, hoping that her expression contained some of the confidence she actually lacked. Today would be the first time she'd see these creatures. Her anxiety grew with each passing second as she waited to face what she had once been.

She jumped as the APC's side door locks activated with a series of loud clicks. Amanda glanced around at the scientists and doctors and saw the raw fear and apprehension dwelling in each of them. Even though they'd all been in this situation before, they were still terrified of the monsters that waited inside that big vehicle. Even the soldiers—people who'd faced these creatures numerous times outside the city's walls—displayed worry in their expressions. Their eyes were haunted by the lingering fear of the living dead.

Amanda glanced down at her watch. She'd contacted the

professor a half hour ago. It would be unreasonable to expect him to be here already, but she wished he was. She wondered where Adam was right now. Had his team been informed of what was going on already? It wouldn't surprise her to later discover that news of the arrival of three subjects had already made its way through half of the city.

The soldier whistled from where he stood behind the others.

"Three of 'em," he actually sounded excited. "We're going to be real busy these next few months."

"I wonder where we're going to keep them all if more are brought in," Emma interjected. She sounded very troubled with the thought of more and more of the undead being housed in the facility. None of the others could blame her. They all shared her feelings on it.

The middle-aged man who first exited the military transport vehicle, was a large man by anybody's standards. Major Alex Tower reminded her very much of the commanding officer of Sparrow Company, Thomas Black. The stern way in which he carried himself told everyone that he was a man in complete control and craved it. The way he looked around the loading bay and everyone standing within it, was the steady gaze of a skilled and patient hunter. A permanent scowl etched into the stone wall surface of his face. The Major was a man not to be trifled with and, as he made his way out of the APC, the soldiers before him straightened their postures as a clear sign of the respect they shared for him.

Major Tower carried his rifle on his person. Amanda wouldn't be surprised to find the gun's safety off.

Alex shot Amanda a quick cursory glance and although his eyes were hooded, she saw clear recognition in his gaze. He shifted his powerful stare towards Jesse Columbus, the senior-most scientist in the professor's employ. As the Major made his way towards the gathered brain trust of the initiative, three more individuals exited the side of the vehicle behind him.

All three soldiers were of varying age and race, and all looked noticeably tired. Amanda could only imagine the ordeal they'd been through attempting to capture these three new subjects. She'd only heard brief snippets of the story from the others. Apparently there was a violent firefight against a swarm of the undead. Alex and his company had almost been completely lost in the struggle.

Several other soldiers converged upon the company and relinquished them of their shared burden. The three undead were secured to mobile, metal stretchers adorned with clasps, bindings and chains. To Amanda, they appeared to be more like mobile torture racks.

Amanda had feverishly studied the professor's long list of requirements. At first glance it appeared all three of these monsters could actually serve as viable subjects.

"Good work, Major," the young scientist congratulated Alex.

The pair exchanged a firm handshake. Amanda half expected to see the much taller soldier lift Jesse up and down like a doll as they shook hands.

"Thank you, Doctor Columbus," the Major replied with a deep-throated voice that even sounded a little bit like Thomas. He nodded towards Emma, Jesse's wife, in acknowledgment. His gaze passed over Amanda briefly with a look that seemed emotionless and cold. "My men and I are tired and hungry," he continued as he shifted his attention to the doctor. "It's good to be back in the city."

"Well, you know your way around this building as well as anyone that works here," Jesse chuckled. "Please take whatever you want from the cafeteria. I think I might even join you."

Alex nodded his thanks, turned to whistle at his company and gave them a 'thumbs up'. The soldiers shared a brief, but raucous cheer amongst themselves and began to make their way towards the exit of the bay.

"Clint," the Major called out to one of the three men. "Make sure to get that bruise checked out after lunch."

"After lunch, please," the man named Clint grinned and put the palms of his hands together in mock prayer.

The Major laughed to and motioned for him to go.

"What's wrong with your man?" Amanda inquired.

Alex's unreadable gaze raked over her, and like before it was like walking into a solid wall.

"He hurt himself during the attack." His answer was clipped. "Clint slipped and bumped his head pretty hard on a broken slab of concrete."

"I'm sorry to bother you about it," Amanda frowned. "But are you sure that's all that happened to him out there?"

Agitation entered Alex's eyes for a brief moment, before he dashed it away. He let out a long sigh before answering, as if he struggled to contain some outburst. "I examined his bruise myself afterwards. There were no visible cuts, He does have a pretty nasty bruise. None of the walkers even got close to him, or any of my men, so I promise you that none of us are going to suddenly turn into one of them."

"I'm sorry, Major. I just wanted to be sure."

Alex stared at her for a short while before his hardened expression finally softened.

"You're right to ask, ma'am," he said. "None of us can be too sure—or too safe—in this day and age. I promise I'll make sure he does go and get his wound checked, just to be sure."

"You're both right," Jesse interjected. "C'mon, Major. I'll walk with you to the cafeteria. You can tell me all about what happened out there."

"Of course," Alex nodded, then regarded Amanda one last time with a somewhat sobered look. "Ma'am."

Amanda didn't know the man as well as Jesse obviously did, but she sensed she could trust him. Something continued to nag at her, however, and it persisted even after Jesse and the Major left the bay. It wasn't anything in particular that troubled her. Rather, it was a feeling, almost like a sixth sense, that warned her that something was wrong. She wished the professor were here. His presence always calmed her whenever she was afflicted with troubling thoughts and uneasy feelings. She also wished Adam was here. She knew she would feel a lot safer with him around.

* * * *

Clint, having stuffed himself full of food within seconds, excused himself and fled to the cafeteria's washroom, where he spent several minutes leaning forward against one of the four sinks. He let the water run from the tap and shut his eyes in an effort to control the nausea in his stomach and the pounding in his head. Every time he opened his eyes, his vision shifted in and out of focus. The floor tilted under him, as if he was in a ship in rough break water, rocking back and forth uncontrollably.

Although the fall hadn't cut his scalp open, the concussion hurt him far more than anyone realized. As the blood continued to flood his brain, he felt consciousness begin to slip away from him. He couldn't think clearly, couldn't remember how he'd gotten to the washroom in the first place. The world around him lurched one way and tilted the other one last time before he finally collapsed, dead on the washroom's tiled floor.

One of Clint's teammates, Caleb came into the washroom twenty minutes later and saw Clint lying motionless on the floor. He rushed to Clint's side and shook his shoulder.

"Clint...man...Clint? Wake up. You alright?"

Clint's body gave an involuntary shudder and Caleb breathed a sigh of relief.

"God, you're alive."

Clint's bloodshot eyes snapped open.

* * * *

Jesse and the Major looked up at the deathly, inhuman howl that resounded from the far end of the mess hall. Francis, another member of Tower's squad, stopped eating with his fork halfway to his mouth. He lowered the utensil and felt his blood run cold as the monstrous howl echoed once more. Instinctively he looked to his left, stared at Caleb's empty seat.

The cry was joined by another. Alex immediately reached for his sidearm and pulled it free from its holster. Francis watched the Major load a round in his gun's chamber and nearly lost his nerve as he finally understood.

"Go for the alarm, Francis," Alex called to his man.

Francis went for his pistol as well and wished he'd thought to bring his rifle with him instead.

At least, Francis thought, they weren't the only soldiers occupying the mess hall. Five men and three women soldiers armed themselves, and all of them now focused their full attention towards the far end of the room. The cries originated from the general direction of the men's washroom. The crimson alarm button was situated against the wall in between the men and women's doors.

"Move, Francis," Alex barked. "I'll stay close to your side and cover you. Jesse, get the non-military personnel out of here!"

The Major's heart raced madly as he and Francis rose from their seats and began to wind their way towards the seemingly distant alarm button. Shuffling movements told him that the others had sprung to action, moving away from the tables while training the sights of their guns on the closed men's room door.

Alex and Francis moved quickly, their speed increasing as fear fed its way through their veins. The muffled cries sounding from behind the closed door halted without warning, yet they kept moving towards the button. They were less than a ruler's length away from it when the door leading to the men's room burst open.

The frame tore free from its hinges and sprayed bits of drywall and dust in its wake. Two monsters rushed out from the chamber beyond. Their familiar faces—the faces of those that Alex had come to care about as both allies and friends—snarled at him and stared through mad and hungry eyes. Gut-wrenching snarls of starved and deprived wolves assaulted Alex's nerves, freezing his heart and making his hands tremble.

Alex fired twice at Caleb. The first shot missed and the second merely grazed the creature's cheek. Caleb fell upon Francis, who cried out in terror as rows of teeth plunged deep into his left forearm, ripping flesh and spraying blood across the tiled floor. The second zombie lunged at Alex and the Major raised his gun as fast as he possibly could and fired.

Chapter Twenty

The researchers, scientists and doctors working in the main Regeneration Lab froze as the alarm suddenly cut into their daily routines. The siren filled the lab, resonating from wall to wall. Heads rose from behind computer monitors like gophers popping out of their holes to see what was going on the surface.

They all knew the facility contained alarms and a lock-down system in case of an outbreak, but none of those working in the building had ever really believed they would be in a situation that would require its use. They knew an outbreak was possible, but didn't dare imagine it would happen.

Amanda, who'd been going through old research files the professor gave her to study, frowned as she looked up at the crimson lights that flashed repeatedly along the corners of the ceiling.

"Oh, my God," Imogene looked up, her eyes filled with terror.

"It's okay," Emma said. "It's just probably another drill."

The look of deep concern in Emma's eyes, however, spoke clearly of her doubts. Emma had declined the offer of eating with Jesse and the crew, and now looked nervously in the direction of the cafeteria, her face white.

Amanda turned to Emma. "So, what do we do?" she asked.

Before Emma could answer, the sound of the alarms was joined by the sound of distant gunfire. The shots rang out clearly, free of their normal silencers. It wasn't long before they realized that the exploding gunfire continued and didn't stop.

"Shit!" George hissed as he sprang from his chair, knocked over the loose charts on his bench, spilling them across the floor. His face was a caricature of horror.

"Everyone calm down," Emma said aloud. "George, get on the phone and try to find out what's going on. Amanda, contact the professor and see if he knows anything about this. Everyone else, please sit tight. Most of us have run through the drills before, and all of you know that this building is perhaps the most protected and secure location in New Edmonton. We'll be fine. Let's just figure out what's going on and then move on from there."

Amanda reached the professor in less than a minute. A

powerful feeling of relief washed over her when the elderly man's face appeared on her computer screen.

"I'm sorry I'm running late, Amanda," Florentine smiled warmly. Then his good cheer began to crumble when he quickly took note of her fearful expression, the flashing red lights behind her, and the sound of the alarms. "Amanda, what's going on?"

"I'm not sure yet, professor," she stammered as her words came out through slightly trembling lips. "I hoped that you'd know."

"There aren't any planned drills today, or for the rest of the week," the professor's expression hardened. "Amanda, I don't want to believe it's real, but we have to assume that the facility may in fact be compromised. The infection could be on the loose and you have to act quickly.

"The alarm's already been triggered, so that means that the whole facility will go under lockdown. The systems in that building are automated. All exits, including both doors and windows, will be locked and covered under protective steel shutters. You and the others can't leave, so you have to stay in the lab. The doors can only be opened by using the keypad, so they won't be able to get in there. As long as you and the others remain there you should be safe. Triggering the alarm outside of schedule would have already alerted the military. Help is coming for you soon."

"Professor, I'm scared," Amanda's terror haunted her, and she began to feel the same fear she experienced in her dreams.

"Amanda, I'm on my way there now. My driver just told me that we're minutes away. I'll be there soon. You can bet that Thomas and his team are racing there right now also."

And Adam too, she prayed. It was no secret she cared deeply for Adam. It seemed natural that the professor's first two subjects would be drawn to one another. They shared a bond that nobody would understand.

"Do you want me to stay on the line with you?" Florentine asked.

She saw the sincerity in his worried eyes, and she knew if she said yes, he would stay with her throughout this whole ordeal. However, she saw the frustration in his gaze and his need to spring to action and try to do something to help them. It was clear in his expression, even if he was fighting to hide it from her.

"No, go see what you can do out there." She forced a tight smile. "I'll try to help out here, if I can."

"You're stronger and braver than you know," the professor told her. "Good luck. I'll see you all soon."

Amanda nodded and cut the line.

She looked up from her screen to find the others gathered around the weapons locker, located against the wall near the only exit at the back of the room. Emma had unlocked the transparent door and had it swung wide. She handed out pistols to the others and they loaded the weapons.

"It's not a drill, is it?" Emma asked as Amanda approached. She held out a Berretta towards her with a steady hand. "Do you know how to use this?"

Amanda took the weapon, checked the clip before sliding it back in place and switched the safety off.

"Red dot means I'm armed," Amanda referred to the indicator next to the gun's safety.

Emma appreciated Amanda putting on a brave face for the others when they were both clearly on edge. She handed Amanda a couple of extra clips, grabbed a pistol for herself and closed the weapon's locker behind her.

"I'm leaving it unlocked. A few of you know the codes to access it anyway," Emma spoke aloud.

"Um, Emma where do you think you're going?" George called after her as the young doctor made her way towards the exit.

Emma began punching in numbers in the wall-mounted key-pad. The others exchanged worried glances. George walked towards her and stopped suddenly when Emma turned her stern eyes on him.

"Don't try to stop me, George," she spoke. "You know that Jesse is at the cafeteria with Tower and his crew, and I know that he'd run back here first in an emergency. Well, he isn't back and don't you dare think that I'm going to leave him out there to die."

George didn't say anything, except look at her with resignation in his eyes.

Emma looked back at the others before turning back to George. "I'm going to go find him. Please watch out for the others. You're in charge. Just wait here until the professor and the army gets here."

She paused when the gunfire suddenly came to a stop. When they'd heard it last, it had sounded a lot closer.

Emma steeled herself and took in a deep breath. She punched the last string of code into the keypad and left. She said nothing more as the door close shut behind her.

George and the others appeared crestfallen, and the looks of defeat on their faces began to anger Amanda. It was like they were already writing her off as dead. Her mounting frustration bolstered her and washed off much of her terror. Amanda wasn't entirely certain what really convinced her to walk over and start punching in commands into the smooth digital keypad. The professor might be furious with her when he found out later. That didn't worry her as much as how leaving Emma alone to face those things out there might haunt her in the future.

There were already more than enough nightmares keeping her up late in the night.

"Amanda, you can't go out there," George said, aghast.

"And why shouldn't I?" Amanda countered. "My friend is out there. Our friend is out there and she needs help."

"But you're the second subject," one of the others spoke up. "You can't just throw yourself in danger like this. What if you get killed?"

"Listen, all of you," Amanda spoke. "I am going out there, whether you like it or not. Hide in here where it's safe if you want. You have that right. I'm going to go and help Emma. This is my decision, no matter how important anyone thinks it is that I should remain just because of what I am."

Her confident voice surprised them and helped to bolster her courage. Amanda suddenly stopped and frowned. Since the beginning of the emergency something had been nagging at her thoughts. Ever since the alarms started, everyone in the room had been lost in fear and near panic. None of them were really thinking clearly, focussed more on their lives and the lives of those they cared about. She'd been so distracted that she'd lost sight of a few obvious things around her, things that could aid her in this emergency.

Suddenly the answers she'd sought came to her, and she knew what she needed to do. Amanda turned and faced her new friends. As the alarms continued to blare, they all stared at her and waited.

"I know what to do," she declared. "Can someone take care of that alarm first?"

Kenneth stepped up first, raced to his terminal and shut off the bells. With the raucous noise gone, Amanda could think a little more clearly.

"I understand I'm still really new here, but I'm asking you all for a little bit of trust right now. I think I know what we need to do."

George and Kenneth nodded approvingly. Their support helped immeasurably.

"Look around you," she began, and many of them did. "We

have everything we need here. We're the eyes and ears of this city, the heart of the Charon Initiative. We need to use what we have, to help these people. We control all the cameras and the communications in the building."

As she spoke, this realization began to dawn on them all. These were the brightest minds in New Edmonton, and it didn't take long for them to grasp what she was explaining to them. They could help, all of them. And if there were any survivors left in this building, there might be a chance to help them after all.

"Does anyone know where the safest place is in the facility besides this room?" Amanda asked them.

"The loading bay would be," a woman in the back of the group offered. "They designed it in case of an outbreak, in case the military lost control of the walkers they bring inside."

"Good," Amanda said excitedly. "Okay, we need the cameras both inside and outside the facility. Rescue should already be on its way and we need to do anything we can to help them. We need to use the cameras to find any survivors and get on the radios so we can communicate with them. The cameras will help us locate where the undead are and we might be able to lead the survivors either here or to the loading bay. We need someone to find Jesse on the cameras, and throw some eyes on Emma before she gets herself killed."

"What about you?" George asked her.

Amanda raced to her desk and retrieved two earpieces, one of which she inserted into her right ear.

"George, will you keep in contact with me? I'm going to go help Emma, but I need you to be my eyes and ears."

"Of course," he nodded and even managed a weak smile. He clapped his hands together once to get everyone attention. "Okay people, it looks like we have a plan. Let's get to work!"

They rushed to their terminals with renewed hope. Their training kicked in and, in an instant, they were no longer the frightened lot huddling behind a closed door. They knew what to do, and with purpose they moved. Keyboards clicked while others began to talk loudly on their headsets, coordinating with personnel outside. They checked blueprints of the facility and studied camera feeds.

The speed with which they got together and set to work amazed Amanda. It helped wash away her disappointment with them when they saw Emma as lost to them. Now they were strengthened by something that brought out the best in them.

They all found hope.

* * * *

The bright lighting in the hallway was a sharp contrast to the grim reality of what was going on elsewhere in the Charon Initiative. The hallways both behind and in front of Amanda were completely empty. Normally it was bustling with people, scientists or military personnel, walking back and forth the long stretches of corridors as they carried out their duties.

Now the emptiness was haunting. The fear of what might have happened to Emma, and the reason for the security trip, weighed heavily on her shoulders.

"George, are you there?" she spoke as she pressed a finger on her earpiece to better hear his reply.

"The military just arrived and Stan's communicating with them right now," he answered into her ear. "We haven't found Jesse yet, but there's some good news."

"Go ahead," she urged him to continue.

"A lot of people made it to the loading bay. They're holed up in there right now and there are a lot of military personnel there as well as our own people. But it's pretty bad everywhere else, Amanda. It looks like we've lost a lot of people, and...oh, God...I know some of those people."

"George...I'm sorry."

George coughed away from his mic. "It's okay...we have a job to do and right now, I'm going to focus on that first. We need to get these people out of the building. There are a few holed up safely behind locked doors, but they'll need help to guide them to the loading bay."

"Can you communicate with them through the intercom?" Amanda asked. "If they don't have weapons or don't want to risk going out into the halls, we can at least assure them that help is on the way and that they should stay where they are."

"That's a good idea," he agreed. "I never even thought to use the intercom system." He turned away from his mic to shout orders to someone.   "Stan and Kenneth are on it. There's some bad news, Amanda. A lot of the dead are already starting to turn. It doesn't look like there's any of them ahead of you, but there are a few on the floors above. Wait...there's good news. We just found Jesse. He and a few others are stuck in an office two floors above you. That's the same place where this supposedly started. From what we've ascertained so far, this began in the cafeteria. There are lurkers outside the doors trying to hammer their way in."

"Oh God," Amanda breathed.

"The door seems to be holding so far, but they're in an office and those doors were never designed to stand up to that kind of force."

"I'm on my way. How far ahead is Emma?"

"She's a few meters in front of you, just around the right corner."

"Thanks. I'll contact you back soon."

The sound of hurried footsteps drew her attention down the corridor in front of her. Against her better judgement, Amanda sprinted across the tiled floor and raced quickly around the sharp corner to her right. She immediately came face to face with Emma and her gun, whose dark gaping barrel was raised towards her face. Amanda raised her hands in front of her in shock, trying to look as harmless as possible.

Recognition dawned, and Emma lowered her weapon and let out a heavy sigh.

"Amanda? What the hell. I could have shot you!"

"I'm sorry," she apologized quickly, her heartbeat slowing.

"Are you here to help me look for Jesse?" She frowned.

"Yeah, I guess I am," Amanda nodded. "He's alive. We saw him on the security cameras."

Relief flooded across Emma's face as she let out a heavy breath. "I guess there's no point trying to convince you to go back."

"Nope."

Emma stiffened at the loud crack of a gunshot from somewhere close by, followed by a single, terrified shriek. It stopped just as abruptly as the gunshot a second later. Silence followed. It had come from somewhere nearby, someplace on the next floor directly above them.

"You're going to need this," Amanda said as she took out a spare earpiece from her pocket and handed it to Emma.

They moved down the hall with caution in every step. Beside Amanda, Emma's face was a mixture of worry and fright. She was obviously not confident with her weapon, but as Emma walked beside her, Amanda admired her all the more for being out here. The way she held her gun told Amanda of her inexperience in handling the weapon. Amanda herself never once fired a gun in a combat situation, but she'd logged enough hours on the practice range.

At the same time, she envied her colleague. She envied the strength of the love this woman shared with her husband, and how it was powerful enough to override her naked fear. It had even been enough to bring her out beyond the safety of the secured lab.

Emma's arms trembled as she walked. Her lower lip quivered from time to time and Amanda understood that she was on the knife's edge of losing her nerve and succumbing to a panic attack.

"We'll get to him," Amanda whispered.

The cafeteria was located two floors above them. As the two women made their way to the nearest elevator, Amanda's concern grew when she came to realize that they hadn't run across a single person since they'd set out on this quest. Where had they all gone? Worse yet, what had happened to them?

The duration of the infection varied drastically between the time of the person's death and when they rose once more. It was impossible to tell when someone who was infected was going to change. According to George, a few of those infected had already started to rise. In a few hours more of the infected would come back as well. If left unchecked, the facility would be completely overrun by the undead. If they somehow managed to get out, there was no doubt that it could mean the end of New Edmonton.

A soft, short tone in her ear alerted her that George needed to talk to them. Emma put a finger to her earpiece.

"George," she whispered, "how's Jesse and the others?"

"They're holding out and the office door seems to be hanging in there," he answered.

"We're heading to the elevators right now," Amanda said.

"That's a good idea," he spoke into their earpieces. "The power throughout the facility is still up, so it should work fine. You don't even want to think about taking the stairs. There are a few of them there, wandering up and down the steps aimlessly."

A cold feeling tore into Amanda as she walked. Hearing him say that there were walkers on the stairs, made their situation all the more real to her.

They pressed the elevator call button and waited as the car slowly descended to their level. Directly to the left of the closed silver doors was the door leading to the stairwell. Amanda listened for a long time, anxious and frightened as she prayed for the elevator to arrive soon. As she listened, she heard something coming down the stairwell, shuffling sounds of dry flesh and loose cloth being dragged over the surface of the floor.

"Do you hear that?" Amanda whispered.

Emma looked at her. "Hear what?"

Amanda frowned as she focused her attention on the closed door.

The elevator bell chimed and Amanda spun around to face it as the silver doors slid open. Nothing lay waiting beyond. Of course there wasn't, she reasoned. George would have seen it in the elevator cameras if there was and would have informed them already. Terror slowly ate away at her rational side and filled the empty gaps with irrational fright.

They entered the lift and as it rose to their desired floor, Emma turned towards Amanda.

"I don't know what to do," she spoke in a loud whisper, as if the dead beyond the door might hear them.

"We find your husband and anyone else who's still alive," Amanda reassured her. "Everything's going to be fine."

"But it isn't fine is it?" Emma's voice rose in panic. "What if we run into one of them, one of the dead? They'll be people I once knew, people I either cared about or just knew in passing."

"You shoot them in the head if they aren't one of us," Amanda injected a cold tone into her voice, trying to lend her friend some of her strength. "If it's not alive, kill it."

Emma lowered her gaze to the cabin floor.

"I've been working here for a lot longer than you have. I know pretty much everyone in this building on some level. It's not so easy for me to just point and shoot someone I used to know in the head. I don't know if I can be as strong as you."

"Your husband is counting on your right now. Even if you don't believe you have it in you—you have to lie to yourself for a little while and pretend that you're strong. Right now nothing else matters. Your personal demons don't matter. If you don't do what it takes, Jesse will die today. So please, get it together and get ready, because we're almost there."

Emma continued to stare at Amanda for a while, fear and regret in her eyes.

The cabin shook gently as it reduced speed. By the time the doors slid open, both women had their guns pointed towards whatever might lie in wait beyond.

The hallway was empty, and the both of them breathed sighs of relief as they relaxed their tense bodies just a little bit.

"Okay, let's go find Jesse and the others and get back to the lab," Amanda spoke as she raised a finger to her ear.

Through the facility's camera's George laid out for her the

locations of the undead that appeared on his computer screen. Amanda and Emma moved down the hall quickly, trusting in their eyes in the sky as they passed through several vacant offices and meeting rooms. Blood marred the wall to Amanda's right as they rounded a corner on the right. A body wearing a military uniform lay beneath the crimson stains. He lay face down, and Amanda saw the wide bite mark that made a ruin of the left side of his neck.

"Jesus," Emma breathed.

Amanda thought of firing a round from her gun and shooting the dead man in the head, just in case. She decided otherwise because the gunshot would surely be heard by the living dead who wandered this floor. An axe stood to her left, encased behind protective Plexiglas.

Amanda went to retrieve the axe. She moved to stand before the corpse. Uncertainty clouded Emma's eyes, but she nodded, knowing what had to be done. Amanda lifted the axe above her head and drove it down swiftly with strong arms. A loud *thunk* sounded as the blade drove through the back of the man's skull. A fresh splatter of blood jetted upwards from the wound. Brain matter oozed from the gap when she pulled the axe back out.

Amanda stared down at the dead thing for a time. It had been surprisingly easy and almost anti-climactic. The body hadn't moved or stirred after the blade had gone through its skull. A part of her expected it to writhe in agony, but it lay there...still.

She spun to stare behind her suddenly. She thought that she'd heard a voice. It was only Emma standing behind her, and Amanda frowned. She thought that she'd heard a man's voice, a whisper of it close to her ear, so low she hadn't been able to make out the words but enough for her to know that it was someone speaking to her.

There was nobody else besides her and Emma, but the voice had sounded so real, so tangible.

Amanda shook her head in frustration. Her head suddenly felt dizzy and she had to focus her thoughts to keep herself together. For a moment it felt as if the floor had suddenly tilted beneath her and, if she hadn't caught herself, she would have fallen.

Emma eyed her strangely as she came closer. She held out Amanda's gun in her left hand, which she took without even being aware that she was reaching for it.

"You don't look so well," Emma commented.

"Just a little dizzy," Amanda explained.

Together they proceeded down the hall. The banging sounds of fists beating on a door grew steadily louder as they drew closer. They turned the corner and froze.

Five of the undead surrounded the door to the office where Jesse and a few others had holed up, and all clambered over one another as they mercilessly beat against the door leading to the office beyond. The sounds of the undead wails and pained moans grated against Amanda's heart like sharp metal shards scraping on a marble surface. Emma's breathing quickened as she stared at the scene before her.

They knelt low behind a wall of bookcases, situated in the middle of the large room, which housed several doors leading to separate offices. Papers and various other belongings littered the floor, spilling from the already cluttered desks.

Amanda's earpiece crackled softly as George reconnected with her and began to speak.

"I know you can't talk, so just listen. I can see you both on the camera. Jesse and the others are still behind that door, but as you can see it's starting to buckle under the constant strain."

Amanda saw that the door was beginning to splinter and break apart. A large crack was beginning to form from the top, and the fracture was slowly spreading down towards the entire length of the door.

"The military's gotten through the front of the facility and Sparrow Company is leading the charge. They're headed towards you right now. That door should be able to hold until they get there. You should both wait until—"

A large section of the door broke free and disappeared into the room beyond. Audible shouts rose from those hiding within the other room. The undead, seeing the fruits of their labours, grew more excited as they lost themselves in a wild frenzy. With increased vigor they tore away at the hole, widening it within seconds. The sharp splinters drove and tore into the monsters' hands and rivulets of blood soon covered the door and handle, but the creatures continued on, unfazed.

"Damn it," Amanda hissed as she instinctively rose and charged towards the living dead. Her fear evaporated and what replaced it was a cold and calculating mind that knew exactly what needed to be done.

She raced across the carpet and fired her gun with one hand, the other hefting the heavy axe. Two of the monsters fell as their heads exploded from bullets that reduced their skulls to mush and gristle. The remaining creatures spun to face her and began to lurch towards her with surprising speed. One of the undead was a face that she recognized very well from about an hour ago.

The monster that bore the face of Alex Tower groaned as it bared its teeth in anticipation towards its coming meal. She raised the barrel of the gun and fired several shots at it. Most of the bullets found their mark in the chest and shoulders. One nicked the monster cleanly through the right side of its temple, but it wasn't nearly close enough for it to destroy the brain.

An empty, terrifying feeling slammed into her when she pulled the trigger and fired a dry shot. The gun was empty. She stopped mid-charge realizing she had no time to reload. She was simply too inexperienced and had miscalculated how fast the undead could move when their bodies were this fresh and motivated. Amanda dropped her weapon and seized the handle of the axe in both hands. As the remaining three charged for her, shots rang out from behind her.

Emma's streaking bullets took another one right between the eyes in an amazing shot that surprised both of them. The creature groaned once, exhaling its final breath before falling dead upon the carpet. Alex and his companion stumbled awkwardly over the body. Their struggles bought the two women some time and Amanda charged forward with her axe held high above her head.

With a scream that resounded from the depths of her soul, she brought the blade down in a whistling arc before it chopped and cleaved the second creature's head in two. Alex reached out towards her. She tried to wrench the axe free but discovered to her horror that it was stuck inside what remained of the ruined head.

Emma fired three more shots, two of which found their mark in the creature's skull. Alex's head whipped back from the force the two rounds drove into it. It regained balance, lowering its head as it stared at them fury in its feverish eyes. Two bullet holes, one high on its forehead and another to the left of its nose, bled like miniature crimson waterfalls. Despite this, the creature was still on its feet, driven by the unnatural life that kept it alive.

It continued towards Amanda, reaching out with its arms towards her neck. A sliver of panic shot through her and she desperately tried to pull the axe free. Unlike before, this time the axe was stuck in zombie's head. The creature was almost upon her. She abandoned her weapon and backed away. It moved around the two corpses and stumbled towards her.

Emma fired. The bullet plunged deep through its temple and

out the other side. Red gore showered a nearby desktop and the zombie fell dead between the two women.

Fresh tears streamed down Emma's face as she allowed herself to lower her gun and stare at the lifeless thing.

Amanda heaved deep, frantic breaths as she fought to calm herself. It had moved so fast, and just wouldn't stop. If it hadn't been for her friend's lucky shot, it would have torn her to pieces.

The office door opened and the survivors hidden behind it stepped out tentatively onto the scene of the massacre. Emma lifted her gaze, wiped the wetness from her cheeks and ran into her husband's arms. A look of relief flooded Jesse's face as he held her tight against him, burying his face in her shoulder. He didn't hold back the tears from his eyes. Emma, transported away from the nightmarish scene, closed her eyes and bathed in her husband's warmth.

Amanda studied the couple for a short time before turning her gaze away to let them have their happy moment together. Her thoughts were of Adam.

A voice spoke to her, the same one from before. She couldn't hear clearly what it was trying to say to her.

Thinking that it was coming from her headset, she placed a finger to her earpiece. "Can you repeat that, George?"

A dark feeling settled upon the pit of her stomach when she listened to his reply.

"What are you talking about? I'm trying to coordinate the rescue and relief efforts with the others."

Had she just imagined the voice? Amanda shook her head, thinking that perhaps the tense situation was just getting to her, making her hear things that weren't there.

"Sorry," she spoke into the headset. "It's nothing."

Amanda, suddenly feeling out of place amongst the others, quietly walked out of the office and found herself once more out in the vacant hall. She leaned back to rest against the wall and stared off into nothing. For a long time she lost herself in her deep thoughts. Memories of her nightmares, flashes of the things she'd seen in her sleep, came to her then, haunting and taunting her even in her waking life. Her right arm trembled and she wasn't sure why.

Terror filled her veins, feeding thoughts of paranoia and fear into her soul. The voice she thought she'd heard seemed so real, but George insisted that it wasn't him who'd spoken.

Amanda glanced up and down the length of the hall and found

she was truly alone out here. Her headset crackled to life once more as George's voice poured through.

"We've checked the camera's on the rest of that floor. We don't see any more traces of the undead. It looks like you guys are safe there. Just hang on until help arrives."

"Thanks for letting me know," Amanda sighed and closed her eyes.

She didn't feel safe. She felt as if something was watching her from some dark corner, hiding and keeping an eye on her even now. She lowered her head and screwed her eyes tight. The attack she'd just survived was bad enough, putting her on edge, but now there was this. Thoughts began to swirl in her mind, in her soul, pulling and tugging at her with unseen fingers. What was wrong with her?

She suddenly felt so dizzy she thought she might vomit. Something spoke to her then, close to her ear but seemed to re-sound in the inner confines of her head.

Once more she couldn't understand what the whispering voice was trying to tell her. This time she fought with every ounce of will to ignore and banish the voice from her mind. The strange voice began to fade but the lingering effects of it continued to un-settle and frighten her.

She breathed hard and wished Adam was there, at her side. The sound of rushing footsteps racing up the fire escape shed light on her shadowed soul. She smiled weakly and allowed body to slide down the length of the wall until she sat comfortably on the carpeted floor.

* * * *

"What you did back there was amazing," the professor told her where she sat on the edge of the APC's open door.

A warm blanket draped over her shoulders, but somehow she still felt cold—inside and out. She only half listened to the profes-sor's words.

"Amanda, you saved a lot of lives today," he continued. "I hope you know that."

Soldiers and doctors raced across the snow covered front lawn outside the Charon Initiative facility. Escorted survivors were brought to ambulances, or gathered together, covered in thick blankets. Distant gunfire could occasionally be heard from the inside of the facility. The clean-up crew was still hard at work and every single time a bullet was fired, Amanda noticed the survivors jump in fear at the sound. Their eyes would hover back towards that building and she somehow understood these people would be haunted by this day forever.

How many sleepless nights would be had by everyone here? How long would it take before the initiative could rebuild and begin anew?

"Is there anything I can get you?" the professor asked her.

Stiffly she shook her head. "I just want to go home," she said in a hollow and distant voice. Her stomach rumbled loudly and she realized for the first time that she hadn't had anything to eat all day.

She looked up as footsteps approached her. Adam walked up and put a comforting hand on her shoulder. Much of her anguish vanished the moment he put his hand there. Amanda looked up at his concerned face with gratitude. Her thoughts slowly came into focus as they homed in on this man...and this man alone. She was glad that for now that voice had become an afterthought in the back of her mind.

"I can take her home," Adam said to the professor. "I'm sure the sergeant won't mind. I think Amanda needs the rest."

"Of course," the professor agreed.

Adam helped her to her feet and led her towards where a line-up of vehicles waited at the side of the road, including a few taxi cabs.

"Thank you," she whispered into his ear and meant it. She wanted to go home so badly and get as far away as possible from here.

In her pants pocket she carried the communicator she'd neglected to return, hiding it away and making sure no one had seen her do so. A part of her felt ashamed for having stolen it. She felt more ashamed of the reasons why she'd hidden it in her pocket, and why she wasn't going to tell the professor or Adam why it was there.

* * * *

"I still think you shouldn't be alone right now," Adam protested as they stood together outside her apartment door.

The look in his eyes was sincere and Amanda stared at his face. She felt something in her heart tremble. She wanted to be with him, and she wanted to invite him into her home. She'd just gone through a harrowing ordeal, and perhaps right now she should seek comfort from the one man who actually wanted to be with her. She was on the edge, ready to ask him to stay for a while.

Something inside of her drew her back. Dark thoughts haunted her, thoughts of the voice lingered in her memory. Something bothered her greatly, something she didn't think even Adam could help with.

"I need to be alone for a while." She shook her head.

The hope quickly extinguished from his eyes. It looked like he wanted to argue some more. If she continued to listen, she knew she'd give in.

"Please," she placed a palm on his arm. "Just for a while...I need to be left alone."

It was clear that Adam didn't agree with this, He nodded with a disheartened look on his face.

"Please let me know the moment you need anything," he said.

"I will," she smiled.

He surprised her when he suddenly drew her close against him and held her tight in his strong arms. Amanda was stunned for only a moment before she let herself rest her forehead against his. This felt good, and a large part of her didn't want the moment to end. Eventually she gently pulled away from him and turned to open her door.

"Good night," he told her.

"You too," she replied as she entered and slowly closed the door behind her.

Alone in her apartment at last, Amanda quickly stripped herself of all her clothes and leapt into the shower. She remained there for a long time, letting the hot, steaming water rain down on her and cleanse her from head to toe. Her thoughts mingled with what happened on this insane day. The city of New Edmonton would be reeling from the aftermath of the outbreak. Many would be spending the night in fear.

For a while she completely forgot about the item that lay in her pants pocket. She emerged from the shower an hour later. Wrapped in a fresh green towel, she walked into her living room and noticed the pants lying haphazardly on the floor. She grimaced at the dark stains that now stained the carpet and wished she'd thought better than to leave her clothes lying there instead of stuffing it in the incinerator.

Her dark tresses, still damp from the long shower, cascaded down her back into the slender curve of her waist. She stared at the pants for a long time as everything that had happened that day came flooding back.

Amanda walked across the carpet and reached for her clothes. Quickly, almost with desperation in her movements, she fished into her pocket and pulled out the tiny communicator. She was too far away from the initiative's systems, so there would be no way of connecting to anyone from here. The earpiece was pretty much useless. She placed the device into her ear, held down the button and listened.

There wasn't even the faintest noise of static. Dead quiet filled her ear, but still she stood in the middle of her living room for a long time and waited. What was she waiting for? The voice? She was terrified she would hear the man's voice whispering to her. At the same time, a part of her longed for it. Perhaps she wanted to hear it so she could reaffirm she wasn't crazy. It dawned on her that if the voice did begin to speak to her, it would only confirm she had gone insane.

No voices came, but for a long time she listened.

She jumped when she heard a knock at the door. Her gaze swung to the door and for a moment, an unsettling feeling lingered. A part of her wondered if perhaps the voice had somehow taken physical form and was now standing in the hall outside her apartment. Of course, that couldn't be the case, but still she wondered.

"Who is it?" she called out, too frightened to think of anything else.

"It's me," Adam's muffled voice spoke through the door.

The dark feelings were swept away in an instant and Amanda quickly walked over to open the door. Adam stood there, dressed now in a simple shirt and dark pants. His eyes widened in appreciation as his gaze swept over her . She was so excited to hear his voice, she'd forgotten she was only wearing a towel. Amanda tightened the towel around her, feeling a little foolish since it didn't help to conceal her any better. Adam coughed as he forced himself to lock his eyes on her face.

"You don't give up, do you?" She smiled weakly, her brow furrowed with a hint of annoyance.

"You shouldn't be alone after what happened today."

She cast her eyes down and sighed. Only then did she realize that the mic was still clutched in her hand. She dropped it behind the door where he couldn't see it and nudged it away with her toe. Paranoid fears taunted her but with great effort, she pushed them all away.

Once more she was on that edge between wanting to open up to him and pushing him away. It was Adam who'd helped pull her all the way to the other side.

He entered the apartment without asking and embraced her like he did before in the hall. This time, when he pressed his lips against hers, she resisted for a fleeting moment before she began to kiss him back.

She let the towel fall away from her as she lost herself to him. Amanda didn't know if being with him would help with her, but she was willing to give it a shot.

Chapter Twenty-One

The open ocean stretched out in front of him. It was a long time since he'd dreamt of this place. The hot sun beamed down on him from above, making him break out in a sweat. He squinted as he looked out across the surface of the ocean. Sure enough, Adam found exactly what he expected to see out in the vast and constantly rippling waters.

A familiar boat sailed upon the azure surface. On board stood the dark-haired woman and young boy. They waved at him, trying to get his attention.

A ripple of fear rolled across his back, making his hairs stand on end. For a while he'd begun to suspect who those people might be, but at the same time didn't want to contemplate what that might mean. Adam began to believe that they once were important to him. These phantoms visited him from time to time, except his dreams of this beach and the distant boat had begun to occur less and less. He'd started to dream less about these two since his relationship with Amanda began to develop.

A shot of guilt drove itself into his heart and he couldn't explain why. Adam had come to accept that he might be in love with Amanda. That he cared for her so deeply that when she'd been in the center of the facility's outbreak, he hadn't been more scared in his life. Yet his feelings towards this amazing woman were also accompanied by a numbing guilt he couldn't ignore.

The outbreak had occurred over a week ago now, and the city was still trying to recover from the harrowing experience. Sleep had been rare and short for him, but this was the first time this week he'd dreamed of the beach. He felt comfortable being there somehow...and a part of him longed to remain in that peaceful and beautiful dream.

The figures, which he believed might be the phantoms of his wife and son, stopped waving at him. They stood on the deck of the small boat with their arms at their sides, and the looks on their faces registered as naked fear. They raised their hands up to their mouths and cupped their lips with their fingers as they began to shout something at him. He could actually hear their distant cries. Previously he'd never been able to hear their voices, and hearing it now sent a powerful feeling of pain to lance into his heart.

But why were they crying out to him?

What were they saying?

He glanced down at the sand beneath him and realized that his shadow wasn't alone. He spun to face whatever might be waiting behind him, and in his dream he screamed as he looked upon the ravaged face of the thing that had crept so close to him without making a single sound. The undead thing was rotted and dark, and it was a glaring contrast to the brightness and the life that surrounded it. The creature stood, swaying gently from side to side like a dead leaf that barely clung to the branch. Its tattered clothes blew in ghastly streamers to the side, and its long dark hair hung in tangled curls of black waves.

Adam recognized the face of the creature. It was her face, Amanda's face, exactly as he remembered it when he'd found her the first time a few months ago. The hunger in that gaze was unmistakable, and here he stood in front of her with everywhere to run but lacking the will to move.

He stammered as he tried to say something to her, to plead with her perhaps.

Amanda lunged for him and drew him down hard on his back against the rough sand. When she bit him in the side of the neck it felt all too real to him. As he screamed in his nightmare, she tore at his flesh with her jagged and rotten teeth.

* * * *

He shot up in bed, gasping at the cry of the woman who lay in bed beside him. Amanda's eyes were wide open and terror filled her gaze as she stared emptily at the bedroom ceiling. She continued to scream, her mouth a wide gap that strained at her lips as her horror leapt from her throat. Adam reached over and shook her firmly by the shoulders.

"Amanda, wake up," he urged her.

It was like the image of a woman in a horror movie, possessed by some kind of demon. The look on her face sent chills down his spine.

"Amanda!" he shouted at her louder.

Finally she stopped screaming and blinked several times as her breathing tried to catch up with her. The rise and fall of her chest lessened in intensity as she began to climb from the dark pit she'd been lost in, before slowly turning her gaze towards him. The look of loss and of surprise on her face told him she was back, but the lingering worry remained in the back of his mind.

"You were having a nightmare, I think," he gently told her. He tried to ignore the sharp images of his own dream and tried to instead focus on making sure Amanda was alright. "Amanda..."

"I'm okay, Grimm," she said in a breathless voice that was almost a whisper.

Adam frowned as he looked down at her. Amanda shook her head and looked confused for a long moment.

"I'm sorry, Adam. I don't know why I just called you that."

"It's okay," he told her, even though he was more troubled now than ever. "Are you going to be okay?"

"I think so," she said as she forced herself up into a sitting position, her back resting against the headboard.

He couldn't help thinking how beautiful he found her, even now. Her hair was a mess, a remnant of their lovemaking from earlier, but it only added to how attracted he was to her. The whispers of his swiftly fading dream left him with some feelings of guilt for being in a relationship with her. He quickly shook these thoughts away, knowing that there was nothing else he could do in life now but move forward. It was all any of them could do, to continue to stay strong and simply keep living. He looked at Amanda and moved to sit beside her with his own back against the headboard. They sat close to one another and he felt the comforting warmth of her arm against his.

"Do you want to talk about whatever it was?" he asked her.

Amanda drew her legs up and raised her knees up so she could wrap her arms around them. She looked down into the shadowy place between her ankles and seemed to drift off to somewhere else.

He saw that she was either unwilling to tell him, or was just having a hard time trying to open up about it.

"I dream about this beach a lot," he told her, his mind reaching back and grabbing a hold of familiar images and sensations. "In my dream there's always this woman and a young boy. I think they might have been my wife and son."

The revelation drew Amanda's full attention, but the mention of a possible past wife didn't upset her. Instead she looked at the man at her side with patience and understanding.

"This woman," he continued. "She has dark hair like you, but

I think she might have been a little older." Adam smiled before he went on. "The boy kind of looks like her, He also has features I recognize when I look in a mirror. I think he has my nose and my eyes, but I can't be a hundred percent sure. A lot of it fades when I wake up, but sometimes I remember specific details more than others."

"And the three of you are on a beach?" she asked.

"Sometimes it's the three of us. Other times, I'm the one that's standing on the beach. I see them standing on the deck of a boat. They're always waving at me, and sometimes it looks like they're trying to urge me to join them on the boat. Sometimes I feel like I should wade deep into the water and try to swim to them, but every time it gets to that point I wake up."

Amanda moved closer to him, looking deeply now into his eyes.

"It sounds nice and sad," she said. "Tell me more about the beach."

"Oh, it's beautiful." He shook his head as he contemplated the dream. "It stretches out from each side of me like an endless lane of sand. The sand is light in color, almost white. The sun is always strong as it hangs in the sky, and the air carries this warm wind that blows against you gently in an inviting way. The waters reach out into infinity, stretching out in a vastness of blue that is so deep and so rich that I think that particular shade only exists in the dream.

"There's this rocky outcrop far to the right in the distance that reaches out far into the water. It ends at a sharp point almost five meters over the water. A vast jungle sits at the back of the beach and there's a wide area of lush grassland that leads up to that point. The forest is covered in shadows because of how thick and dense the leaves are.

"The whole area seems familiar to me somehow, even though I can't remember where it might be or if that place even exists at all. Sometimes I wonder if the dream is a memory of a place I visited once in the past. If that were true, does that mean the beach is out there somewhere in the world? I always wonder if it actually exists somewhere."

Adam lowered his head slowly and Amanda placed the palm of her hand against his back.

"Maybe we'll get to go to that place together, one day," she told him.

It was an empty promise. Adam knew this, but the thought

that one day he and Amanda would stand on that beach lent a sense of hope he needed. He drew from this and looked up at her with a smile on his face that put one on hers as well.

"I dream of a dark basement," she explained with a frightened tone. Then her smile faded slowly, like the night creeping in to steal the day. "In this basement I'm always sitting in the corner, watching as this man begins to descend the steps coming down from the floor above."

"You don't have to tell me if you don't want to," he said. "If it hurts too much, you don't have to talk about it at all."

"It's okay," she smiled weakly. "I want to tell you about it. I feel like I should. I don't know if that makes any sense, but..."

"It does make sense to me."

He waited for her to continue and let her collect herself before she did so. But then she stopped, looked up at him and the grief in her face spoke volumes of the sorrow that now tortured her soul.

He wrapped his arms around her and held her tight against him. He held her close as if this might be the last time he would, as if this was the last chance he was ever going to get to hang onto the woman he now loved. Amanda wept bitterly as she held him and sobbed into his bare shoulder as she let out the grief building up inside of her. Adam realized that he wanted to take care for her always, that he truly loved her and never wanted to let her go.

When she'd been in the center of the outbreak, he had been so terrified for her safety that he'd almost pushed his way past the sergeant just to be the first to enter the building after they'd disabled the front door's security locks. Adam would have waded through a sea of the undead, torn and shot his way through a horde of their kind to save her.

"I love you," she whispered into his ear and he returned her sentiment with a kiss on her trembling lips.

She hadn't been back at the Charon Initiative since the incident a few days ago. Only a handful so far had returned to continue their work. Many had taken some time away, while others grieved over friends or loved ones who'd lost their lives on that day.

Amanda had chosen to remain in her apartment and no-one questioned her reasons for it. He and the professor had come to visit her on several occasions. Even Emma and Jesse, thankful for what she'd done for them, had come twice so far to see if she was alright and if she needed anything.

Four nights ago, Adam had visited her late in the night, and on that particular night she kissed him and asked him to stay until the morning. He didn't have it in him to deny her request.

"Adam, what's going to happen to us?" she asked him.

He pulled away from her slightly so that he could look at her.

"What do you mean?"

"I mean, you and me. What's going to happen to us down the road?"

"I don't know. We just have to keep hoping that things will get better, that we'll always be safe within the city walls. As long as we keep working to make the professor's dream a reality, we can hold onto the hope that there will be a better life for us on this world someday."

Amanda nodded, He noticed that a part of her seemed to hold back from fully accepting his words. Perhaps she was hesitant to simply trust that everything was going to turn out okay for the both of them. Unlike him, maybe Amanda was a little bit more of a realist, who needed to see the facts before making a decision on anything about her life and the future.

"Please listen to me, Amanda," he spoke to her in almost a whisper. "As long as we're together, we'll be fine."

She smiled at him and this time Adam felt the smile looked true.

* * * *

Adam slipped away from the bed and headed towards the bathroom after Amanda had fallen asleep. He came back into the room a few minutes later, and stumbled on something small and hard hidden in the pile of clothes strewn over the floor near the foot of the bed. Confused, he almost chose to continue on and head back to the bed, but what his foot had landed on had felt familiar to him.

Against his better judgment, Adam knelt down and began to search through the pockets of her jeans. Sure enough, what he pulled out and held in his hand was an earpiece. What was Amanda doing carrying an earpiece around with her? He couldn't figure out why she would have it in her possession. Maybe she'd accidentally kept it after the incident, forgetting she had it. Adam thought back and recalled that she hadn't been wearing jeans that day. He remembered how tired she'd looked in her bloodied blouse and beige pants. So why had she taken the device from the facility and what purpose could it serve her now?

Adam glanced up and towards Amanda's sleeping form and

continued to wonder. He returned the item back where he'd found it, making sure it was back exactly where it had been before he'd taken it out.

As he lay awake in bed with her, he couldn't figure out why it troubled him so much.

Chapter Twenty-Two

Florentine hid it well from everyone else, but the truth was that what had happened to the Charon Initiative wounded him deeply. He'd been stuck outside the locked doors and windows of his own facility and he had felt completely helpless. What else could he have done?

Wracked with guilt, and blaming himself for something beyond his control, he felt compelled to place the fault on his own shoulders. Somehow he felt that he could have done more to protect the people who had devoted so much of their lives to seeing his dream become true.

If it hadn't been for Amanda and her quick thinking, so many more would have died. The professor knew she didn't see it now, but what she did had perhaps saved even all of New Edmonton.

Even as he sat in his old leather chair, in the far end of his vast personal library, he felt he should have been able to do more.

The library was bathed in shadow and he sat with his back facing his wide desk as he stared out the room's single, tall window and looked upon the night sky beyond. The house was empty, and he himself felt like a ghost, wandering the halls. He spent most of his time in this library now, locked away with his books, his thoughts, and his memories.

Here he felt the most comfortable, surrounded by the things that now helped to define who he was. Books had always been an important part of his life, and in this day and age a collection like his was one of the rarest in this world. He'd collected as many as he could from the ravaged world beyond.

From the works of Homer to the more modern writings of King and Keene, he'd been able to preserve some books whose origins were more than five hundred years old. He felt this was very important because some of these works, the ones particularly that were hundreds of years old, were the preserved thoughts of intellectual minds that had once lived and breathed in this world.

Some of these books might in fact be the last copies of those people's works, and if those were to be destroyed, it would mean those authors and all their works would be gone forever.

Florentine let out a heavy sigh as he leaned back in his comfortable chair and closed his eyes. The night was still young, He hadn't slept well in days. Perhaps he did deserve a little more rest. Many of his nights had been spent sleeping in this library on the second floor and every time he did, he slept soundly without a single nightmare to disturb him throughout the night.

* * * *

Danny and Isaac walked along the wide walkway on top of the southern wall on the outer fringes of New Edmonton. Over a hundred meters below, beyond the wall, were the heavily forested lands that sloped downwards to a winding river. The river separated the city from the lower lands, where the rest of the older parts of the city lay.

In the old world, Edmonton had been a much larger city, but now only a fraction of it served as a home for the last of mankind. Situated atop a vast stretch of land that had a slightly higher elevation than the area to the south, New Edmonton was protected by the surrounding walls that stretched all around the city.

The walls were just under twenty five yards thick, and had been a massive undertaking in its construction many years ago. The wall was built to protect the people living within from the undead, and so far it had served its purpose well. Still, it didn't take away from the natural fear all humans felt towards the creatures that lingered eternally beyond these borders.

Isaac himself felt the slight chill of this fear as he walked alone beside his companion and friend. The rifle slung over his left shoulder still wasn't enough to banish the dark thoughts of the things he'd seen and experienced first-hand out in the rest of the world. You could never be too sure about the safety of those you cared for when it concerned these monsters.

He'd been born into this world, and all his life he'd heard of how things were before the collapse of mankind. Before the cataclysm, it was said that the world was a far more beautiful place. He longed for a life without fear of being eaten by these creatures; he wanted to experience what it was like to explore the world beyond these walls without having to carry a rifle around with him all the time.

"I wonder how Jenny and the sergeant are doing in Himura?" Danny commented.

"I wonder if the wall around that city is as busy at this one is tonight," Isaac spoke with a slightly worried tone.

Even from all the way up here, the pained cries of the living dead could be heard from below. A swarm of almost twenty walkers had emerged from the woods a few nights ago, and they'd since been scratching and pounding at the impenetrable walls. Sometimes a herd of them would migrate to this area.

Herds of the undead were known to wander the landscape aimlessly, and at times they would come across the walls of New Edmonton, climbing up the hill and stumbling up the slope until they reached the wall. Large groups were rare, and so far this one was nothing to be concerned about. Though it was not normal that there were so many of them gathered together in this cold weather. The dead normally strayed away from the cold. It was something to do with the freezing temperatures affecting and inhibiting their already dead bodies.

From where they were on the top of the wall, Isaac and Danny could shoot them from up along the top of the wall; snipe them off one at a time with their high-powered rifles, but the noise could potentially draw more of them if there were others wandering nearby.

Isaac took a long look over the edge of the wall and shuddered. There were only twenty of them, but the sight of them gave him a bad feeling in his stomach. Something didn't seem right, and it was clear to Danny that his friend was very troubled with the herd.

Thomas and Jenny had taken the train over the Romero Bridge to visit the distant city of Himura Valley. They were to escort a few of the scientists and doctors from the Charon Initiative whose job it was to help set up a new facility in the city. The prospect of the initiative branching out beyond these walls was an exciting one, because it meant that there was more to hope for now in ridding this world of this deadly virus.

Jenny and the sergeant were due back in a few hours. Adam had taken some time off to be with Amanda. It was no secret to the others, or perhaps even the whole city, that the two of them had formed a relationship with each other. A wistful smile played across Isaac's face. He was happy to know that Adam was starting to really find a place for himself in this city.

A part of him was a little jealous of the man because he hadn't ever experienced what it was like to be with a woman. Isaac sighed and wondered if he would ever find someone to fill that empty place in his life. Being in the army just took so much of his time, and he was left with little of it to spend on forming other relationships outside his known circle of friends.

The truth was that he was a little frightened of the idea of trying to meet others and introduce himself to them. He imagined he'd just stumble over his words and make a fool of himself in front of a beautiful lady. Being up on this wall tonight, on patrol with his friend, suddenly seemed less of a problem for him now.

"So, are you and Adam okay with each other now?" Isaac asked.

Danny's expression darkened and the young man instantly regretted having asked.

Danny nodded. "Yeah, I guess we are. The man did save my life and all. I just don't know, Isaac. I know he's cured, He was one of them."

"Not by choice," Isaac frowned, not liking to have to remind Danny yet again.

"I know that," Danny said a little bit more forcefully than he'd intended. "It just bothers me that he might have killed and eaten other people. I don't know. I can't imagine what goes through the guy's mind when he thinks about stuff like this, He has to be wondering from time to time if he'd ever fed on...well...the living."

"I bet the guilt haunts him," Isaac said.

"Yeah," Danny commented as a look of sorrow temporarily overshadowed his face. "I can't imagine what he goes through sometimes. At the same time I can't help how I feel about him. I just miss my wife, Isaac. I miss her so much. I know that he didn't do it, that he didn't kill her, but..."

"It's not because of him," Isaac suddenly spoke in a firm voice. "Damn it—it wasn't his fault, and you can't blame him for something that wasn't his fault. Adam's proven himself to us so many times that he's our friend. I do trust him with my life. I wouldn't trust anyone else out there as fully as I do everyone in this company. I think he's been through enough as it is, and so have you. Please, you have to let this anger go. "

Danny was silent for a long time and he lowered his head as he continued to walk on his patrol. Isaac quickened his step to catch up to him and they walked beside one another for a while in silence.

Isaac thought about his desire to find a nice woman he could call his girlfriend, and he remembered that there was something between Danny and Jenny. It was pretty obvious that they had feelings for each other, that they'd harbored these feelings in secret for a long time, but neither had taken that extra step to make it anything more.

He wondered if their hesitation to further what they had was partially due to Danny's past, and the lingering pain that remained in the man's heart. There was so little left for any of them to cling onto in this life and it seemed like such a waste to Isaac that neither of his friends saw that they should seize the time they had now before it was gone.

He looked down as a few more lingering ghouls wandered from the forest and began to scratch on the wall's outer surface. A few of them glanced up and looked at Isaac directly. Some of them were now so desiccated, so decayed, that the faces he looked down upon were like skulls with thin sheets of dry flesh covering bleached-white bone.

What horrified him were that these skulls still contained their eyes, and these eyes looked up at him with such need that it shook him to his core. What also bothered him was the emergence of a few more of the creatures.

He hadn't counted them out before, He was sure that they'd increased in number significantly in the last few minutes. They shouldn't be out here in such a large group, especially in frigid weather like this. Was it just coincidence that they were gathering now out of the blue?

Isaac was reminded of vultures that circled around the dead below. The troubling thought only served to add on to his already mounting anxiety. The feeling that something was coming, something big and something terrible, continued to follow him throughout the rest of his patrol and throughout the rest of the night. The chill winter wind blew against him, but it wasn't because of the cold that he shivered under his thick jacket.

* * * *

Adam tried knocking one more time and waited patiently outside Amanda's apartment door. He waited until the watch on his wrist told him that another five minutes had passed. Amanda wasn't home, and tonight they were supposed to go out and watch a movie together.

He enjoyed the time he spent with Amanda, but lately she seemed distant. What had happened to her over a week ago had affected her greatly, and he wanted to be there to help her get through this hard time in her life. It bothered him to think that she'd left her home without letting him know where she was going.

He also feared that she might be home and was ignoring him for some unexplained reason.

Adam sighed and understood that he wouldn't be spending any time with Amanda tonight. The wind howled and whistled as it blew against the closed windowpanes, and sometimes it was so strong that it made the glass rattle in their fastenings. The lonely winter night filled his heart with emptiness. Dressed, and with no other plans to spend the evening, Adam walked down the apartment's winding stairs and out into the street beyond the front door.

The street was particularly busy this night. Several vehicles motored down the icy road past him, and even a few individuals and couples had chosen to brave the cold night and walk down the snowy sidewalks.

He wondered for a moment what month it was and realized there was less than a month until Christmas. The thought of the coming holiday season filled him with little warmth. It only served to remind him of Christmases that he might have lost in his past. Adam hoped that he and Amanda could find a way to enjoy the holidays together. He saw some of that good cheer on the faces of the couples that walked past him, and it made him smile to himself because it meant that the city was finally moving past the recent events that had put everyone on edge.

Adam had heard from the professor himself that the initiative was already well on its way to rebuilding what they'd lost. Despite this, the subjects that the late Major Tower had brought in had since been relocated to the new facility in Himura Valley.

Every single one of the undead had been taken care of, and the bodies of loved ones had been laid to rest in a large funeral that had been attended by thousands. Adam was shocked to find so many people gathered in and out of the cemetery grounds, all come to pay their respects to the dead and the fallen.

None of those killed during the attack had survived to be considered as specimens for the cure trials. The army had moved in quickly on that day and had ended the unnatural lives of any of the walkers that prowled the halls of the facility. There was simply not enough time to try and take any of them down alive. The losses of those poor souls were felt by all, and Adam knew it was perhaps the professor who felt the great weight of that guilt on his shoulders.

And that was where he was headed tonight; to meet with the professor. It was a long while since Adam had found any time to visit the old man in his home. He'd learned enough of Florentine to know that the man's home had once been filled with laughter and family. On a lonely and cold night such as this, Adam decided that perhaps the professor could use a little company. Adam knew he needed it as well.

A short cab ride later brought him to the front door of Florentine's home. The delighted look on the elderly man's face when he opened to door told Adam that he'd been right in his guess. The professor led him to the large dining room where they spent a couple hours laughing and talking over several hot cups of coffee.

His worries over Amanda faded a little, but continued to linger in the back of his mind. The howling winds outside the professor's home reminded Adam of how cold it was outside this night. The branches of nearby trees waved like skeletal arms outside the dining room's windows. The sight of it made him shiver. He shook his head as he focused on what the professor was telling him about his family, and how the first settlers had come to live in this region. Adam had heard this story before and read about it in books, He liked hearing the professor tell it to him.

Afterward, they took a tour of the man's private library, and like every time he'd seen it, Adam was astonished at Florentine's incredible collection. Adam was one of the few people the professor allowed to borrow books from his place. He walked along the line of shelves on the west side of the room and ran his fingers gently across the hardbound tomes in front of him as he moved past them. There were so many, and Adam wondered if the professor had read them all.

"The weather's getting pretty bad out there," the professor commented as he glanced out the room's single window just behind his desk. "You're welcome to spend the night here if you'd like, Adam. There are more than enough rooms and extra clothes around here."

"I might do just that," Adam smiled.

The weather grew visibly harsh outside the window. The freezing winds cast billowing clouds of white snow all over the city and seemed to pull so hard on branches that it looked like the trees might actually be ripped from their roots. The howl grew into a hollow cry that seemed to reverberate throughout the large home, lending it an even more ominous quality than before. Adam began to doubt that there would be any more couples walking the streets in this storm. The storm had become so strong that the clouds of snow made it impossible for him to visibly see the night sky.

"Where's Amanda tonight?" the professor asked him as he took another sip of black coffee from his mug.

"I'm not sure," he answered with more than a little worry. "I think she just wanted some time to be with herself. I hope she's okay."

"As do I. She's proven herself to be very strong, so I'm sure that she's alright."

"It's pretty amazing how quickly she organized the people back at the facility," Adam turned to face the professor.

"Yes, she's becoming more intelligent every day, much like you."

"Have you noticed anything else about her, any other changes like the ones that we've both noticed in me?"

"She's exhibited an increase in mental capacity. That much is for sure. Her coworkers have noticed how quick she is to grasp even the most complicated subjects. Also, as you probably know by now, bones are harder to break than people really believe. The damage she caused to a few of the undead, with the axe alone, is incredible. She was able to cleave through a skull all the way down to the collar bone in a single stroke. I'm almost surprised that the handle of the axe didn't break in two because of how much force she would have had to exert to do what she did. Emma even noted in her report that Amanda had been able to hear some of the dead moving down the fire escape long before she did. There is no doubt that she is developing like you, but at an even faster rate."

"What does this mean then?" Adam asked.

"The ZF-93 serum can destroy the virus in those infected with it. Along with the use of our equipment, it can regenerate a person enough so that they...well, they become like you two. But there is a definite side effect to this serum, and it's gotten me thinking about the reasons why the two of you are showing such drastic developments and changes in your genetic makeup."

"What do you mean?" he frowned.

The professor regarded the room they were in and observed the books he'd collected over the years. The look on the man's face appeared solemn and contemplative. He'd come to a conclusion that he'd been wrestling with for some time, and only now it seemed he might finally have some evidence to prove his theory.

"I think I know how this all started, all those years ago," Florentine Mena said. "The origins of the plague are shrouded in mystery and, after all this time, I'm sure that little evidence survives to this day to tell any of us for sure how it all began. I think I have an idea how it did start, even though I think I'll never know for sure who started it."

"So someone did create this virus?" Adam mused.

"More like a country's military might have," the professor declared. "I've talked to you about this before, months ago, and I'm starting to think that maybe I'm right. Adam, what if they were trying to develop a drug to increase a person's performance, to make them strong and smarter than anyone else that's ever been? What if whoever it was who designed this chemical, had come very close to figuring out how to synthesize such a formula? What if they'd made a slight mistake in their calculations and thus created a mutation in their formula that caused...all of this?"

Adam was silent for a while, letting himself have a chance to digest this information.

"What if it doesn't matter anymore?" he suddenly said to the professor.

The professor swung his gaze over at him with a dumbfounded expression written all over his face.

"I beg your pardon," the professor said in a low voice.

"What if they did try to create some kind of ultimate soldier? Maybe you're right and even though your serum has cured us of the disease, perhaps it did leave us with the original design of this virus. But does it really matter, professor? After all these years, who's to say what really started it all anymore? What's important is that we figure out a way to stop it, or at least continue slowing it down enough so that one day one of our future generations might find a way to permanently rid the world of it forever. Whoever started this is long dead by now. We're all that's left, and we have to keep moving forward if we're to survive."

Florentine closed his eyes for a second and smiled.

"My boy, I really wish I could have known you in your previous life. The thing's that you've faced so far, the revelations that you've discovered astound me. You've weathered through it all and come out on the other side stronger than ever. I am very proud of you."

Adam grinned back at him, feeling good that he'd come here after all to visit with the professor. His gaze lingered around him, and he caught sight of some old family photos. In many of them he saw a young man that was unmistakably the professor in days long past. He smiled at this and wondered who the other people were in the photographs. They all looked so happy.

"I've always wanted to know, professor," Adam said, turning to regard the man who would be his father. "You have a very interesting name. Do you know what nationality it originated from?"

"Indeed I do," Florentine smiled. "Much of my family are of Filipino origin. I've longed to see the country where my ancestors came from. From my books I know it was very beautiful."

"It sounds nice."

"Maybe one day, I will get to see it with my own eyes," the professor said.

The winter night outside continued to howl with a fury rarely seen in these parts.

Again that night, Adam hoped that Amanda was okay, wherever she was.

Chapter Twenty-Three

The frigid snowstorm blew all around her in torrents and waves that blinded her to what was going on in the night. How had she come to find herself out here, in the blowing winter, far from the safety of her warm apartment? Why was she out here?

Amanda couldn't answer those things, nor could she explain this strange feeling inside that she was being watched by something. It lurked in the shadows around her, this thing that stalked her in the night. She knew it only existed in her mind, but the feeling of it was so real and so tangible that she began to question her own sanity. She moved along the sidewalk at a slow pace, wrapping her arms around her tightly as she tried to garner some warmth from the terrible storm.

She passed by an alley and almost came to a stop. A part of her dared to look down the gloomy stretch of the alley, to see if there was someone standing there watching her. She resisted the urge to stop and continued to move on, but she was haunted by her thoughts nonetheless.

She stopped when she found a small glass shelter situated on the edge of the sidewalk. The bus station was empty except for a single bench, and she stood for a while, protecting herself from the blowing snow and the pulling winds. Amanda stared out across the street before her, but she could barely see much through the storm. It had increased in intensity, and the howling winds shook and jostled the small bus shelter around her. She stared out into the night and she could somewhat discern the building across the street in front of her.

It looked like an old structure made of red bricks and dark grey mortar. Empty windows loomed out upon its four floors like darkened eye sockets. It looked like some of the buildings she'd seen in photographs of this very city in the old world. Perhaps it was a derelict building, left behind from a world long since gone and reduced to nothing more than memories and ruins.

Stray memories flooded into Amanda's mind. She trembled as she continued to wrap her arms across her chest. The images of the basement came back to her, teasing her and filling her with feelings of sheer terror.

She closed her eyes and tried to will away the thoughts, but the more effort she put into blocking them out, the stronger they came back at her.

Her heart yearned for Adam, and she wished so desperately that he was here right now. So what was she doing out here in the storm?

The answer came to her when Amanda realized that she was running from her nightmares. It didn't make sense that she was trying to run away from her dreams by fleeing into this stormy night, and now she was alone and far away from the very man she hoped could comfort her during this time.

Memories and images of the now familiar basement assaulted her senses. She could almost hear the sounds of the man's heavy footsteps as he began to descend the stairway towards the lower level. The heavy boots the man wore clumped and thumped along the old wooden boards as he took each step with excruciating slowness. Amanda was once more a little girl, crouched in the far corner of the basement, trying to use the shadows to hide from this terrible man.

She knew she wasn't alone down here, in the cellar. She usually never was. There was always someone else here as well, bound, tied and gagged. The muffled cries of the latest prisoner filled the air with the woman's frightful struggles. Amanda, who wasn't bound in the same fashion, shuddered as she wept in the near darkness. Only a single chain bound her to a drain pipe that ran along the wall behind her.

The chain was attached to a single metal cuff that dug into her right ankle. Its edges had dug and cut into her flesh over the many months she'd pulled on it and tried in vain to wrench it from her ankle. Fresh cuts from her pointless efforts stung as they came in contact with the metal binding.

Amanda blinked her eyes and found herself once more in the storm. For a brief moment she felt a strange disoriented feeling that she'd jumped from her dreams and the real world. Quickly she adjusted herself back to where she truly was, and she tried desperately to shed the horrible images that had momentarily taken over all of her senses.

The earpiece she kept hidden in her jacket pocket squawked to life. Amanda froze; her body rigid. Her eyes widened as she stood and wondered if the sound she thought she'd heard had in fact been real. What is sounded like was the earpiece suddenly activating with a loud electronic stutter. She knew it couldn't have been real, that it must have just been her imagination.

Despite this fact, it had sounded so real...

Amanda fished the small device out and slowly lifted it to her ear. Emptiness greeted her. There was not a single sound from the fragile object. Not even the sound of empty static formed from the device's tiny speaker.

She was about to put the damn thing back in her pocket when she thought she heard the faint sound of a whisper coming from it. She froze and listened. Fright flooded through her veins and the feeling of an electric jolt rushed up along her arms and along the back of her neck. Amanda continued to listen Heard no more from her illusive phantom.

Then, on instinct alone, she looked back out towards the building across the street. The storm picked up outside of her small shelter, but she could still see the darkened windows beyond. Upon the third floor, on the window that was fourth from the furthest right, she thought she saw a shape. The shape changed in the night, taking on different characteristics against the faint light of the street side lamps. She squinted her eyes and tried to focus.

Amanda looked upon the dark shape behind the window and began to see it as the shape of a man. It almost looked like someone was standing at that black window, staring back out into the night, staring down the street and at her and her alone.

She felt a part of her mind begin to drift, as if her sanity had suddenly become partially unhinged. What she was seeing couldn't be real, but no matter how much she tried to blink her eyes, the shadow standing just behind that fourth window continued to take on the shape of a grown man.

"Aren't you hungry?" A voice spoke beside her.

Amanda jumped, and for a moment it felt as if her heart could actually leap out of her throat. She quickly spun her gaze to her right and was immediately filled with dread when she saw no one standing there. Then she realized where the voice had come from, and she looked upon the device in her hand with total and paralyzing horror. The world around her felt as if everything had suddenly taken on a surreal quality. None of this could really be happening, could it? Was she really out here, hearing this voice coming from the earpiece she should never have taken from the Charon Initiative?

Against her better judgment, Amanda brought the earpiece back up to her ear.

"It's been so long, Megan," the voice, ringed with static, spoke back at her. "It's time to wake up."

Tears had begun to flow from her eyes. She wept because she feared she was indeed going mad. It was impossible she could be hearing this ghostly voice speaking to her, but she couldn't deny it. It was speaking to her, and deep down a part of her understood what the mysterious voice was trying to say to her. She couldn't explain how she knew, but she just felt that something inside of her was now stirring, as if rousing from a long and deep slumber.

She looked up at the window and saw that the shadow was still there. It hadn't moved an inch from its spot but it had seemed to take on more definition now. The darkness that comprised its form appeared even blacker.

"Time to wake up, Megan," the voice continued to speak to her. The voice had a touch of mirth to it, as if the speaker were toying with her somehow and enjoying every minute of it. She was immediately reminded of the nightmares of the basement, and the man that kept coming down the stairs to deal with his latest victim. "We have a lot to do tonight. You are hungry, aren't you? No matter how much you cry, you have to eat if you want to live."

Another image flashed through her mind. She doubled over in the bus stop as the recalled memory stabbed at her cerebellum as if a sharp knife had just been stabbed into her skull.

She briefly saw the cellar once more. She knew the man had come downstairs and had already dealt with the bound and weeping woman. In front of her, the killer knelt. In his hand he held out a spoon, and within that spoon was held a dark crimson substance that made her stomach roll.

"You have to eat if you want to keep your strength up."

"God dammit!" she screamed. This time she threw the small device. She tossed the earpiece out into the night, outside the tiny bus shelter. The howling winds beyond sucked the small object into a vortex of wind that cast it out into the darkness, and there it was instantly lost to her forever. Cast away into the storm, she hoped that she would never look upon the wretched object ever again.

She looked up at the gloomy window, and to her relief, the figure was gone. She smiled and chuckled even though she still felt so very far from safe.

"Let's go outside. You haven't been outside in a while, have you?"

She spun towards where she thought she'd heard the voice.

Amanda was still alone in the bus shelter, but at the same time she knew she wasn't alone. She never would be alone, as long as the killer continued to whisper these words against her ear.

The bitter tears cooled on her trembling cheeks, and she sobbed as she began to lose herself to her insurmountable fear. Amanda fled from the bus shelter, daring to venture out into the storm once more. The biting winds tore and clawed at her as she ran. She didn't know where she was going, only that she had to escape from that voice. To her, the undead were no longer the most feared things on this world.

"This is the world as it is now, Megan," the voice continued, just behind her ear. "This is how things are like for every single one of us who are still alive. Do you know what that means?"

"Stop it," she whimpered, even though she was speaking only to herself, even though her words were instantly lost in the torrential storm.

"This means that we have to change how we deal with our lives and those around us. We have to do everything we can to survive. Mercy and remorse have no place in this world. If we don't make ourselves stronger, numb to things our ancestors would have considered crimes, the monsters will get us. They will never stop because they don't have any remorse or regret. We have to be the same if we want to survive in this world, if we want to survive them."

"You don't just do it to survive," she spoke with vehemence. "Maybe at first you thought you did, but you started to take enjoyment from it. You liked to hurt people, and you used survival as an excuse to keep doing what you did."

The voice was silent for a long time. The harsh howling cry of the winds called out to her, beckoning her deeper into the heart of the city of New Edmonton. After a long while, her ghost eventually replied.

"You're no different, not anymore."

The words hit her hard, and her steps faltered as she contemplated why she sensed truth in the phantom's words. Her past, whatever had happened to her in the past, was coming back. Amanda, who'd once desired to know who she was in her previous life, now desired for nothing more than to remain as she had been, living her life with Adam in this wonderful city. She would prefer to wonder who she was than face this horror.

There was more to what had happened to her and more to the man from the basement. She felt herself, her personality, beginning to weaken somehow. Her old self was fighting to reach the surface of her mind, desiring for her to return to the way she was before this second life.

"When I found you, I could have killed you," the voice continued. "I could have taken you downstairs and tortured you as much as I wanted to until I was ready to finish you off. I kept you alive because I sensed that you were like me. You've seen how bad it could get out there. That's why I kept you alive, even after I killed the rest of those people you were travelling with. Don't think they were trying to protect you, Megan. They would have eventually hurt you, or used you for whatever carnal desires their twisted minds would later think up.

"Me? I want to protect you, make you stronger, help you become like me so that you could be a survivor. Maybe you're right; maybe I do enjoy hurting others, but eventually you will be just like me."

Amanda slapped the palms of her hands against her ears, fighting to keep the man's words out. Where was it coming from? Why couldn't she stop it from saying these horrible things to her?

She felt the other person inside of her. This time it wasn't the man from the basement whom she could sense. No, this was another presence, and one that was closer to her heart than any other in this world. Somewhere deep within her, the memories of the woman named Megan were slowly beginning to surface. Somehow, Amanda understood that if her past was allowed to overtake her, then she would become fundamentally changed.

The personality that made up the courageous, loving, and kind woman she was right now would cease to exist. This other person, this Megan, would retake what was rightfully hers, and there would be nothing Amanda could do to stop the transformation because in essence they truly were the same person. Her new life in New Edmonton was simply a temporary placeholder, saving her for when her true self was strong enough to the point that she could once again become whole.

Amanda wailed into the winds, but there wasn't a single person around who heard her. A few of the buildings nearby held lit windows, but she knew her cry of terror wouldn't be heard by anyone in this storm. Amanda fell to her knees, crashing hard into the snow packed sidewalk.

With her hands pressed tightly against the sides of her head, she screamed as the multitudes of images and thoughts began to flood into her mind.

Adam. Her thoughts drifted to the man whom she'd fallen in love with in this new world.

I don't want to lose you.

In her mind she saw herself as an older woman, reaching the age of maturity. She was in the basement once more, but no longer was she the person cowering in the corner, waiting for the familiar sound of the heavy footsteps from upstairs. This time she was the one descending those now familiar steps, going down into the cold bowels of the earth with a leisurely pace that surely terrified her prey all the more.

The numbness in her mind helped to block out any lingering feelings of remorse or guilt over what she'd become. A wistful smile played across her lips as she caught sight of the young man who was bound and gagged at the far end of the cellar. Her belly rumbled, and she knew she'd held out long enough, and now she was hungry once more.

Amanda screamed and screamed at the top of her lungs, and she mumbled words of sorrow as she sought forgiveness for the things she'd done in the past. The realization of what she was slammed into her like a fist to the gut. She was struck with such a feeling of loss and guilt that she knew now there would be no escape from this nightmare.

She felt a hand press down gently on her shoulder. She knew in reality she was all alone out here in the snowy streets of New Edmonton. The hand, however, felt real. There was weight to it and there was tangibility. She was alone, but at the same time she wasn't.

"It's too late, Amanda," a woman's voice spoke to her. "It's time to wake up."

Amanda opened her eyes and looked up at the person who stood mere inches in front of her. What she looked upon was a twisted reflection of herself. Megan looked down at her with the same face that she shared but with eyes that were so very different.

Amanda screamed, and she knew no more.

Chapter Twenty-Four

Jason and Price stood on watch, even during the terrible snowstorm. Neither of them believed the powerful gale force winds they'd witnessed outside the safety of their shelter. Their shelter was a bunker nestled at the base of the wall's eastern sector. Their zone was a key position in the security of the wall, because these two were guarding one of the four gigantic gates that led in and out of the city.

The bunker was a fifty square foot building, with its own power generator and running water. Price was glad it had come furnished with its own heating system, as well as a decent coffee machine. He sat in front of the window, staring out into the night. In his hand he held a steaming mug of coffee, black just the way he always took it.

Jason was still in the washroom, suffering from a stomach ache. Price had laughed that it was probably due to his wife's cooking, and that he shouldn't have tried to man up and eat something he knew he shouldn't be putting in his body.

Price chuckled and continued to look on as the mighty snow drifts continued to blow and swirl before him. The powerful winds rattled the window frame, and the howl it created lent an eerie quality to the rather plain interior of the bunker.

He sighed, took a long sip of his beverage, and winced from its bitter flavor.

He thought that Jason was lucky to have a wife and a home. Price would have taken an uncomfortable night nursing a painful stomach just to know that he was coming home to a nice woman. And Jennifer was a nice girl. Price had met her a few times on occasion, usually at work functions and parties.

Price had always thought of himself as a good judge of character, and when he'd been first introduced to Jennifer, he was instantly struck by both her good looks and her charming personality. He told Jason as such when they had been on watch shortly after that first meeting. Jason was a lucky guy, stomach ache and all.

Price once had a serious relationship with a woman before.

Even now, the memories of her brought him down a little, even after all of these years since he'd last spoken with her. He missed her so much, and he wished he could have spent more time with her before she'd passed away.

She'd been killed within the walls of this city while he'd been out in the field with his squad. Apparently she'd been walking to work at the time when she passed nearby a construction site where they were expanding the housing sector of New Edmonton. An accident had ended her life when an overworked and overly tired operator lost control of his crane carrying a heavy load of steel beams. They told him that she'd died instantly when the beams fell on her, crushing her underneath all that weight.

Price shuddered at the thoughts and images that swirled through his mind. The hand holding the coffee cup shook, and a few droplets fell to the tiled floor.

There hadn't been enough of her left to become reanimated. Perhaps that was a good thing, but the thought of what had happened to Melissa always horrified him even to this day.

The sound of the toilet flushing in the bathroom interrupted his troubled thoughts. A groan of pure pain and discomfort followed shortly after, and it somehow brought a grin to Price's face. This was the third time in the past half hour that Jason had flushed the toilet. Whatever Jennifer had made for him last night had really done a number to his system.

"Hey buddy, you going to be okay in there?" he hollered across the wide room.

"Fuck me," Jason spoke with a heavy groan. "I think I might be dying in here, Price."

"Take your time buddy," Price chuckled. Then, in a lower tone of voice, he whispered. "It's a slow night anyways."

The bunker shook slightly from a mighty gust, and Price's fears mounted for a moment before the structure around him settled back to normal. He didn't like this storm. There was something dangerous and foreboding about it that he couldn't explain. He felt out of touch with the rest of the city, even though the closest residence was only a couple of blocks away, and the closest convenience store was even less than that. His view outside the window was so obscured that he could barely discern the street lamp and sidewalk across the street.

Price paused and his eyes widened when he caught the sight of something out there that he hadn't expected to see in this kind of night.

A shadowy figure stood beneath the faint lamp light upon the sidewalk across the street. He blinked a couple of times, thinking that maybe he was crazy, but the stranger continued to stand there. The figure's long hair and shapely figure suggested that it was a woman, but why a female—let alone anyone—would be standing alone out in this weather.

His first instinct was to assume that it was one of them, one of the undead, but that decided against it because the wall was still secure, and he hadn't received any radio calls of anything out of the ordinary in the other sectors around New Edmonton.

"Hey Jason, I'll be right back," he called back towards the bathroom. "I gotta go check out something."

"What?" Jason called through the door. "What's going on?"

"I'll be right back." Price reached for his rifle on the nearby table. He walked over to the locked bunker door and donned his winter jacket as quickly as he could.

"You can't just go out there," Jason shouted, cracking open the door. "It's a fuckin' hurricane out there, the worst I've ever seen."

"There's a woman out there, and I think she might need some help," Price argued as he made sure that his sidearm was loaded and ready. "I won't be long, but we might be taking in someone in a bit here. We can't just leave her out in the cold."

"Are you crazy?"

Price shook his head, keyed in the proper codes into the door panel's keypad, and exited out into the blizzard. He stared out through the snow drifts and saw that the woman was still there. He hesitated.

The woman had turned to face him, but she continued to stand underneath the lamp light. The shadows hid her face from view, but for some reason he thought that she seemed familiar. He shouldered his rifle and began to make his way towards her, fighting against the mighty wind.

Even though the howl of the blizzard raged all around him, he thought that he heard the faint murmurs and moans of the undead beyond the gate and the wall. It chilled him to the bone knowing that they were out there, amassing in their ever growing legion just a few yards away from where he was standing right now. None knew why they were beginning to crowd around the city's perimeter.

It reminded Price of crows flocking around a corpse. Gathering birds had always been a sign of danger nearby. The very idea of it frightened Price, but then he steeled himself. He was a soldier in one of the last bastions of mankind, and he'd always been a proud member of the armed forces of this city. No matter how hard things got for him, he'd always managed to get through it all and come out alive in the end.

The sight of the woman standing beneath the streetlight unsettled him. What was going on in this strange night?

He got to within arm's length before he recognized who was standing beneath the lamppost.

He recognized Amanda's face well. He was there when she was first revealed to the masses of New Edmonton as the second person to have been brought back from the undead. He remembered the terrified look on her face that day, the worry and fear she held in her eyes when she looked upon all those people gathered around her. Even then he thought she was beautiful.

Amanda's face now showed none of that hesitation and worry. Somehow, even though she was still so strikingly beautiful, she seemed different. Before he said anything, before he could ask her if she was alright, she rushed towards him and wrapped her arms around him.

Shocked, completely at a loss, his body instinctively caught her in an unexpected hug. Price was perplexed as he found himself holding this very famous woman. She clung to him with desperate need, as if something terrible had just happened to her and she needed someone to hold on to—to remind her that everything was going to be alright.

He never realized until then how long it had been since he'd held anyone in his arms. Price wanted to keep holding on to her, but something in the back of his mind suddenly began to warn him. It was a familiar feeling, and sometimes that feeling had saved his life a few times outside of the city walls. He pushed Amanda away from him, and his arms instinctively went for his rifle. He drew and aimed the weapon at her, sensing now that something was terribly wrong with this entire situation.

Amanda stood before him with a wicked smile on her beautiful face. In her right hand she held a very familiar pistol, its muzzle pointed towards his face. He realized only then that there seemed to be something missing on him, and looked down to the empty leg holster where his sidearm should have been resting.

"Oh, God," he whispered.

"God doesn't exist," she said. "He couldn't save you now anyway."

There was a crack of thunder as a bright flash erupted from the muzzle, and he knew no more.

* * * *

Shivering in the cold, Megan waited in the shadows next to the bunker's single entrance. She hadn't thought of torturing the code out of the first man when she'd shot him point blank in the face. She regretted the decision. She should have let the man live a little longer so that she could rip the door's codes out of him one digit at a time. Now she waited, hidden in the darkness, as she listened patiently for any movement from within the bunker.

There was always a chance that whoever else was inside would send word to other soldiers about his missing partner. In Megan's experience, that was a rare occurrence. People generally didn't want to raise a potential false alarm because it put them under an embarrassing light somewhere in the future if they were wrong. No, she believed the second soldier would come out to investigate what happened himself before calling it in to his superiors.

Random thoughts and emotions flitted across her mind. The memories of the woman she'd been living as for the past few months tugged at emotions that she herself found strange and foreign. The truth was that Megan retained all of the memories and experiences that Amanda had gained in her short existence on this world.

Yet Megan was her true being, and when she thought about how scared she'd been less than an hour ago as Amanda, when she had been running through the streets like a mad woman, Megan thought about how strange it was that she had been scared at all.

She understood that she had been terrified because she hadn't remembered the truth about herself, but now that it was all back, she could resume being who she was before the undead had come crashing into her home, killing both her and her partner, Grimm.

What had happened to Grimm, she wondered? Last she recalled, her mentor, surrogate father, and lover had been trying to defend her as the horde came crashing into their home. She remembered fleeing into the basement while his shrill screams of pain rang out through the entire house. Megan had fled to the cellar and found a familiar place in the corner of the shadowy basement, where she knelt and waited for the end.

Grimm had tortured her, fed her death and despair until she knew nothing else but this. When she eventually succumbed to the truth that only he could offer her, she truly became something like him. She had become a monster in her own right, far more savage and perhaps even more frightening than the undead that now ruled the world. For a time they had lived together, luring hapless victims into their home and enjoying the screams of these poor souls.

Then the dead had come, pouring into their lives and into their home without abandon.

She still remembered how it felt when they started gnawing and pulling at her flesh. An involuntary shudder ran through her entire being at the thought of what had happened on that terrible night. She couldn't shake how afraid she'd felt when she heard their wet, slapping footsteps begin their descent down the dusty old stairs.

Her thoughts snapped back to the present when she heard movement from beyond the sealed door. There were shuffling footsteps, a jacket's zipper pulling up, and the familiar sound of a fresh magazine being loaded into a rifle. The muffled sound of the beeping keypad was soon followed by a loud click as the door unlocked. It swung open, and just as the second man's face poked over the door's edge, Megan moved.

She used the harsh torrents of the blizzard to her advantage, and raced up behind the second soldier and quickly pressed the barrel of her stolen pistol between the man's shoulder blades. The man's body stiffened, and she swore she could taste the fear that radiated from him and leapt into the air.

She had always been right about Grimm, when she'd told him that he killed people for more reasons than just his survival. He did it because he enjoyed hurting others, to see the sheer emotions of terror and the desperate desire to live completely consume their eyes.

Megan grew to see this for herself, and after a while, the guilt over killing grew duller. The cries of pain that erupted from someone she hurt filled her with the sense of power. She was the one in control of their lives, in total control over whether or not they lived. Megan lusted for that sense of power and strength. Even now, she wanted to feel it again.

This city was unlike anything she'd ever seen before. It stunned her that such a place could exist, let alone the fact that there was a sister city linked to this one by an elevated railway known as the Romero Bridge.

Outside of the city's protective walls, the shuffling undead continued to hunger for human blood.

Megan hoped that this man knew the key codes for the wall's sealed gate. She also hoped he'd last through the forthcoming interrogation.

Chapter Twenty-Five

Nestled in a small bunker situated on the top of the wall, the four soldiers waited with apprehension as they listened to the storm. They looked up as they heard what they thought sounded like a gunshot. Unsure if what they heard was firepower or the endless storm, they waited. A few minutes later a second shot sounded, and they began to arm themselves, ready to go out into the storm to investigate.

Terror settled in at the unmistakable creak of the wall's gates beginning to swing open. Alarmed, they raced out into the night, and through the torrential storm, they squinted their eyes as they tried to see through the heavy gloom and the blowing drifts of snow.

There was no mistaking it now. The gates in their sector were opening, and soon *they* would be coming in. The horrifying moans and pained cries of the undead mixed with the shrieks of the snowstorm, intensifying as if signaling their notice of the opening.

A shadow moved below the soldiers, somewhere close to the foot of the wall. It shuffled along the piles and mounds of snow in a swaying gait. The soldiers took aim and fired. The bullets tore through the creature, spilling its hemolized blood and strips of dry flesh all over the snow. The creature fell face first in the drifts, but it was soon replaced by more of the undead.

They swarmed through the gate, and the soldiers began to fire, raining down a hail of bullets to the ground below. The intensity of the blowing snow, coupled with the darkness of the night, made it impossible for the squad to spot them all. There were just too many, and the conditions were not in their favor.

The soldiers' panic began to rise, and no matter how many they killed, more replaced the ranks of those that fell. How many were there? How had so many gathered together outside the city?

Megan emerged from the shadows carrying the rifle of her latest victim. The first soldier she shot gasped as wet holes were ripped outwards through his chest cavity. The snow and the darkness, mixed with the terror that began to trickle in through the gates, blinded the remaining soldiers to what had just happened to one of their own.

Megan snuck up behind the remaining three members of the squad and quickly pulled the rifle's trigger again and again and again.

* * * *

Alfred had lived in New Edmonton all his life. He'd grown used to its nature, its culture, the way the city lived and breathed as if it were alive. He'd been from one end of the city to the other, from one wall to the opposite one. There was nothing that he didn't know about this city, and he always appreciated that he'd been born and raised in such a wondrous and safe place. The only thing he regretted, in the fifty-seven years in which he'd lived behind the safe walls of New Edmonton, was that he'd rarely ever ventured outside.

He'd heard stories of the hardships from those who had lived in the outside world, and he'd read everything on the subject of what it was like to try and survive in their world. He was happy to be behind these walls, but at the same time he'd always harbored a child-like desire for more.

Alfred wondered what it was like to go out there, in what he'd often thought of as the wastelands, and journey on foot from one place to another. What was it like to fight to survive day in and day out? He knew because he'd been cooped up in this city for most of his life, he'd developed an almost romanticized view of what it might be like to go on an adventure out there.

Alfred wasn't an idiot, and he knew people out there suffered. He knew, and on occasion, had seen what an undead was like when it went on a rampage for flesh and blood. One time, one had been found in the apartment room directly across the hall from his. The thought that he'd been so close to one of the undead at one point made him shiver even to this day.

An old man had passed away alone in his apartment, and when Alfred had heard the scratching sounds of the man's fingernails against the inside of the man's apartment door, he'd immediately called for assistance from the military. They'd arrived in less than five minutes, and when they burst into the man's apartment to finish him off, Alfred had caught a brief glimpse of what had happened to his old friend when the soldiers broke down the apartment door.

The creature that jumped out at the soldiers had the face of his friend, but the eyes...the eyes were completely different. They were empty, soulless, and they were filled with a strange mixture of pure hatred and suffering.

Despite everything, Alfred had always dreamed of one day travelling beyond the walls of New Edmonton, to experience the outside life for himself. He understood that he was now an old man, and he'd probably never get the chance to live this strange dream for himself.

He lay in his bathtub, surrounded in white hanging curtains, soaking in the warm, soapy waters as he continued to read his book. He leafed through a strange story about parasitic life-forms that took forms that looked human . He was so engrossed in his story, surrounded in his little world of white, that he almost realized too late that the water he was soaking in had begun to grow cold.

Groaning, he reached out with his feet and nudged the tap on, and a waterfall of hot water began to cascade down into the tub. The pipes in this apartment had always been loud. Alfred grew tired of complaining to the landlord about the rattling pipes and the inhuman squeals that issued from them whenever he turned on the bathroom taps.

He settled further down into the water, until his ears were submerged, muting the groaning plumbing and thrashing storm.

Something that sounded like glass crashed and tinkled to the wood floor in the foyer. Snow flew in on strong winds and dotted the room with a dusting of silver. A ragged figure pushed through the broken window and lurched across the hall. A wet, slimy hand pushed against the unlocked bathroom door, swinging it wide.

The zombie pushed aside the drapes. Alfred dropped his book into the warm water, looked up at the thing with widened eyes, and all thoughts of living in the outside world left him completely when he looked upon the soulless eyes. The eyes reminded him very much of his friend's from across the hall. The face was nothing more than a skull covered in thin layers of dark brown tissue and muscle fiber, and the lipless mouth pulled back into a maniacal sneer. Loose twigs stuck out from places all over its body, as if at some point it had rolled down a forested hill, and what flesh it had was covered in dirt and moss.

The creature opened its mouth and roared, dropping a trio of wriggling maggots into the warming water.

Alfred screamed.

* * * *

"What the hell is that?" Jesse exclaimed as he was roused from his sleep by the sounds of rapid gunfire.

Beside him, Emma stirred as well. The fog of sleep slowly left their minds, as they looked about in alarm. Their home, located a few blocks away from the eastern wall, was the closest structure to the main gates. Neither of them wanted to move so close to the wall, but housing was scarce when they first came to this place, and beggars couldn't be picky about the accommodations offered to them.

So, they sucked it up, chose to accept their new home at the edge of the city, and for a time it wasn't such a bad place to live after all. Even though they were amongst the senior most members of the Charon Initiative, this was the best place they could find. After having settled down, they'd grown to love the house so much they had decided to remain there, close to the wall.

Now, the sounds of gunfire going off in the night stirred fears that the both of them had long since grown to accept. The gunfire could only mean a few things and the first thing that came to mind—somehow the eastern wall had been breached. The memories of their recent ordeals with the undead filtered through both of their minds. The horror of their near death experiences awoke terrible imaginings in both of their minds.

They had just narrowly escaped death not too long ago and now that familiar feeling of dread they'd felt them was renewed in their souls. What was going on?

How or why didn't matter to them. Jesse and Emma had long ago prepared a contingency plan in case they ever woke up to the sound.

That plan was to get dressed and run.

Jesse and Emma glanced at each other for a moment as they sat in bed. They exchanged a few words of love and kissed. Shortly after that, they leapt out of their bed and quickly slipped into their clothes. They fled from the bedroom and down the hall, donning their coats and boots as they made for the front door.

Emma opened the door of their once lovely and peaceful home, and a decayed hand shot forward and clutched at her jacket's sleeve with gnarled fingers. Emma screamed as she was pulled over the threshold as if she were a lifeless doll. The monster opened its jaws and tore right into her face, ripping away her left cheek and lower lip.

Jesse bellowed with a mixture of fear and anguish as his wife disappeared beneath a swarm of mangled bodies, and others rushed through the door and reached for him. The powerful strength in their arms and jaws ripped him apart, and he screamed aloud as he was torn asunder by these terrible monsters.

* * * *

The massacres continued throughout the night, leaving nothing but death and ruin behind. The army of the undead surged into the snowy streets, completely oblivious to the raging storm. They went into houses and buildings, tearing down doors and windows with their incredible strength. Their endless hunger spurred them on, driving them to kill whatever they could find.

The late hour in the middle of the blizzard caught the city unaware, and within the first hour, hundreds already lay dead. Those killed would soon rise, to join the ranks of the already massive army of living dead.

* * * *

Megan watched from the shadows, observing the carnage that she alone had allowed to happen. The sense of power was greater than anything she'd experienced before. A large part of her couldn't believe how naïve she was when she'd lost her memory and tried to live as one of these people.

For a long time she watched from atop the wall, surveying the carnage that spread below. The bodies of the soldier's she'd slain lay scattered around her. It was so easy to take them down since they were completely taken by surprise. Her sense of blood lust remained strong and she continued to look down with a sinister smile slowly spreading across her lips.

Finally, she descended the wall and began to move through the shadows in the street, using the snow drifts to mask her presence from both the living and the dead. Like a wraith, she continued to bear witness to the end of New Edmonton.

Megan watched as a woman was dragged from the front door of a small home and out into the cold night.

The creature pulled on her hair and ripped handfuls from her bleeding scalp. The woman thrashed madly in panic, but the creature easily ripped at her wrists and arms, tearing them apart. The zombie's violent howls and cries filled the night air. Other creatures shuffled closer to join in on the impending feast.

The growling and screeching sounds of the horde beginning to eat the woman alive sent chills up Megan's spine. She enjoyed the thrilling feeling of electricity that surged through her body. She moved from shadow to shadow and continued to watch as this once proud and great city was being systematically torn apart at the seams.

Megan smiled and fled into the storm. There were other things for her to do, other tasks that she wanted to cross off her agenda. The one thing that she wanted to do right now was to visit the good old professor. She wanted to show him what he'd done to this city by bringing someone like her back from the dead. She wanted to see the anguish in his eyes when she told him this, and then she would kill him with this last thought lingering in the man's skull.

Megan's smile grew wider.

Part Four
The Fall

"When our descendants look back, I hope they remember what we started here."

Chapter Twenty-Six

"How come you don't remember us, Dad?" the little boy asked him.

The warm air blew in from the ocean, cascading across Adam's face as he stood upon the now familiar boat from his dreams. He'd envisioned this vessel often, but this was the first time he'd found himself standing upon its deck. He didn't know how he ended up standing upon these wooden floorboards, He stood here now, resting his weight against the railing on the side of the boat.

The feel of the warm winds calmed him, made him feel good inside. The cold waters lapped against the sides of the boat, spraying his arms in a cool, salty mist. For the first time in what felt like a long time, Adam smiled and felt as if there was nothing wrong with the world.

"Dad, why aren't you listening to me?" the young boy urged.

Adam looked to his right and upon the youthful face that seemed so familiar to him even though he couldn't place the boy's name. There was love in the kid's face, love towards him, and inside, Adam felt the stirrings of the same feelings he felt towards this nameless child.

He smiled down at him and brushed his fingers through the boy's dark brown hair. The gesture was very familiar to him, and he felt that he must have done this many times over, a long time ago. Adam's smile widened, and he felt the stirrings of oncoming tears welling in his eyes.

He was sure now that this boy was his son, and his heart was gladdened to be standing on the deck of this boat with him. He felt the strange sensation that he'd finally come home.

"Clark," Adam spoke. The name had come to him from out of the ether, and yet he instinctively knew this was the boy's name. "That's your name, isn't it?"

He choked out the last few words, but it was sheer happiness that made him stutter.

"That's right, Dad," Clark said. "How come it took so long for you to remember?"

"I honestly don't know," he laughed out loud. "I don't know

why, but I remember it now? I'm so sorry. I wish I knew what happened to you and your mother."

"We're fine, Dad," his son smiled up at him. "You saved us, don't you remember?"

"I wish I did," Adam answered.

He felt slender arms encircle him from behind. They were gentle arms, soft and smooth, which embraced him warmly from behind.

"You did save us, Jack," Gillian said to him as she rested the side of her head against his back.

He felt her warm breath fill his shirt and brush up against his skin; felt her embrace tighten in a moment of desperate need. Adam's wife held him tightly, and when he turned around slowly to regard her, he looked down at her face and almost broke down in tears. He couldn't remember everything, He did remember her.

This was his wife in his previous life, this was the girl he'd dreamed of for so long and now finally understood he'd once loved her more than anything else in the world.

Her dark hair blew softly against the ocean breeze, and the green tint of her eyes looked like twin gemstones swimming in seas of white.

"I did?" he asked her.

"Yes, Jack," Gillian said. "Thank you."

"I don't remember anything, just your names. I wish I could remember more, but I don't. So much has happened, Gillian. I don't even know how long ago it was when I lost you both. I know this is a dream, but I know now that you were both real. It kills me that I don't know what happened to either of you. Oh god, what happened to you and Clark?"

"I don't have those answers," she shook her head. "I'm so sorry."

"I've missed you both so much," the tears streamed down the sides of his face now. "Oh God, I wish I could hold you both again."

"You can hold us," she said to him. "At least here you can. At least here you are able to, even if it's just for a little while. We're a family, Jack, and no matter what happens, we will always find each other. Somehow we always did."

"Except when I died," he choked.

"Don't," she shushed him, stroking his face softly with the fingers of her right hand. "Just stay here with us for a little while. It's so good to know that you finally remember us."

Clark tugged at his father's pant leg, and Adam extended his arm so that his son could be included in their embrace. He dropped down to one knee and held them both close to him, tightly in his trembling arms, as if for the last time. He wept, but his tears were due to a mixture of sadness and pure joy.

Even though this was all in his head, Adam held onto this delusion as if it were real. At least for a little while, he wished to indulge in this fantasy. Right now, he couldn't let them go. At least not yet. Not so soon.

"Find us," Gillian whispered into his ear. "Maybe we're still out there, somewhere."

He kissed the top of his son's head and then kissed his wife tenderly on the lips.

"I will, Gillian. I promise I'll try."

Chapter Twenty-Seven

When Adam woke, it was with the startling realization that his entire life was different now. No longer was he fumbling in the darkness trying to find answers to his illusive past. He didn't yet know everything, He'd discovered the most important parts of his forgotten history. His real name was Jack. He had a wife named Gillian and a son named Clark.

The fog of sleep lingered with him as he roused himself from his slumber. Before he lifted his fingers to his face, he felt fresh tears drying on his skin. Adam found he was filled with both incredible joy and insurmountable sadness. New questions lingered in his mind, foremost of which was what had happened to his wife and son.

Then he remembered Amanda, his feeling towards her and how far they had moved on in their relationship. Guilt gnawed at Adam's heart and, though his circumstances should have allowed for everything that had occurred since his resurrection, he couldn't help but feel this terrible guilt for having found love in another woman.

He lay on a couch in the professor's vast and shadowy living room. He'd fallen asleep here after the storm had intensified so much that they both decided it would be safer for him to spend the night. How much time had passed since he'd fallen asleep? The howl of the powerful winds outside told him that the hurricane hadn't abated. In fact, it sounded to him like it was raging with even greater fervor than it had before.

The darkness of the room surrounded him. Adam groaned as he fought to wrestle the last of the lingering sleep from his mind.

Something tugged at his right foot.

Confused, Adam's body stiffened and he suddenly felt that he was no longer alone in this room. The pale light from the high windows to his left wasn't nearly strong enough to illuminate much of the living room. Adam felt the urge to whisper to the shadows, to ask if the professor was there, He hesitated, and he wasn't sure why. A sharp pang of fear invaded his soul. A feeling of cold pinpricks raced up the back of his neck and arms.

"Adam, are you awake?" a voice asked him.

His heart jumped. "Amanda?" he asked the darkness.

He more felt than saw the smile that stretched out across her face. He felt it as much as he could now feel the extra mass that weighted down on the couch's cushions near his feet. Amanda's soft hand was on his foot, and he felt the warmth from her palm through the fabric of his socks. He was instantly glad that she was here with him.

Then he wondered why she was here, in the professor's home. How had she gotten in?

He remembered that she hadn't answered her door when he tried knocking on it earlier. Adam wondered if maybe she'd gone out, He couldn't for the life of him figure out why she would have been out in the city in a night like this. He also noted that she hadn't answered him, and for some reason that feeling of unease grew just a little bit inside of him.

"Hey, what's wrong?" he asked, hoping to elicit some kind of a response from her.

"You have no idea how weird this is for me, Adam," she finally spoke. Amanda moved her hand away leaving him feeling completely alone in the black. "I still remember everything that's happened to me since the Charon Initiative brought me back, and that includes how I feel about you. I still love you, and at the same time I don't want to. I can't help it. These feelings...they're there, and I can't get rid of them. I still love you, Adam, and I wish so much that I didn't."

Shock filled him, and his worry intensified like the blizzard outside.

"What are you talking about? What's going on, Amanda?"

"I really wish you'd stop calling me that," she said.

Adam picked up on the strange way she spoke, its subtle differences and the changes in how she intoned certain words. It was still her voice, there was no denying that, but there was something very off with the person that was speaking to him now.

In seconds it hit him, and as he processed everything she'd just said, his keen mind unraveled much of what must have happened to her since the last time he'd been with her. She remembered. How much of her past she'd recalled, he didn't know, He couldn't figure out any other reason to explain her rather bizarre behavior. Amanda remembered her past, and it didn't escape him that it was a little strange that the both of them had experienced these sudden revelations at around the same time.

What had triggered it? Was it the sudden change in the weather, perhaps, or could it be something else that was coming? The real answer could be it was a mere coincidence. Adam's mind already went to work, trying to figure out what had brought about their sudden revelations.

"Have you noticed how different we are from the others?" she continued to speak.

"What do you mean?" he asked her, hating the sound of hesitation in his voice.

"We're stronger than the others. I can hear things before anyone else can. There are other things also, but I'm guessing that you know all about this already, don't you?"

"We weren't sure how to tell you. We didn't even know if you would have the same abilities. I found out while I was out there, right around the same time as when we found you. The professor and I watched and waited to see if you would develop the same strengths. We wanted to make sure what I had wasn't an accident of some kind. Now we know."

"It's okay, Adam," Amanda spoke. "I have to say, it is strange knowing a little bit about what I can do now. Can you imagine how I must feel, finally waking up and finding out that I'm stronger and faster than everyone else out there?"

"Something did happen," he gaped. "Amanda, did you remember something about your past?"

"Did I ever." The joy was evident in her voice. "In fact, I got it all back. So you can imagine my surprise to find myself here, with all these new memories of a life in this city, of a life with you."

"This is great!" Adam beamed, trying desperately to ignore what she'd said about wishing she didn't love him. "If you really do remember everything about your past, that's amazing. We have to go tell the professor. I have some good news of my own. I remember a little bit about myself as well. I don't recall nearly as much as you, obviously, but I'm starting to believe that I will get it all back eventually."

"Don't worry about the professor. I promise I'll tell him myself when the time comes."

Adam squinted into the gloom, concern growing within him once more. He struggled to sit up.

"Who are you?" he asked. The words fell like a dead weight, silencing the room and muffling the gale that raged outside.

"I'm still me, but also I'm more now," she told him. "My name is Megan."

He whispered her name, tested it on his lips and felt a sudden hint of fear fill him.

"What's your real name, Adam?" she asked him.

"Jack," he spoke, the name sounding both strange and familiar coming from his mouth.

"Hello, Jack. Look, this is very difficult for me and this is becoming a rather awkward situation. Maybe we can discuss this further later. What do you think?"

"How did you get in here?" he asked her, and then another thought entered his mind. "The professor doesn't know you're here does he?"

She didn't answer him, and for him this was answer enough.

Adam craned his head to the left as he gazed out the tall windows at the far end of the room. He thought he'd heard something...sounds...the faint popping sounds that reminded him of distant gunfire muffled by the powerful wind. There was something else he thought he heard that even his heightened senses found it difficult to pick up. What he thought it sounded like was the distant sound of human screams.

"What's going on out there?" he asked.

He felt Megan's weight shift on the couch, and then something hard, something made of metal, slammed into the front of his scalp. Adam's world suddenly went black.

Chapter Twenty-Eight

Danny and Isaac had exited the small bunker located on the top of the wall. They both thought they'd heard gunfire coming from the east end of the city. The city was nearly impossible to see through the heavy snow, and as they stood atop the wall looking towards the east, their hearts darkened with the terrible thoughts that began to circle through their minds.

They were tired, having shared a long night on watch duty during one of the worst storms they'd ever experienced in their lives. They were the only two patrolling the top of the wall in the southern area, and as they stood and stared out into the night, a great sense of loneliness and separation fell upon them.

The distant sound of gunfire came from within New Edmonton's protective walls. The ramifications of what this could possibly mean weren't lost on the two soldiers from Sparrow Company. Isaac was on the radio immediately, pressing his fingers onto the small device in his ear as he began to try and ascertain what was going on.

Danny stared out into the gloom for a little while longer before he ripped his eyes away from the shadows and checked to make sure that his rifle was armed. He radioed down to the soldiers stationed below and they reported in that their gate was still secure.

A sudden thought hit him and Danny raced towards the outer fringes of the wall. He looked over the side and down into the forest beyond the city. It was difficult to see anything at all in this terrible weather. He turned on the torch mounted on his rifle and trained its beam down towards the ground. The light helped somewhat, and a shadow fell across his soul when he saw that the ground below was empty. Not a single one of the undead lingered out there, when earlier a growing mass had begun to form. Where had they gone? Instinctively, his attention was drawn towards the east, and he began to wonder...

He locked eyes with his partner, who'd lowered his finger from the earpiece. Danny noted that the young man's hand was trembling, and he guessed that it wasn't from the cold. The look in Isaac's dark eyes told him that his worst fears had come to pass.

* * * *

Chaos reigned through the streets of New Edmonton. Much of the populous had become aware of the undead invasion of their once safe metropolis. The second last bastion of mankind was being overrun by seemingly endless waves of the undead, and there seemed to be little anyone could do to stop them. Even the military, trained through all of their existence to deal with these savage creatures, fought and died in the streets. The blowing snow and the darkness of the night hampered their ability to combat the living dead. The lights from their torches illuminated some of the night, but the storm was so fierce that they could still see little around them.

It always surprised the soldiers how fast some of them could move. The ones more whole and intact than the others couldn't run, but they were faster. Coupled with their terrifying strength, the stronger of the undead became one of the most deadly predators that world had ever seen.

Wilson, a middle-aged shopkeeper, ran through the snowy streets, retreating in any direction just as long as it was away from the hungry jaws of the dead. He gaped as bright headlights suddenly turned the corner in front of him. He rolled to the right, narrowly avoiding being crushed by the military APC as it rumbled on past him. The large vehicle's passing churned up clouds and waves of snow, partially covering him as he lay on the ground.

Out of breath, he drew in deep gulps of air as he lay on his back and tried to reorient his jarred senses. He'd almost been crushed by a military vehicle, and he honestly didn't think that the occupants of the infernal machine had even seen him.

He wondered where they were headed and he soon realized that they were travelling in the direction from where he'd just fled from. Even though he'd almost been accidently run over, he felt pride towards the brave soldiers who were now heading towards the maw. Wilson hoped that they would survive this night. He prayed that they would be able to help the others who were still out there, trying to escape from those things.

Aware that he wasn't safe yet, Wilson flipped himself over and pushed himself up onto his feet. His bare hands chilled from the cold touch of the snow piling atop the street. He almost screamed as a family of four suddenly raced past him, running past him so closely that he felt a skirt brush against the back of his hand. He looked up and saw the face of the girl who'd brushed past him. She couldn't be more than seven.

As her father dragged her away from him, the little girl turned around and looked upon Wilson. There was unmistakable fear written all over her gaze. Tears glistened on her cheeks, reflecting the faint lamp light on the sides of the road. A dark splotch of blood marked the left side of her face, where he also noticed what appeared to be deep scratch marks that looked like they'd been left behind by sharp fingernails.

Horror filled him as he realized that the little girl was infected and that the father had perhaps not noticed. The girl's eyes looked tired and strained, and dark veins had begun to spread around her irises.

Someone else bumped past him, almost knocking him forward and off his feet. The figure stopped and turned to face him.

Wilson gasped as he looked upon the ruined face of the creature that no longer had a mouth. Its lipless mouth looked like a malevolent smile, a smirk from a creature who was overjoyed to have discovered its next meal. Wilson's heart froze to solid ice when he looked upon the creature.

He backed away from it, only to fall into the waiting arms of a dead woman who quickly sank her teeth into the soft flesh on his neck. Wilson screamed as the thing's teeth bit deeply and painfully into his flesh. He roared in rage as the other joined in. It grabbed his right arm and began to tug with terrifying force. His shoulder popped, and he felt the bones in his arms break under the creature's impossibly strong grip.

Before death finally took him, he looked up and saw something that added to his horror. The ground beneath him actually shook as a giant zombie strode towards him, its massive size encompassing most of his view. The monstrous thing reached down, swatting a few of the other undead aside to clear a path. Wilson never heard of a ghoul as large as this colossus. The sheer magnitude of its size temporarily banished his terror, replacing it with awe.

The giant reached down for him, and when its mouth opened, Wilson looked deep into the darkness between its jaws and despaired. Wilson closed his eyes and waited for the end, praying that it would be quick.

* * * *

The hordes of the dead continued to push back the human

resistance. Before long they'd invaded past the eastern side of New Edmonton. They drew closer to the heart of the city and from there they would branch out in different directions, invading the metropolis like a virus. Those left behind soon rose to replenish the ranks of the ones that had been slain by the outnumbered human soldiers.

Within the first hour of the counter attack, nearly a hundred members of the armed forces had perished. The deaths had stacked up at an alarming rate, greater than any of the city's leaders had ever estimated. The generals scrambled to try and achieve some order from this chaos, but even their communications systems were taking a heavy toll from the weather.

* * * *

Danny and Isaac watched from their place atop the wall, and without orders, neither of them knew what to do. They contemplated going out there, driving themselves into the snow to try and help, but they knew was basically a death sentence for the both of them. They couldn't just leave their post and abandon it to go haphazardly into the fray.

The sounds of gunfire intensified in the distance, drawing closer to the city. Sparks of light flashed in the dark; the rounds from the soldier's rifles blinking as they tried to combat the seemingly endless numbers of dead.

The cold winds chilled them to the bone, but neither of them really noticed. All of their focus was rooted to the horror that was going on out there, the nightmare that was still beyond their view. They were mesmerized by the sweeping terror that had somehow found a way inside.

Both Danny and Isaac knew they were witnessing the fall of New Edmonton, the destruction of their home. They knew this outcome was always a possibility, but they'd become so used to life behind these walls that neither of them believed that it could possibly happen.

"Oh God, what are we going to do?" Isaac whispered.

"I don't know, Tennant," the gun felt heavier in Danny's hands. He felt useless, standing here and just waiting. This wasn't right, they needed to do something. It was their duty to try and help those people out there.

Their earpieces crackled, and they heard a voice they hadn't expected to hear.

"Danny, Tennant, are you both reading me?" the Sergeant's voice bulled its way through the layers of static noise caused by interference from the storm. "Come in. Do you read me?"

The sound of the Sergeant's voice instantly filled them with hope, and no matter how small that hope might be, at least it was something to latch onto.

Danny's hand shot towards his earpiece, and when he spoke it was with great excitement.

"Sergeant, goddamn it's good to hear you, sir!"

"You too, Danny," the man's gruff voice spoke to him through the tiny speaker. "Is Tennant with you?"

"Yes, he's right here beside me. We caught watch duty on the wall tonight. Do you know what the hell is going on out there?"

"I know just as much as the top brass does," Thomas growled. "Jenny and I just got off the train from Himura Valley. We're close to the point where they broke in."

"How the hell did they get in here?" Danny shouted.

"That's just it. From where our snipers are, they tell me that the gates look perfectly intact. Maybe the electronic locks failed somehow and released. I don't know. We have safeguards to prevent that kind of fuck-up."

"What are you thinking, sergeant?" Danny asked.

"The same thing that Jenny is thinking," he paused before he continued. "Some asshole must have let them in."

Danny cursed aloud.

"Yeah, but the how or why doesn't concern us at the moment. The situation is a disaster show, and when I showed up, our fearless leaders were running around like headless chickens. Thank god they had the sense to listen to me."

Excitement blossomed in Danny's troubled heart. "What's the plan?"

"We're abandoning the city. The storm is too strong, and it's making securing the city an impossible task. The other squads are already rounding up survivors and readying them for transport to Himura Valley. We've secured and fortified the Romero station, but I can't guarantee that we can hold this position forever. Have you two seen them yet? Do you have any idea how strong their numbers are?"

"We haven't seen them, sir," Isaac answered. His voice was laden with worry.

"It's okay, Tennant," the sergeant tried to sound hopeful. "If we stick to the plan and stay together, we can get out of this.

Evacuating as much as we can out of the city is our top priority right now. There are squads being sent to the Charon Initiative to extract whatever data and personnel we can."

"What about us?" Danny asked. "What are our orders? Please don't tell me that we're going to sit up here on this damn wall all night."

"The soldiers stationed beneath you are already being informed of their duties by their superiors. I'm ordering you and Tennant to find a way to through the city to the professor's mansion. Jenny and I will be making our way there as well. Our job is to secure the professor and make sure he gets to the Romero Bridge's central hub in one piece."

"Yes, sir," Danny said, empowered now that he had something to do, a task to perform.

"Sir, do you know where Adam is?" Isaac asked.

"No, I don't. In fact, I was about to ask you two the same thing. We haven't been able to get a hold of him. He could be back at the apartment. For now, we have to stick to the plan and get Professor Mena to safety."

"Sir, I'm sorry, but Adam is our squad mate," Isaac said with some hesitation and worry. "He's also our friend. We can't abandon him and leave him alone out there."

There was a pause on the other end of the line. Isaac's face screwed up with worry, but when he looked up at Danny he was relieved to see the agreement.

"Sir, I volunteer Tennant and I to go on a search and rescue mission to find Adam and Amanda," Danny spoke to his superior.

Another pause ensued, and when the sergeant spoke once more into their earpieces, it was with a voice that was laced with regret.

"We already have evacuation squads making their way to that sector. When they find him, they'll get him up to speed and maybe he can help them evacuate everyone else in that neighborhood. Your orders still stand. Get to the professor's mansion. Jenny and I will see you both soon."

"Got it," Danny replied and signed off.

He understood the reasoning behind the sergeant's orders, but it didn't help to alleviate the sense of guilt he felt inside. Danny was surprised with how close he now felt with his newest squad member, and it killed him to know that they were effectively leaving Adam to fend on his own without their aid. He honestly believed that Adam could take care of himself, but that didn't lessen his worry.

In the distance, the sounds of gunfire continued. Soon the carnage was close enough that he and Isaac heard the screams.

Chapter Twenty-Nine

It took less than twenty minutes for Jenny and the sergeant to make their way through the chaotic city in their military APC. The streets were crowded with fleeing civilians and battling soldiers trying to save their lives. Further beyond the downtown sector, closer to where the professor lived, the streets grew empty. Heavy snowdrifts blew with powerful gusts against the sides of their vehicle. The storm was so great it shook and jostled the heavy machine.

Jenny fought against the wheel as she battled to keep the vehicle steady on the slick road. She feared for the safety of her friends, but more so she feared for Danny's life. He was out there somewhere, making his way towards them, but both he and Isaac were alone in this terrible situation. Even now she couldn't believe what was happening, but she steeled herself, gathered her courage, and tried to focus on her job.

Thomas sat in the seat beside her, staring out into the night. His face was a blank slate of hidden emotions and troubled thoughts. She marveled at how strong the man was even now during the fall of New Edmonton.

Unlike the rest of the crew, Jenny actually knew quite a bit about the man's past. He'd lost his family-including a mother, father, and two sisters-during an attack years before the sergeant had ever laid eyes upon this city. He and his family had lived amongst a large group of survivors; nomads who travelled from place to place, always on the run and never able to settle down because of the threat that chased after their heels.

The attack had come during the night, when a large herd of undead had descended upon their encampment. Life amongst the nomads was all the eleven-year old had ever known, and though his family had been a part of this group for many years, their tent had always been relegated to the outer fringes of the camp.

The guards must have been killed before they could raise any alarms. The undead had fallen upon his family's tent in a frenzy, waking them all up from their otherwise peaceful slumbers. His older sisters had dragged him bodily out of his cot, pulling him into the darkness. He never found out what had happened to his mother and father in the chaos that ensued, but the end result was easy enough for him to imagine. His sisters ran, pulling him along between them. They shielded him and tried to protect him when the living dead ambushed them, surprising the youths when the creatures had emerged from between other tents.

Thomas Black had somehow survived that massacre, and the events of that night left his soul perpetually scarred. He was never the same after that, and he once conveyed to Jenny how he still remembered what it was like when he used to smile with innocence and earnest joy.

Even though he lived out in the wastelands, living day to day in this dangerous world, he found happiness amongst his friends and family. He had explained to her once that when he looked back at that unsuspecting youth, it was strange for him to comprehend that he once felt so happy. That innocence he used to possess was something very foreign to him now, and when he looked back at his younger self, all that he saw was a stranger who saw the future as a slightly brighter place.

"We're almost there," Thomas growled. "Make a right on this corner."

Jenny nodded as she turned the wheel. She wondered how the sergeant saw anything through the heavy snow. She could barely make out the street lights that passed by, let alone the dark shapes of buildings and homes that lined the empty streets. Perhaps he'd been here enough times to know this area of the city like the back of his hand. Maybe he was just that good at what he did.

She turned, and the area grew a little bit more familiar. A wide swath of front lawn revealed itself, and she slowed to a stop before the front gates. Beyond this was the large mansion. She saw the building faintly through the tall black fence, sitting atop a low hill covered in mounds of snow. The place was dark save for a single illuminated window on the second floor.

Jenny angled the APC towards the front gates when something large and something powerful crashed into them from the right side.

Jenny cried out as the vehicle was thrown far to the left. The inside of the cabin rocked violently, and her hands instinctively gripped the wheel until her knuckles went white. Time seemed to slow, and for a moment Jenny felt weightless as the APC floated in the air. The vehicle crashed right through the professor's fence, tearing through it as if it were wet tissue. The APC shook as they spun on the snowy grounds, churning up snow and mud, before finally coming to a stop facing the distant street.

Thomas looked up from the dash and out through the forward windows. "Shit."

Jenny looked up just in time to see something gigantic and dark charge towards them.

It was perhaps the largest of the undead she'd ever seen, and it was undoubtedly the most powerful. It threw its decayed mass upon the front of the vehicle. Its blood splattered in sopping, sludge-like spatters across the windshield as the APC was once more rocked to the side violently. The muffled roars of the creature could be heard even through the heavy armor and the vehicle groaned beneath its weight.

Thomas snarled as he glared outside the window and moved to unbuckle his seat belt.

"What are you going to do," she cried, frightened. "Go out there and fight that thing?"

She felt the floor beneath her shudder and the tremors increased as the creature drew closer.

"Damn it," Thomas roared, lost now in some kind of mad rage.

He rose from his seat and quickly moved towards the back, where they kept their rifles secured against the wall. Jenny spun to face him, gawking that he was so willing to go out there and face that thing on his own.

She would follow him, of course. She knew she would lay down her life for him no matter how futile the outcome might be. Since she'd joined the military at a young age, she had doubted her place amongst the men. She only came to understand that she might be more than she was making herself out to be when Thomas had selected her to join Sparrow Company.

By that time, the sergeant had become something of a hero, or perhaps even a legend, amongst the military. To be recruited by him opened up her eyes to the possibility that she might be something special after all, and for that she owed him her life.

She was about to rise from her chair to follow after him when she noticed headlights outside the forward viewport, slicing into the darkness of the night. The lights bobbed as the unknown vehicle jumped the curb and began making its way across the snowy grounds of the Mena estate.

"Sergeant, wait," she called back, and waved for him to look out the window.

The vehicle appeared to be a pickup truck of some sort, and it roared through the night as it moved towards them. Jenny's heart raced as the lights approached, and then veered off toward the colossus creature standing in front of the APC. The giant slowly turned around and faced the oncoming lights. It opened its lipless jaws and roared.

The truck sped up as its driver gunned the engine and ploughed head first into the giant. The truck's front end crumpled like a toy accordion, and the front windshield shattered and broke apart, sending glass and bits of metal flying in all directions. The monster shrieked as the metal bumper enveloped its torso and arms.

* * * *

Danny and Isaac were able to find the truck just a block away from where they'd been stationed at the wall. Danny used the end of his rifle to shatter in the driver's side door, and with a little bit of quick wiring work, was able to get the black pickup started up.

The cold wind blew through the broken window beside Danny, He ignored the chilly winter's breath as they sped through the streets of New Edmonton. Something nagged at Danny, telling him that he had to hurry. Something was wrong, and he couldn't explain it beyond the obvious fact that their city was crumbling all around them.

That was when they pulled onto 111th and saw the broken section of the fence through the blowing snow. The APC had come into view after and, for a second or two, he wondered how the hell the vehicle had ended up on the side of the front lawn. Then he saw the gigantic zombie making its way towards the APC, and that was when he pressed his foot down hard on the gas.

"Hang on, Tennant," Danny had shouted.

Isaac grasped the handle hold hanging down from the ceiling just inside of the passenger side door. Danny gripped the steering wheel tight as they jumped the curb and slid over the sidewalk. He lost control momentarily, and for a brief moment he feared that their vehicle would spin out of control. Miraculously, however, he was able to keep the truck steady and he hit his foot down harder on the pedal as he raced towards the beast.

The impact shattered the front end of the truck like Styrofoam. If they hadn't been wearing their seat belts they would have both smashed through the windshield and flown out into the night. The breath was knocked right out of his lungs as he was thrown forward against the constricting seat belt.

Everything around him was filled with the grinding and smashing noise of metal. He felt the world tilt on its axis as the truck slammed down on its left side. Drifts of snow flooded through the broken window and shattered front windshield, drowning him in mounds of white.

He was vaguely aware that something, or someone, was tugging on his right sleeve. Danny coughed, tasted blood in his mouth, and looked over to where Isaac had been sitting moments before. His vision, blurry and clouded, soon readjusted itself. Isaac was kneeling on the right side of the truck, which was now pointed up towards the black sky. Isaac knelt down and pulled hard on Danny's arm, calling for him with a voice that seemed to cry out from a great distance.

He suddenly wanted to be away from the confines of this ruined machine. He struggled and fought for purchase on the smooth leather seats as his friend began to help haul him out. The cold bit him in the face as he emerged from the passenger side door, dragged along by Isaac, who'd already descended to the ground below.

Danny grunted as he pushed and pulled himself up and out of the broken vehicle, still clinging to his rifle.   He stumbled out of the truck and landed on his hands and knees in the snow. Isaac fell on his back, and then quickly rolled to his feet before moving to help Danny to his own. Both of them backed away from the ruined vehicle, staring, as the remnants of the truck suddenly shook and trembled. A sharp roar rose from the front end of the pickup, coming from the creature that was beyond their view. The beast, alive somehow, thrashed within the ruins of steel and electrical wiring.

Danny and Isaac stood beside one another and readied their rifles. The truck was suddenly flung to their right, and it hung suspended in the air for several seconds before coming to a crash behind them in the snow.

The undead monster's body was torn and ravaged from the crash. Its right arm was missing, shorn from its body at the shoulder. Half of its face was simply gone, and there was a gaping section where its right cheek and eye once was.

Despite its terrible injuries, the thing still lived. And it moved towards them now on lurching steps that suggested to them that both of its legs had been shattered and broken from the vehicle's impact. Pure hunger drove this thing now, as it forced itself forward even on its ruined legs. And it moved towards them faster than either had anticipated.

Danny fired off four shots from his rifle before the thing reached him.

The creature swung its remaining arm wide, catching him in its outward arc. The arm caught Danny full in the side of his face and body. Isaac watched in horror as the man's body was flung to the side, arms and legs flailing like streamers in the wind. The body landed in the thick snow, but the angle and the speed of his descent unsettled Isaac.

For a long moment he stared in utter shock at the slumped and lying form of his friend. Then his fear was replaced with rage, and he raised his rifle and began to fire into the beast. He was barely aware that he was screaming out loud until the rifle's magazine ran out. Only then did he see that the giant was still standing, more than a dozen smoking holes pock marking its body in several locations.

It moved forward, slower this time, but still active. Isaac quickly released the spent magazine, and slapped in a fresh one in one successive motion.

He heard the unmistakable sound of moans behind him and to either side. He quickly scanned his surroundings and found that he was no longer alone. From out of the shadows, a teeming mass of the undead emerged. A large group of them lurched towards his downed friend, and Isaac lost himself in fury as he blasted away at them with his rifle. The sharp impacts of bullets hitting home flung the creatures back and away from Danny's body. More soon came to replace the fallen.

He was surrounded and they were coming in from all sides. The giant moved towards him, raising its remaining arm with outstretched fingers. Its mouth opened in a sickening and unnatural way, stretching open wider than any normal human being could. Isaac saw only pure darkness between that creature's jaws.

A small dark shape, the size of a baseball, sailed towards the giant before landing somewhere between its feet. Isaac heard a familiar voice bark at him, telling him to duck and the young man dropped low to the snowy ground. The grenade exploded with a raucous noise that tore into the night.

The giant blew apart from the crotch up, its long decayed body ripping to shreds from the grenade's powerful blast. Its upper half sailed from the blossoming bonfire and landed somewhere beyond his view. The rest of it burned even after falling in the snow, filling the air with the terrible stench of seared flesh.

Jenny and the sergeant emerged from the APC and began to fire into the surrounding hordes of the living dead. Isaac shook himself from his numbing state of surprise and joined with his comrades as they began to fire away at the approaching dead.

Isaac glanced over at the fallen Danny, and fresh tears warmed his cold cheeks as he continued slaughtering the enemy without remorse. His rifle ran empty, he reloaded, and he continued firing into them all, almost enjoying the sight of their bodies exploding and blowing apart from the powerful rounds he launched at them.

The winds continued to blow powerful wisps of snow everywhere by the time Sparrow Company had finished dispatching the last of the surrounding dead. The mansion's grounds were littered with the remains of more than three dozen decaying bodies, along with the scattered pieces of the giant.

Through the thick snow the three of them slogged. When they reached Danny's body, Jenny's heart went still as she fell to her knees. She wept. Isaac and Thomas wanted to look away, but at the same time they couldn't turn their attention away from the unbelievable thing that had happened to one of their own. They hoped that his end had come quick. What remained of his face, after being shattered by the giant's powerful swing, suggested just that.

It had happened too suddenly. They felt cheated because they hadn't even had a chance to say goodbye. Jenny, who'd grown to care for him the most out of all of her team, wept and didn't mind the frost that clung to her skin as she let the bitter tears flow.

Danny Keene was dead.

All of them knew at any moment any of them could die, but it didn't make the reality of what they saw before them any easier. Danny had come to Jenny and the sergeant's aid without a single thought to his own safety. His bravery cost him his life, and they knew nothing they could do could bring this man back. What remained of his face...the giant had simply destroyed too much. Even the virus would leave this man's poor body alone.

Eventually Thomas turned away, hiding behind his gruff exterior the emotions that tore at him from inside. Isaac was not so stubborn or strong, and he sunk down beside Jenny and cried.

The sergeant let them have their time to grieve. Hell, he knew one day in the future he would find himself in some locked room alone, and only then would he allow himself cry for the man's death. That time was not today, and he knew he still had a job to do. He stared up at the mansion and gazed upon the single lighted window through the blowing snow. Was the professor somewhere behind that window and did he even hear the wave of gunfire that had erupted so close to his home?

Thomas turned and regarded his fallen friend one last time. He nodded in respect towards the dead man, released the magazine of his rifle to check how many rounds he left, then slammed it back home with a loud and decisive click.

Chapter Thirty

Adam woke to the familiar and terrible sound of the living dead.

He pulled himself out of unconsciousness just as the gender-less creature bit down on his foot. The creature's blackened teeth sank through the fabric of his sock and clamped down hard on his right foot. The creature took a powerful bite, and a sharp sting of pain lanced up the length of Adam's leg.

The teeth pierced his flesh and drew blood.

Horror instilled Adam with a disorienting feeling of disbelief and dread. He cried out, screamed to the top of his lungs as he kicked the corpse in the center of its face. A normal human's strength wouldn't have been enough to dislodge the monster's teeth from its catch, but Adam's strike shattered its skull, killing it instantly. The horrid thing slumped down on the cushions in front of him, silent and still, but the damage had already been done.

Already he began to feel the unnatural sensation of burning heat moving up the length of his foot. He realized that this wasn't the first time that he'd felt this, and this time was no less terrifying than the first. The virus was in his bloodstream, and it was already making its way up towards his heart.

Sweat beaded on his brow. A thousand terrible and frantic thoughts race through his mind as he tried desperately to come to grips with the situation. What was going on? Amanda had betrayed him, knocking him out and leaving him here alone in the living room. Because of what she'd done this creature had been able to do this to him. What was the creature doing in this mansion at all? How did it get beyond the walls of New Edmonton? Where were both Amanda and the professor?

Panic threatened to settle in his heart. He had to get to the professor before Amanda. How long had he been unconscious, and had she gotten to the old man already? Was it too late?

Adam glanced down at the dark blood that began to seep into his torn sock. A wracking sob took him, and Adam pressed the palms of his hands hard against his forehead and pushed hard until it hurt. Adam knew he was going to die again, and this time there might be nothing that can bring him back.

His mind felt numb, but Adam forced himself to his feet. He immediately stumbled under his own weight and the nauseating feeling that suddenly took him. The virus had already made its way far into his system, and he was shocked by the rapid spread of the disease. He felt his lungs labor for breath, and his vision swam with crimson swirls.

He wondered how long he had until he was gone.

"Not right now," he shouted to himself.

He steadied himself on his feet and felt the pain of the bite remind him of his situation. Adam forced breath into his lungs and he began to move for the door leading to the hallway. For the first time in his second life, there were thoughts of murder on his mind.

* * * *

Florentine received the call from the generals only a few seconds before and he raced toward his library in search of his hidden store of weapons. Years ago his father told him of this secret store of weapons. Florentine never believed that he would be the one going to it now. Sparrow Company was on the way to extract him from his home, and what he'd heard of what was going on in the city rattled his tired heart. In the back of his mind he realized that he forgot to report Adam's presence to the General on the radio, He knew there was no time to waste in trying to call the man back.

The city his ancestors helped build was falling apart all around him and the professor didn't know what he could do to stop it.

He focused on the fact that he'd been so close to perfecting his cure for this plague, so close to stopping it all.

What happened? What was his mistake?

Florentine burst through the door leading to his library and he quickly made his way to the western wall of shelves and books. The bookshelf swung aside easily on its cleverly concealed hinges like a pantry door.

Behind lay a steel wall safe that was nearly as wide and as tall as the same shelf that had concealed it just moments ago. He'd memorized the electronic keypad's code long ago, and he pushed in the proper commands now and waited for the ensuing beep to signal that he'd gained access to these hidden stores. Automatic lights switched on within the shallow section hidden in the wall revealing wall-mounted rows of automatic weapons and ammunition.

Florentine hoped that the other personnel that worked with him in the Charon Initiative had already made it safely on the other side of the bridge to Himura Valley. They had already gone through so much, including the years of work they'd spent on the serum and the recent attack within their own facility. All hope wasn't lost yet. There was still time for him to start over in Himura Valley and continue his research in perfecting his cure.

A terrible sound issued from somewhere downstairs and his stomach dropped out when he recognized the scream as Adam's. He momentarily forgot about the secret arsenal and spun towards the door, determined to help the young man.

He heard a loud crack, and saw a flash from a shadowed figure standing before him as something hot entered his stomach. Florentine staggered back from the force of the slug into the open safe door, knocking over a few of the books that sat on the shelf on the other side. Something warm spilled from his stomach, and Florentine felt a sudden rush of panic as he looked down to see blood spreading across his shirtfront.

The shadowy figure walked towards him, and the faint glow from the lamp sitting on his study desk illuminated his attacker's legs, then torso and then face as she walked into view.

"Amanda?" Florentine choked.

The woman who stood before him appeared to be the person he'd grown to care for and love, but the eyes that glared at him were not. This person, whoever she really was, tossed her rifle aside and drew a knife that she'd tucked between her belt and her pants.

Florentine tried feebly to raise his hands to protect himself, but she batted aside his arms with her free hand before she plunged the glimmering blade into his gut.

The fire that bloomed from the new wound raced through the professor, blinding him with pain. Florentine gasped as she pushed her weight towards him, driving the knife up to the hilt into his flesh.

To his horror, he could actually hear his blood splatter on the carpet like running water. He stared long and hard into the woman's strange eyes as she slowly let him collapse to the floor. She followed him as he fell, going down to a kneeling position beside him while she kept the blade lodged in his body.

Florentine sputtered. "Why?"

She took a moment before answering him. She looked long and hard into his eyes. Florentine saw the delight in her eyes, and his heart collapsed when he realized the mistake that he'd made.

"Haven't you ever considered who you might be bringing back with your cure?" she asked with mirth in her voice.

"No," he rasped. He tasted copper blood on his tongue, nearly choking him. "I just wanted to cure you. I wanted to save humanity."

"Well, you won't have to worry about it anymore, professor. But, honestly, thank you for bringing me back."

"Why are you doing this?"

The woman looked up, away from his eyes, and for a brief moment she stared out through the high window located behind his desk. What can she see through the storm? It seemed like she listened to something he couldn't hear but only she could.

"Can you hear them, Professor?" she asked.

She twisted the knife slightly inside of him and he screamed.

Something cold and numbing crawled up the professor's body, filling his arms and legs. He felt himself growing tired, and he came to the realization that he was dying.

"I can't hear anything, Amanda." He took a shuddering breath. "What do you hear?"

"I hear your people crying," she answered him, returning her full attention to his gaze. "I hear their screams of terror and rage. I can hear the dead lumbering after them, calling with their familiar call, the moans of damnation and oblivion. Your city is dying all around you, and I wanted you to know that it was all your fault. Because you brought me back, this happened."

"No," he shook his head feebly. "Everything you do is your choice. You did this. I just don't understand why."

Her resolve faltered for a moment and the professor saw that something, perhaps a glimmer of the woman that he knew resurface just a little bit in those eyes.

"When the survivors hear that you are dead, they will grieve over you. They will despair. I want them to feel it. I want them all to hurt, and know that hope is lost. This is me, lashing out at the world because I've been so wronged in my life. I guess you can say that I'm addicted to it now; I want to make others feel pain, because through their suffering I feel alive."

"Amanda, please...please stop this," he begged. The coldness had reached up to his neck now. He knew he wouldn't last much longer.

"Can you hear them, Professor?" she asked once more as she leaned closer towards him.

"All I can hear is you," he said. Twin trails of tears made their way down his wrinkled cheeks, mingling with the blood spilling from his trembling mouth. "All I can hear is you, and it saddens me. You were so good. You were given a second chance. For a while, you were so beautiful."

Florentine closed his eyes, and his body went slack where he lay on the floor.

Megan, feeling her arms tremble now, pulled the knife out of the old man's corpse. She couldn't remove her eyes from his face. Within her she felt her heart begin to beat faster and faster. An overwhelming sense of guilt stole its way into her dark soul, and this feeling filled her with great pain. The hurt that she wanted others to feel over this man's death was experienced by her alone. Megan knelt beside the old professor and began to weep.

No matter how hard she tried, she couldn't staunch the tears. No matter how much she wished to, she couldn't stop this terrible feeling from taking control of her.

Damn Amanda's memories! She wished now that she came back to life aware of her true past. Instead she lived with this other past, this other life, that wasn't her own. She experienced the feelings of torment as if she were still the woman named Amanda.

Megan, the cold-hearted killer forged from years of suffering and murder, broke down and cried for the death she'd just brought to someone who had been so good to her.

The sound of something crashing loudly outside momentarily broke her from her grief. This was soon followed with the sound of raucous gunfire. The roar of some frightful and unnatural creature rose from the din. It sounded gigantic and unlike anything she'd ever heard before.

"Megan."

Megan turned and looked up at Adam's emaciated and weary face, and he looked down at the professor's corpse with sheer dread. Then those eyes, those accusatory and angry eyes, looked up at her with smoldering rage. Megan watched him, unable to move from her rooted spot and he bent low to quickly retrieve the rifle she'd discarded earlier. Adam lifted the gun and pointed its barrel towards her. He did so with steady, unshaking hands.

"Adam?" she spoke, her eyes pleading.

"Don't you dare," he spat at her, barely holding himself together. She wondered what had happened to him to cause that strange lack of color on his face. He looked like he could barely stand on his own feet. It didn't take long for her to realize what must have happened to him and her stomach twisted with regret. This was something else that she had caused. She had killed the man she loved as well.

Megan shook herself from her paralysis and she rose from the floor. Adam pulled the trigger and she heard the loud rounds explode from the rifle. One bullet lodged itself on the wall next to the window. Another found its home in her left thigh muscle.

Grunting in pain, Megan raced towards the back wall and threw herself at the window. Without abandon, she crashed through the window and exited into the cold night air. All that she could think of was to run, to get away from what she'd done. The guilt followed her into the darkness as she rolled off the roof and landed hard on the snow below. With incredible strength and resolve, she pushed herself back up onto her feet and ran as fast as she could across the snow covered landscape.

Chapter Thirty-One

Adam heard the sound of the living dead thrashing out in the hallway, throwing themselves from wall to wall and from door to door in their frantic search for food. He barricaded the door to the study, quickly lifting one end of a bookshelf and toppling it over on its side right in front of the closed portal. The professor's prized collection of books spilled across the carpet in a loud crash that surely alerted the hungry beasts. The sounds of their grunts and pained cries moved closer towards the study. Its sound sends tremors up along the length of Adam's spine.

He turned to face the body on the floor, and he knew without a shadow of a doubt that the professor was dead. He'd come too late.

As the creatures began to pound their decayed fists upon the library door, Adam moved and knelt beside the professor. Grief temporarily stole away the anger he felt towards Megan. This was a pain deeper than anything he'd felt in a long time. The death of Florentine Mena left his heart barren and dry.

He remembered the first time he'd met the professor, and the memories felt so old to him now. It was the professor who first came to him, reading to him from his many books, helping to draw Adam back to humanity with his gentle, guiding hand.

Now, he was dead, and his killer was still somewhere out there.

"I'm sorry I couldn't save you," he whispered down to the dead man.

A large piece of the door suddenly broke away and dropped to the floor. Greyish, decayed arms snaked through the opening, and gnarled fingers grasped at the air, trying with futile efforts to reach for him. The roar of their cries grew louder, and through the cracks he saw some of their feverish eyes.

His eyes would soon mirror theirs.

Before that happened, Adam intended to avenge the professor's murder.

Without hesitation, he stood and retrieved a rifle from the professor's hidden store of weapons. He refused to take the one Megan left behind with him; he refused to use a weapon that had been used to end Florentine's life. Then he dropped down next to the professor, unlaced his shoes, and slipped them on. He made a mental apology to the professor before he collected himself and turned to face the broken window.

As the creatures shattered what was left of the door, Adam leaped out of the window and descended down to the ground below. He winced from the pain in his foot, and he scanned the gloom for any sign as to where Megan may have gone.

There was a faint trail of blood in the snow before him, disappearing into the darkness. He followed this trail, moving as fast as his legs could take him, aware that the storm would soon cover any evidence of Megan's passage. .

His vision blurred, and for a second he couldn't see the blood trail at all. Then his sight cleared, and he continued on. Before long he reached the outer fringes of the mansion's vast grounds. A tall fence blocked his way. Megan must have come this way on her way out. Her passage was marked by the thin dark streak of blood left behind on one of the metal posts.

Adam tossed his gun over the other side and began to climb. The exertion and effort weakened him further, and by the time he landed on the earth on the other side, he felt his pulse beat loudly in his ears. Adam felt death slowly creeping closer up from behind him, almost close enough to put its hands on his shoulders.

By the time he crossed the road and made his way to the edge of an unfamiliar neighborhood, he'd lost her trail. The snow had covered up the rest of her trail, and now Adam was lost with no direction as to where to go. He closed his eyes in frustration and tried to think of where she might go now.

Megan was lost as well, and when Adam had entered the room and seen her kneeling over the professor's body, he noted something strange in her demeanor. What had it been? What did he notice from before that he hadn't considered at the moment but seemed very important now?

Through the fever and the heat blossoming in his head, he tried to focus and think.

He opened his eyes wide.

She'd been crying. Megan had looked at him with eyes that momentarily looked like Amanda's. Somehow a part of Amanda's memories, perhaps a part of her lost soul, resurfaced and wept over what she had done to the professor.

Adam didn't think that she'd go back to her apartment because there was really nothing for her there. Other than that, there was only one other logical place that he could think of as to where she might have gone.

Adam began to walk towards the city, hoping that he was right about his assumptions. The darkness of the night enveloped him as he passed through the middle of the street, avoiding the light from the roadside lamps.

* * * *

The all too familiar building of the Charon Initiative stood before him. Along his journey here, Adam had run across a few groups and clusters of the undead. He'd killed them all, shooting them down with his rifle and checking that they were indeed dead before he moved on.

Adam crossed the outside grounds, shooting a couple more of the creatures that lingered outside, before he made his way through the open front doors of the facility. His heart skipped as he saw that the trail of blood continued inside, and he followed it down the winding halls.

His heart beat faster in his chest. He knew the excitement that coursed through his veins would only serve to spread the disease faster throughout his body, He couldn't help the adrenaline pumping his heart faster as he neared his destination. His every step became a tortuous labor, and he wondered how long he could keep this up before the inevitable finally caught up with him.

He traversed the familiar and empty halls of the Charon Initiative. It looked to be completely deserted, its staff having evacuated hours before in a hurry, as evidenced by the strewn mess they'd left behind.

Several of the offices he peered into on passing suggested that they had tried to gather as much intel and research as they could as they were leaving. There was little doubt that the military had been sent here to aid in the evacuation procedures. Hopefully they'd been able to collect enough to continue their research in the newer facility in Himura Valley.

A familiar door lay open before him, and he entered into the once sterile room filled with computer terminals set about on rows and rows that descended down towards the main floor below. A single stairway, cutting through the four levels before him led down to the base level. More computers lined the half circle wall at the far end of the large room, and in its center hung suspended the glass chamber that had brought him back into this dark world.

The glimmering tube was empty of the curative fluid that brought life back to the undead. It hung above the metal grate on the floor, suspended by a large robotic arm that protruded down from the ceiling.

Adam still recalled what it was like to be floating in that cylindrical prison, watching from within as the scientists worked on their terminals outside. Vague recollections of his final days as one of the living dead surfaced in his burning mind. He remembered trying to scratch at the glass frantically, trying desperately to break through.

Kneeling in front of the cylinder was a lone and familiar figure.

Loose dirt stuck in the treads of his shoes crunched against the smooth stairwell as he stepped closer and Megan twitched. Adam froze, knowing she heard, yet she remained kneeling without turning.

Adam turned to the control panel mounted to the wall beside the door keyed in specific commands handed down to him long ago by the professor. The electronic keypad accepted his commands, and the large metal door slid to close off the room's single exit behind him, locking shut with a loud and brief hiss.

Adam descended the stairway slowly, and the sound of his footsteps shook Megan from whatever trance she'd been lost in. She turned and stood. The look in her eyes was that of fear, laden with a mixture of sorrow and utter confusion. She winced with every step he took. Something about his descent down these stairs startled her for some reason, and he couldn't fathom why.

The look of terror seemed to lessen the closer Adam got to her, and by the time he'd made it down to the main level of the laboratory, the look on her face was that of the killer who'd taken the professor's life. Megan stared at him coldly, her expression as impassive and as still as a viper's. He couldn't have imagined Amanda's face to ever contain such a chilling look, but then again, this wasn't the woman he'd fallen in love with in New Edmonton.

He noticed the bloody dagger still gripped in her right hand. Megan's face twisted in some kind of inner conflict, and for a moment his Amanda stared back at him with complete and utter fear.

Who was this woman before she was killed and brought back as one of the living dead? What had happened to her in her past life to twist her into this monster?

Adam knew he would never find out the answers to these, and many other questions, so there was no point in dwelling on what-ifs. His borrowed time was running short, and he had to make the best use of it. There was only one thing left he needed to do before he himself returned to being one of them.

"Adam," Megan spoke.

Adam wasn't sure who it was who had said his name.

He didn't know if he cared any more. Then he saw a sinister glint in her eyes, and her mouth twisted with what almost looked like a smile she was trying to hold back. This wasn't his Amanda. That person was gone.

He pulled the trigger of the rifle once and shot her dead center between the eyes. The sharp crack of the rifle echoed loudly in the lab, rolling in waves to slap back at Adam as he stared at Megan through the scope.

A spray of red and bits of bone shot out of the back of her head in a rush, and a thick line of blood dripped from between her eyes and down her nose before she collapsed. Her flowing dark hair whipped around her face, covered the wound as she fell dead on the cold floor. Adam lowered his rifle and felt a heavy weight descend upon his heart. Numbness replaced the rage that he'd felt earlier. Amanda's death rewarded him not a single ounce of satisfaction.

His fingers released the handle of the rifle, and the weapon clattered loudly on the ground beside his feet. Adam finally let his weariness take him as he stumbled back against the front end of a table and slid down to a sitting position on the cold floor. He sat and stared upon the glass tube that had brought him back from the dead, and in a moment of pure madness, he smiled to himself and let out a nervous laugh.

The room around him was silent. Everything was as still as a tomb, and he was alone now, separated from the madness of the world outside. Cut off once more from the rest of civilization, Adam took some solace in knowing that when he did turn he would be trapped in this place and would never have the chance to kill another person.

He let out a heavy sigh and thought about everything that had happened to him since his rebirth. Adam also thought about his lost wife and child, and he wondered if by some miracle they might be somewhere out there, older perhaps, but alive and well. He prayed that this was so, and in his final moments of life he allowed himself to indulge and truly believe in this fantasy.

At last, Adam closed his eyes and let himself rest.

Chapter Thirty-Two

When Adam woke, for a moment all that he saw was covered in a wash of crimson. Then he blinked his eyes, and slowly color returned to his surroundings. Adam breathed heavily as he gasped as if for the first time in what felt like years. He shook himself awake, and in his shock, fell on his side upon the cool surface of the laboratory floor. He blinked once, twice, then perhaps a hundred more times. He heard the faint hum of the room's lights above him, and for a long time he lay on the floor with wide eyes, trying to piece together what was going on.

When it all came back to him, his eyes roved up and along the floor and saw that Amanda's body still lay where he'd left it. The glass tube hung on the grasp of the robotic arm. The heart in his chest continued to beat with a normal and steady pulse.

The feverish heat that had been spreading up his legs toward his heart and lungs was gone as well, and this was perhaps the most startling revelation of all. He slowly pushed himself to a sitting position and shook his head. The pulsating pain in his skull was gone. When he stood he was surprised to find that the wound on his left foot no longer hurt. Confused, he removed the shoe and the bloody sock.

"What the hell?"

The wound on his foot was gone, completely healed as if it never been there in the first place. He turned his ankle, trying to inspect his foot from every angle. There were no signs of teeth marks, no broken skin, no bruising.

He was healed.

Adam's gaze lifted to the empty class cylinder, and then his eyes widened.

"It can't be."

He crawled to the glass tube and glanced down at his reflection in the metal grating. His eyes looked tired, but they also looked alive. For a time he'd been undoubtedly sick from the virus, but if he felt the way he did now, there could only be one explanation. The ZF-93 cure had done more than save him from death.

The cure itself truly was what it was called: a cure. Could it be so? Did Adam dare to believe that somehow the professor had stumbled upon the true cure for the virus? In his blood resided the last living specimen of the cure that could save the world.

Adam looked up and studied the silent room around him, and then smiled for the first time in what felt like eons. He smiled and looked around him in awe as if the world had taken on a new dimension. Adam was alive, and his body could now fight off the disease.

As if on cue, Adam heard gunshots ring from somewhere outside of the lab. This was followed by the muffled sounds of a familiar voice, growling as he barked orders towards his company. Adam frowned, wondered what was going on, and he moved towards the flight of steps that led up towards the room's single, locked door. Before he could reach it, however, he heard someone inputting commands in the control panel located on the other side of the door, and with a sharp hiss, the metal portal opened.

Thomas, Jenny, and Isaac stood on the other side. Each of them held smoking rifles in their hands, and their faces registered both surprise and shock.

The sergeant raised his rifle halfway up Adam's body and quickly studied him with hardened eyes. Those eyes peeled him open, bore deep into his sockets and searched for any sign that Adam was still alive. When Adam smiled, the sergeant's tense shoulders visibly relaxed. The others quickly stepped around him and moved into the room, training their weapons around to make sure that the rest of the lab was clear.

Then they all noticed the dead body lying just below the shadow cast by the room's central tube. Adam felt his heart sink once more. He had done this, he had killed her, and even now he didn't fully understand why she'd done what she had. The appearance of the zombies in New Edmonton couldn't have been a coincidence. Adam knew somehow she had been involved in the destruction of their home.

He had loved her, loved Amanda. He had also killed her with little hesitation.

Adam understood that in the years to come he would be haunted by the ghosts that had been born in this place. The smiling face of the woman he'd grown to cherish would always visit him in his darkest nights. Perhaps she would ask him why he had chosen to end her. He didn't think that would be the case, however. Somehow he knew she had truly loved him, except that her dark past had been too much for her, too strong, and too overwhelming.

With great effort, Adam brushed away such thoughts for now. He filed them away, knowing that their specters would likely visit him later.

Adam and the rest of Sparrow Company exchanged notes, sharing short versions of what had happened. Isaac explained that after they'd entered and cleared the mansion, they'd found Florentine in his library. They'd taken the time to bring his body back with them, strapping it in one of the secure beds in the APC. None of them had it in them to put a bullet in the old man's brain, even though they knew eventually he might rise.

Adam's spirits fell when he heard of Danny's death, He felt a sense of sheer pride for the young man who'd thrown himself in the fire to save his friends. He couldn't help but glance at Jenny as Thomas related this part of the story. The look of grief in her eyes ran deep, and he understood the feeling of loss that she held in her heart.

"I'm so sorry," he said to everyone, though his eyes were for Jenny.

Jenny glanced over at the body of Amanda, and then back to Adam. The look in her eyes said she understood as well.

Thomas shook his head as he followed Jenny's gaze to Amanda. "Think she did it? You really think she let them in?"

Adam sighed. "Maybe an investigation in the future will explain things better, make things a little clearer for all of us, but the truth is the damage has already been done."

Most of the city was abandoned now, and thousands had needlessly lost their lives. Thomas had confirmed that the evacuation of the rest of the populous to Himura Valley had been successful, and the Romero Bridge on that end had been secured and was now under heavily armed watch. The station in New Edmonton, however, was still overrun by the dead. Sparrow Company had little hope of catching a train at this point. It was likely that not a single train was left in the station anyway.

Adam jumped as Jenny laid a hand on his arm. Her eyes were rooted to his face. "I can't believe it. If what you're saying is right, then the professor did find his cure after all."

"It's the best news I've heard all day," Isaac added.

"Right now, you are our top priority," Thomas said.

Adam almost laughed at the man's gruff tone; it was a voice he suspected would never change.

Thomas ignored him. "We need to get to Himura Valley, behind its protective walls. Then we can form a plan on how we can take back this city. Maybe we can still rebuild our homes here."

Looks of hope crossed all of their faces. The sergeant was right, and that perhaps they could find a way to one day come back here and retake their homes in this place.

Adam's jaw dropped, and his eyes suddenly went wide. "Oh my god."

"What is it?" the sergeant asked, instinctively raising his rifle to his side.

"You said that the professor is strapped to a bed in the APC, right?"

"Yes, but what does this have to do with—"

Adam raced out of the laboratory in a rush. He raced through the halls of the Charon Initiative, and the faces of his wife and son took form and shape in his mind. He smiled to himself as he ran faster. He could picture them smiling at him, and he felt that they might be proud of him right now, proud of what he'd figured out.

The cold winter air greeted him when he emerged from the front doors. The storm had finally abated, though the winds still churned with power and howling noise. He sped down the walkway, balancing himself as he moved across the icy ground.

The APC waited on the white covered front lawn of the facility. He keyed in his codes and entered the large armored vehicle and maneuvered toward the back.

Lying beneath the pale glow of the ceiling's overhead lights, the professor waited strapped to a steel bed. The virus had already done its terrible work on his body, and the creature that lay on the bed turned its head to the side to regard him.

For a moment Adam felt the world slip out from under him, as the horror of looking upon what had happened to his surrogate father—his friend—stared back at him with its lifeless eyes. The creature thrashed against its bindings, wrenching its entire body back and forth in a futile effort to free itself from its bonds, gnashing its teeth at the frigid air.

Adam froze, his nerves shaken.

The others arrived, filing behind him. They followed him into the interior of the vehicle as Adam made his way closer to the steel bed. His steady approach seemed to aggravate the creature even more, and the thing that wore the professor's face grew angry as it tried and tried again to take a bite out of his flesh.

"What's going on?" Thomas asked, concerned.

"Oh no," Jenny whispered, looking up at Adam.

Adam held up his hands. "Guys, please, I know what I'm doing."

"Do you?" Jenny shouted. "Adam, this is crazy!"

"Crazy?" the sergeant glanced to his side at her. "What the hell are you both talking about?"

"He's talking about the professor," Isaac spoke up. "Isn't that right, Adam?"

"After he bites me, I need you to strap me to a chair, just in case," Adam began to explain. "I'm sure everything will be fine. Well, I think it will be, but I need to try this. I need to try to bring him back."

"Oh my god, Adam," Thomas protested. "I won't let you do this."

"Promise me that you'll strap me to a chair...just in case."

"Adam, no! I won't let you do this."

The sergeant strode forward, ready to do everything he could to restrain the man. Adam moved faster, already prepared to do what he'd come here to do. He moved closer to the professor's bedside and brought the length of his left arm right against the creature's mouth.

The monster bit down hard against his flesh, and Adam felt hot fluid ooze from his wound as a strong feeling of nausea took him. The professor chewed and pulled its head back, swallowing the large chunk of meat it had taken from Adam.

Adam reeled back, cradling his wounded arm. The fire that burned through the wound told him that the infection was already working its way through him once more. It was happening all over again, only this time Adam had allowed it to happen.

The others moved with blinding speed. The sergeant swore as he caught Adam before he could slide against the bulkhead to the floor. As the creature strapped to the bed thrashed and screamed, wanting more of Adam's flesh and blood, Jenny and Isaac quickly helped to move their friend to the closest chair in the back of the cabin. Thomas left to retrieve the bindings.

Adam swooned in his pain. This was worse than before. The wound was larger, He needed to make sure that the professor took a lot of his blood into his system. He didn't know if this would work, He wanted to try.

The venom that coursed through his veins burned hotter than before, and he groaned and doubled over. A hint of fear laced through him. Perhaps he'd taken too much of the virus into himself this time, and his blood might not be enough to bring him back from death a third time.

He heard the others talking to him, trying to keep him awake with their consoling words. Their voices sounded distant, as if he were listening to them underwater. He felt the fire rage through him, tearing and shredding him throughout his entire being, and his lips curled back in an angry grimace. Crimson swirled at the edges of his vision, and his muscles bunched in anticipation.

As darkness enveloped him he saw once more the faces of his wife and child, Gillian and Clark. If this was to be his true end, then it would be a good death. Everything that had led him up to this point had been an adventure, and he was happy that he'd been given the chance to experience it. If this was to be his last moments on this world, he was happy to be able to leave it once more having saved someone else.

Chapter Thirty-Three

The members of Sparrow Company drove the APC out of the city. Even if they could get through the teeming swarm of the walking dead, they didn't want to risk taking Adam and the professor across the Romero Bridge, just in case Adam was wrong about his mad theory.

Sergeant Thomas Black stood just outside the door of his APC, taking in a deep breath of cool air as the sun shone down on his weary and cracked face. The storm had finally died, and the open plains surrounding him were covered in thick layers of rolling white hills. Not a single one of the undead could be seen for miles around, and he'd decided that they all needed to take a stop for a while, to gather themselves and find some rest.

He still couldn't believe what had transpired, He dealt with it, just as he continued to deal with every problem that crossed his path. He carried his rifle with him, which had become a sort of permanent fixture upon his person.

Jenny was inside tending to Adam and the professor. Isaac was at the forward console, checking to make sure there was nothing else damaged during the attack by that giant that had thrown the heavy vehicle so easily before.

Adam had turned, and he sat strapped in his chair, snarling and trying to bite at them from afar. A part of him was furious with what the man had done, foolishly risking himself in some crazy hope that the cure could help both him and the professor.

They could have brought them both to Himura Valley, to the other facility, and given time, they could have formulated a better plan of action. Thomas had always been about proper planning; it was his credo, and the testament to which he abided by. Adam was something else entirely, and truth be told, Thomas still understood why the man did what he thought he had to do.

He thought back to the time when they had first found Adam, before he was even considered as the first of the professor's subjects. Danny had been there at the time. Thomas had shot Adam down with a single bullet from his sniper rifle. None of them could have foreseen that one day that very same creature they captured would be someone they cared about very much.

Then there was Amanda. Who was she before she'd been turned? Why did she do everything she had done? Thomas pondered this for a very long time, and he continued to land upon the same conclusion. Some people were just messed up; some people were just broken. Sometimes those people just wanted to see the world suffer.

He stared long and hard at the serene and beautiful landscape that stretched out before him. It reminded him of why he continued to fight for this world and its last remaining survivors. Why, no matter what happened, he could not give up.

"Sergeant!"

Thomas whipped about at the cry from Jenny. His heart raced as he looked toward the APC.

"Black, I need you!"

* * * *

Adam tested his legs and footing as he tentatively stepped out of the APC's open hatch and was instantly bathed by the afternoon sun outside. He moved away from the large vehicle and raised a hand to help shield his eyes as he waited for his vision to become used to so much light. He glanced up at the sky, stared long and hard at it, and was overjoyed that what he perceived was blue instead of crimson.

It had worked.

He'd been scared, but a part of him had known that his gamble would work out in his favor. The others stood just outside the APC now, watching him as he readjusted himself once more to life. It was impossible, Here he stood, breathing in the cool air and feeling the wind chill his living flesh. He couldn't help but allow a wide smile to spread out across his lips. He turned, faced the others, and he saw that they shared in his joy. For the moment, the horrors of what had happened to all of them were forgotten.

Adam closed his eyes and thought of his long lost family, pictured their faces in his mind, and he held onto them. He swore that he would never forget their faces ever again. He prayed that one day he would regain the rest of his memories. After they made their way to Himura Valley, Adam made a solemn oath to himself that he would begin to really seek the answers to questions that had followed him since the first time he'd been returned to this world.

Thoughts of Amanda and what had become of her filtered into his mind, and a large portion of his joy left him when he pictured her beautiful face in his thoughts. He pushed the image away. Whoever Megan had been in her past was something very dark and very terrible, and the sad truth was that perhaps no one could escape their past.

Adam steered his thoughts away from her and thought of the beach he longed to see with his real eyes. There, in his daydream, he pictured Gillian and Clark waving to him from where they stood on that strange boat that may or may not have existed in his past. Adam stood on the edge of the beach.

The waters crawled up the sandy slope to tickle his toes before receding back into the deep blue vastness. He'd never been able to swim into that ocean before, but now he knew inside he had changed. He was strong enough now to take the chance of swimming into those dark and ominous waters. He was brave enough now to take the risk so that he could once more stand on that boat to be with his family.

It would be a miracle if those two were still alive somewhere out there. Then again, wasn't his very existence now a miracle in its own right?

The sun continued to shine down, and the world continued to turn all around them. The days would continue, as well as their struggles in this harsh and unforgiving world. And Adam would continue living, knowing that he had no other choice than to seize this miracle that he'd been given, and try to live his life to its fullest.

Adam opened his eyes, took in a deep breath, and walked slowly towards his waiting friends.

* * * *

Florentine stirred in his sleep. He felt himself rise out of unconsciousness, and he felt his soul being lifted up from some dark pit he thought he could never escape. Up and up he went, and as he rose higher and higher, he began to feel a strange sensation of warmth take him. He felt his eyes open, and the first thing he noted was both his terrible headache and the harsh brightness that assailed his vision.

The professor groaned as he gently forced his own eyelids open.

He found himself lying on a steel bed. Confused, he stared up at those gathered around.

There, standing closest to him, was Adam's familiar face. The professor noted the large wad of bandages that enveloped the man's left arm. He looked up into Adam's face and he was overjoyed when he saw the life and joy that resided in his son's eyes.

"Welcome back, Professor," Adam said, his voice cracking. "Congratulations. You just saved the world."

Florentine looked up at Adam and smiled.

About the Author:

Adrian Mallabo is a writer and a black belt martial artist who enjoys a good zombie tale or two...or three. His interest in horror fiction was introduced at an early age, and he has since made it his life's goal to succeed in this genre.

Adrian was born somewhere in the beautiful islands of the Philippines. He now lives in the often chilly city of Edmonton with his soon-to-be wife, Andrea.

For more information, please visit his website at: http://www.somethinginthebasement.com

Also from Damnation Books:

Dreams of the Dead
by Jeremy Terry

eBook ISBN: 9781615728121
Print ISBN: 9781615728138

Horror Zombie
Novel of 80,000 words

How do you survive the end of all things?

The dead walk the streets of America. State and National government have collapsed. In the face of the end of all things, a group of young teenagers come together to fight against the hoards and find a way to survive in their new nightmarish world.

Also from Damnation Books:

Better Off Alone
by Yolanda Sfetsos

eBook ISBN: 9781615720514

Horror Zombie
Short Story of 8,741 words

I'm coming 4U

Nell has been forced to leave the safety of her basement. As the dead chase her along the familiar streets of her suburb, she stumbles on a group of survivors who offer her shelter. But all she's concerned about is finding her way to Todd, the only person who's helped keep her sanity.

She intends to ask this group of survivors to help her save Todd from his predicament but changes her mind when she spies the sick and twisted way they ensure their safe existence.

Visit Damnation Books online at:

Our Blog—
http://www.damnationbooks.com/blog/

DB Reader's Yahoogroup—
http://groups.yahoo.com/group/DamnationBooks/

Twitter—
http://twitter.com/DamnationBooks

Google+—
https://plus.google.com/u/0/115524941844122973800

Facebook—
https://www.facebook.com/pages/
Damnation-Books/80339241586

Goodreads—
http://www.goodreads.com/DamnationBooks

Shelfari—
http://www.shelfari.com/damnationbooks

Library Thing—
http://www.librarything.com/DamnationBooks

HorrorWorld Forums—
http://horrorworld.org/phpBB3/viewforum.php?f=134

CPSIA information can be obtained at www.ICGtesting.com
Printed in the USA
LVOW061813220313

325607LV00001B/3/P